MW00640417

"Cyn?" The ongoing keyboard ceased. "I'

Some clicks, some butt[...] [...]ne of the massive screens at the front of the room flickered. Points of light and smears of color swiftly resolved into an image of the moon, recorded from one of many orbiting satellites.

The time stamp read 22:47 UCT. Cynthia didn't even look at the date; she already knew when this had been recorded.

They appeared around the moon's edge. A few at first, a handful more, and then in the thousands, until they blotted out the cosmos. A faint grayish distortion wrapped the base of each, invisible against the darkness, seen only when one passed in front of another, or in front of the distant stars. Cynthia flinched, but at such a great distance, end on toward the camera, the alien lettering on their sides was obscured.

A thousand questions crossed her mind, a thousand reasons she couldn't possibly be seeing what she was seeing, but there it was.

Something else crept slowly into view, something largely obscured by the moon and by the obelisks themselves. Only bits and slivers were visible, but from those alone she could tell it was enormous, the size of a mountain at least. If she could only get a clearer...

The clock on the video clicked over to 22:49, and after a few seconds more, the entire image vanished behind a wall of static.

Copyright ©2023 by Ari Marmell
ISBN 978-1-63789-716-4
Macabre Ink is an imprint of Crossroad Press Publishing
All rights reserved. No part of this book may be used or reproduced in any manner
whatsoever without written permission except in the case of
brief quotations embodied in critical articles and reviews
For information address Crossroad Press at 141 Brayden Dr., Hertford, NC 27944
www.crossroadpress.com

First Edition

OBELISKS

BOOK TWO: ASHES

by Ari Marmell

Author's Note

Getting a book from concept to shelves is a long process. As I write this foreword, it's already been a couple of years since the first draft of this novel.

As I write this foreword, people are dying in Ukraine because the monster who currently rules Russia values his own ego over human life.

I don't know what the situation will be when Obelisks hits shelves, let alone at the near future point where the story is set. I don't know if the invasion/occupation will be over, I don't know what international relations with Russia will look like, I don't know what the Russian space program will look like. I can only write what I know to be the case now, and what I hope will be the case later.

Right now, Russia remains an integral part of the ISS program, their cosmonauts an integral part of the mission crews. I hope that in the near future, the people of Russia and Ukraine both will be rid of the monster. So Obelisks will run with that, and remain as it was written.

Content Warning

Many of you are familiar with my other novels.

Obelisks is very, very much not like those. Very. So, for those who appreciate such things, I'm including a content warning. If you prefer to skip these to avoid spoilers, please page ahead now.

CW: Violence, graphic injury, body horror, drug use, prolonged illness, suicide, dead animals, dead infants, pedo/hebephilia (though anything explicit remains "offscreen"), gaslighting and manipulation, slurs and bigotry, catcalling.

Chapter One

They sat around a table in a high-backed booth, tucked away in the corner of the Starport Café. Her hands warming around a steaming mug of black coffee, Cynthia stared at the glass panels that formed the front wall, peering through her phantasmal reflection at the bare-branched trees beyond.

She looked deader than they did. Pale, sunken, bloodless. Almost as dead as—

No! Stop it!

A few sporadic images were all she'd retained of the moments following their soul-shattering discovery. Natsuhiko doubled over the hood of an abandoned car, vomiting and weeping. Johanna's screams fading into unending moans, a wordless and primal pain. And Grigory...

Grigory, lips pressed tight, grim but determined, lifting, cajoling, *dragging* them back to the Charger. Jabbing Cynthia with a syringe of Dilaudid. Slipping behind the wheel, driving as fast as he dared to the main gate of the Johnson campus. Ushering them inside, gathering coffee from behind the cafeteria counter and retrieving several bottles of stronger stuff from the trunk of the car. If not for him, they might still be out on the highway, mesmerized by the incomprehensible carnage and gradually losing their minds.

Now he hovered over them, half drill sergeant, half mother hen. "I wish you would try to eat something."

Natsuhiko thumped a finger against the bottle of Jim Bean. "This'll do."

Cynthia directed a pointed glance at a trash can across the cafeteria, one everyone but Grigory had visited at least once since they'd arrived. "I'm barely keeping down the coffee right now. I don't... I don't think I'll be eating again this year."

From Jo, they heard nothing. She'd said nothing, done nothing, drunk nothing since Grigory guided her to the booth. Cynthia wasn't entirely sure the woman had even blinked.

If she'd had the emotional strength to worry, that would have worried her.

Cynthia had never seen the Starport Café empty before. It felt sad. The booths, the tables, the glass, the vaguely retro-future rounded light fixtures, the tiled floor... Nothing particularly wrong with any of them, but taken as a whole, without the buzz of conversation and the clatter of cutlery and the scents of cooking, it all proved sterile. Soulless.

The people who had once gathered here to eat, to socialize, to take a few minutes for themselves, had included countless NASA personnel, the builders of what was supposed to be the future. It should have been special.

But then, look at the future we got.

Chiding herself, Cynthia turned her attention back to the windows, to her reflection. Only it wasn't hers anymore.

God, not again!

Again.

Again, as she had so many times since they'd gotten here, she saw not herself, but her mother. Not the trees and grass of the lawn outside, but the sandy California beaches she'd visited so often as a child. And again, as clearly as if cast by a movie projector, she saw her mother, face aglow with a beatific smile, eagerly stroll over to the water's edge. To it, and then into it, the waves lapping up to her knees, her waist, her chest, until she was gone.

She never even liked to swim.

Is that what had happened? Had her mother, had *everyone*, done as the countless dead of Clear Lake? Done as the profane lettering on those obelisks—come not merely from space, Cynthia felt now, but from hell—demanded? She couldn't know, not for certain, but she had no reason to doubt.

Nor could she tell, anymore, if the constant repetition of that image—sometimes her mother alone, sometimes with friends or family, but always with the same outcome—was just her distraught imagination running out of control, or genuine hallucination. Overwhelming grief, or a symptom of her worsening condition.

And God help her, she didn't know which answer she'd prefer anymore.

Her stomach turned over. Cynthia bolted from the booth and across the café, staggering under the influence of the hydromorphone, just in time to empty what little coffee she'd swallowed into the trash can. When she was done, the stench of the earlier vomit wafting from the bin nearly set her off all over again.

"If I'd known..."

Cynthia was halfway back to the table when she, and everyone, stopped to stare at Jo, speaking for the first time since the lakeshore.

"If I'd known," Jo said again, "what kind of world was waiting for them, for us, I'd have driven that bus off an overpass instead of to Marcus's prison. Would've been so much kinder."

Still meeting no one's gaze, never so much as turning her head, Jo rose and wandered out of the cafeteria.

Grigory opened his mouth to say something, closed it. Looked at Cynthia as she wobbled back to the table, at Natsuhiko and the bottle before him. Then, with a sigh, "I should go get her. Please do not go anywhere." Resting the shotgun over his shoulder—even here, the Russian refused to go unarmed—he followed Johanna out the door.

"Where would we go?" Cynthia asked, sitting with a limp thump.

"I suppose we still ought to go looking for answers at some point," Natsuhiko said.

Cynthia froze. In light of the past couple of hours, she'd honestly forgotten why they'd come.

"Do you think it still matters?"

"I think it might be the only thing that does."

She thought on that for a moment, then nodded. It wasn't as though she had anything better to do. "You may want to cut back on that, then," she said.

"I really don't." Natsuhiko pushed the bottle away. "But I will. How does he do it, Cyn?"

"How does...? Grigory?"

"Yeah. We're all disintegrating. I can't think of anyone who wouldn't be. But he's..."

"I have no idea. But I'm grateful for it."

"Heh. As long as we don't run into any kryptonite."

It wasn't much of a smile, but Cynthia was surprised—and, again, grateful—she could manage even that. She decided to risk another sip of coffee, reached for the now lukewarm mug.

And it finally dawned on her.

"What the hell?"

"Cyn?"

"Natsuhiko, look around. What do you see?"

"Um. Tables. Chairs. The counters and cash registers. Why?"

"And *how* are you seeing it?"

"What? I..." His jaw dropped as it sank in. "The lights are on! I've been so distracted, it never even..."

"Yeah." She raised her cup. "It didn't even occur to me to wonder how Grigory made this."

Natsuhiko leaned back. "But that makes sense, doesn't it? We know NASA has backups for their backups. Especially after last year."

"Sure, but... I mean, okay, I don't know the details of the generator systems or other redundancies, but I feel like they'd still need refueling after two weeks? And even if not, wouldn't they be focused on vital systems?"

"The staff would still have to eat, even in an emergency."

"Maybe. Maybe. Still, I can't help but wonder if—"

The opening door, heralding Jo's return, interrupted Cynthia's thought. The good news was that the other woman appeared substantially more aware and alert than when she'd left.

The bad news was that she was alone.

"Grigory?" Cynthia and Natushiko asked in unison.

"Told me to get back here. Said it was *safer*." Her tone permitted little doubt as to how she felt about *that* concept. "Said he'd be along later."

Well, that's odd.

"Maybe he needs a few moments?" Natsuhiko said.

"Yeah, I guess. If anyone's entitled to them..."

All three settled back around the table. Cynthia sipped at her coffee. Natsuhiko switched to water. Jo did nothing.

"How long's it been?"

"About three minutes, Cynthia."

"What? No, he's been gone longer than that!"

Natsuhiko sighed. "I meant since the last time you asked."

"Oh."

More coffee. More water. Several trips to the nearby restroom, though at least they weren't vomiting anymore.

The breeze outside died down, just enough for the distant calls of the birds at Clear Lake to penetrate the walls, carrying memories and emotions with them. Cynthia stood, went behind the serving counters, and turned on several faucets until the running water drowned out the noise. She splashed a few handfuls across her face before returning.

"How are you doing?" she asked.

"A lot more sober than I want to be," the other astronaut said. "You?"

"Not about to fall over with every third step, if that's what you mean."

"Your head?"

"Dull ache. Nothing I can't ignore, and the Dilaudid should keep it there for a good while yet."

Both turned toward Jo, who said, "Doesn't matter."

"Oookay." Cynthia sat. "Ten more minutes. Then we go get him and figure out what the hell we're doing here. Agreed?"

Natsuhiko nodded. Jo, at least, didn't object.

"All right." Cynthia left her seat precisely at the ten-minute mark. Now that they had something to do, she chafed to get to it. It was better than thinking. A quick step back behind the counter to turn the faucets off, and then she made for the door.

They checked the rest of the building first: the restrooms, the exchange store, even the back hallways and the storerooms in case he'd just wanted a place to sit on his own for a while. Nothing.

Outside, then? It was chilly, and even though the wind had picked back up while they waited, the avian calls were still far too loud, far too great a reminder, for comfort. Still, the idea that he might have taken a walk to clear his head wasn't beyond the bounds of credulity.

But the courtyard outside Building 3 was empty of all but trees and a single skittish cat that vanished the moment they opened the outer door. The trio made a quick circuit of the yard and around the neighboring buildings.

Still nothing. No sign of Grigory.

God dammit. She couldn't blame Johanna. Neither Natsuhiko nor Cynthia herself would have been in any emotional state to think this through, to demand that Grigory set a return time, or tell them where he'd gone. But Grigory himself should have thought of it!

Be nice, Cyn. He's gotta be as messed up as you are, inside. He'd just been so unyielding, so in control, it was easy to think him unbreakable.

Still, understandable or not, the upshot was that they hadn't the slightest idea where to look.

"So do we just poke around until we find him?" Jo asked, though she sounded only vaguely interested.

"Over a hundred buildings," Cynthia replied, "on more than sixteen hundred acres? No, I don't think we'll be doing that."

"Got somewhere else to be?"

Natsuhiko casually put himself between them. "Not that I disagree with you," he told Cynthia, "but I do hope you have a better idea?"

"First, we go back to the car, pick up a few guns." Grigory had, after all, walked off with the only weapon the group had carried inside. "Just in case."

"And then?"

"Then we take advantage of the fact that we're briefly back in the twenty-first century."

Moments later they found themselves in Building 4-S, home to numerous Mission Operations support offices. They chose one at random; since the campus actually had power, any room with a computer should do. Cynthia planted herself in the chair, violently rejected the sudden realization that the last person to sit here was probably floating in Clear Lake, and pressed the power button. A quick whine as it emerged from sleep, and the desktop appeared almost immediately.

She raised her hands to the keyboard and froze as her gaze landed on the desk beside the computer.

A child's drawing, four stick figures and a stick dog, labeled "faMly." A dog-eared copy of *The Martian*. An Incredible Hulk bobblehead.

Shaking, she swept the whole collection onto the floor, kicking at it until she'd shoved it all behind the desk and out of sight.

Natsuhiko's hand closed on her shoulder. Briefly, she leaned her cheek against his skin, and then once more let her fingers drift over the keys.

"Cyn?"

"Hmm?"

"Do you actually know how to access the security systems at all, let alone the cameras?"

"Not a clue. Cross your fingers that it's all user-friendly."

Her friend snorted. "A government system? From *your* government?"

"Hush, you. Now, where do I—?"

Both astronauts jumped as a floating text box appeared on screen with a soft chime. Cynthia recognized it as one of several intranet chat programs sundry workers had installed on Johnson's network.

Who are you?

"Uh..."

"Don't look at me," Natsuhiko told her.

"How much do you think we should tell them?"

How about everything?

Son of a... "You can hear us?" Cynthia asked.

You think? Who are you?

"No threat to you, for one thing."

Cool. Ain't what I asked, though

"Look, can we save the twenty questions? Our friend's missing. If you're in the system, can you help us find him?"

Long seconds passed, until Cynthia wondered if whoever this was had decided not to speak to them anymore.

Or maybe we lost connection. That'd be about right, we find someone who can maybe tell us where Grigory is, and the damn intranet...

Big dude? Packing a 12-gauge?

"Yes! Yes, that's him!"

Again the response was slow in coming.

He's in FCR1. But I don't know if you want to go in there

"...what?" Soft. Broken. A little girl's uncomprehending question. Behind her, Natsuhiko's breath caught in his throat, and Jo's aimless pacing halted midstep.

I'm sorry

Chapter Two

Natsuhiko hit the door first at a dead sprint, Cynthia and Jo on his heels. They pounded across the courtyard, breeze biting at exposed skin as the sun dropped in the west, grass crunching underfoot. Windows and stone walls blurred past them, until they hit the entrance to 30, still not slowing. The door slammed into the wall as they passed through it, the echo quickly lost behind them.

More halls. More doors. *Too long, too long, too* fucking *long!*

FCR1. Mission Control.

Half of America had seen that room, in one form or another. Walls covered in images of space, of craft, of astronauts. Line upon line of mission patches and insignias running around the chamber near the ceiling. Multiple enormous screens up front, normally displaying all manner of information and imagery but currently dark, switched off. And of course, occupying the bulk of the room, row after row of computer stations, multiple dozens of them.

Only one was turned on, revealing a grainy picture: a satellite camera, to judge by the numbers and notifications scrolling beside it. It showed nothing but the dust clouds and static-lightning choking the atmosphere, but the coordinates indicated it was aimed at the coast of the Baltic Sea, near Saint Petersburg.

He'd been trying to look in on home. At the shoreline beside his home.

Grigory himself lay sprawled on the floor beside that computer station. The blast that took off most of his head had also knocked the chair backward, half-dumping him onto the carpet.

He still cradled the shotgun in one limp arm, thumb caught in the trigger guard.

Cynthia had nothing left. She should mourn, as she had for Clarence, for JD. Maybe more. Without Grigory, she'd have lost herself out on the highway. He deserved tears, heartfelt words.

They wouldn't come. Neither of them. She felt so numb, so deadened, she wondered briefly if the Crooked Men had found them again.

The upside was, while she couldn't grieve, she also couldn't work up any sense of abandonment.

"I wish you'd told us," she whispered. It was all she could manage. And all she could think of was tree limbs bending in the wind, because any that were too stiff and too unyielding would inevitably break.

She and Natsuhiko carried him into a nearby office and, after moving the computer and other detritus, laid him out gently on the desk. Lacking a sheet or blanket, they scoured the building's other rooms until they found one that had been personalized with decorative curtains instead of blinds. A poor shroud, but once again, the best they could manage.

Cynthia carefully placed the shotgun across his chest like the sword of a fallen Viking. They had other weapons, and nobody relished the idea of wielding this one again.

"Would... Does anyone want to say anything?"

"What's left to say?" Natsuhiko asked, slumped as though he'd been physically beaten. Jo said nothing, stood motionless save for a single tear running down her right cheek.

"Yeah." Cynthia held Grigory's hand briefly. "I think he'd understand."

The curtains only barely covered him; a problem, since they had more than just the corpse that needed covering. Fortunately, several offices they'd already searched contained coats or jackets left behind when everyone had... gone.

One of them, a woman's long trench coat, was sufficient to cover the stains and remains where Grigory fell. They had work to do in FCR1, and staring at that mess would've just been the last straw.

Moving several rows up and all the way across the room,

Cynthia and Natsuhiko chose a pair of computer stations far from that spot and woke the machines. They were here, they'd come all this way, sacrificed so much. By God, if Johnson held any answers at all, they would find them!

The chat box popped up again.

<u>Sorry about your friend</u>

"Thanks." Cynthia kept working, refusing to dwell on Grigory, opening various systems, hunting for files. "Uh, you can still hear us, right?"

<u>Yeah</u>

"Good." How the hell were these directories even organized? She'd never spent any real time on these stupid systems...

<u>So you gonna tell me who you are?</u>

"Depends. You going to answer *our* questions?"

<u>Depends</u>

Natsuhiko looked up from his own computer, directly into the camera high in the corner. Obviously their mystery guest had gotten into the security system, watching the grounds the same way they'd intended to search for Grigory. "How are you pulling this off?" he asked.

<u>Ain't hard. It's what I do</u>

"You're a hacker," Cynthia said.

<u>Network Security Specialist</u>

"Uh-huh. And you expect us to believe you hacked—sorry 'Network Securitied'—NASA?"

<u>Ain't saying it was easy. But I had time and no FBI or NSA to come down on me for messing with a few firewalls. Got my own generator and enough equipment to bounce signal off satellites. Figured I'd find answers here if anywhere. Been in y'all's system a while now</u>

Facing away from camera, Cynthia and Natsuhiko exchanged looks, but neither commented.

Instead, seeing no reason not to, Cynthia came back around to the initial question, still clicking and typing as she spoke. "My name's Cynthia. That's Natsuhiko and Jo. Our..." *Swallow, clear throat, keep calm, keep going.* "Our other friend is—was—Grigory. What's your name?"

<u>How come you ain't swimming?</u>

She came *this* close to screaming, cursing the unseen hacker for treating the topic so casually. But he'd known longer than they had, had more time to sit with it. And he could well be putting on a brave face for them, just as she'd done regarding Grigory.

"We were on the ISS when it happened. Since then we've, uh, been careful." She was not *about* to tell a complete stranger the details of her tumor, thank you very much! "And," she admitted, "we *have* lost people."

<u>So y'all are astronauts?</u>

"Well, most of us. Jo's from a different group of survivors."

<u>WHAT GROUP</u>

Now *that* was interesting. Cynthia leaned back from the screen, pondering. Keep it a secret? It might be wiser, but Marcus had told her that stories of their refuge had already spread.

"Small commune at Travis County State Prison."

Nothing. No response. She decided to take a wild stab.

"*Not* one of Lamb's people, if that's what you're worried about."

<u>Guess you met those assholes too?</u>

So, even here in Houston. Those bastards get around. "We didn't hit it off."

<u>Good</u>

"So, you want to tell us who you are? How you've survived all this on your own?"

<u>Thinking about it. Y'all seem okay but I ain't got this far being careless. I'll tell you there used to be a whole network of us for a few days before the internet went down, so I knew some of what was happening, where to stay away from</u>

<u>And who</u>

Now *that* might be useful. If Johnson didn't have answers, this individual might. If Cynthia could get them to stop being so cagey, to share what they knew.

"Cyn?" The ongoing background clatter of Natsuhiko's keyboard ceased. "I've found something."

Some clicks, some buttons, and one of the massive screens at the front of the room flickered. Points of light and smears of color swiftly resolved into an image of the moon, recorded from one of many orbiting satellites.

The time stamp read 22:47 UCT. Cynthia didn't even look at the date; she already knew when this had been recorded.

They appeared around the moon's edge. A few at first, a handful more, and then in the thousands, until they blotted out the cosmos. A faint grayish distortion wrapped the base of each, invisible against the darkness, seen only when one passed in front of another, or in front of the distant stars. Cynthia flinched, but at such a great distance, end on toward the camera, the alien lettering on their sides was obscured.

A thousand questions crossed her mind, a thousand reasons she couldn't possibly be seeing what she was seeing, but there it was.

Something else crept slowly into view, something largely obscured by the moon and by the obelisks themselves. Only bits and slivers were visible, but from those alone she could tell it was enormous, the size of a mountain at least. If she could only get a clearer...

The clock on the video clicked over to 22:49, and after a few seconds more, the entire image vanished behind a wall of static. The exact same static they'd seen on the ISS cameras.

That the obelisks had come from "out there" was no surprise, of course. But that wasn't what had Cynthia, Natsuhiko, and even Jo gawping at the glowing screen.

"They're *stone!*" Jo finally shouted, as though her objection might somehow change what they'd witnessed. "They can't... How can they...?"

Cynthia, who had risen without realizing it while watching the brief footage, fell back into her chair. "I have no fucking idea." She had assumed, they *all* had assumed, that the obelisks had been carried within something larger. Now?

"Could they have been launched? Moving by momentum?" Even as he asked, Natsuhiko clearly wasn't buying it.

Of course they couldn't. They'd deliberately maintained course to keep their approach hidden by the moon until they drew near. They'd spread across the globe, landed on high ground or open plains or clustered in population centers. And as large as the unseen thing accompanying them appeared, it wasn't remotely big enough to carry even dozens of the damn obelisks, let alone hundreds of thousands or millions.

She knew Natsuhiko knew this, had spoken in desperation or without thinking it through. She did him the courtesy of not answering.

Instead, she said, "That haze? Distortion? Some kind of propulsion, maybe?"

"Propulsion? They're *stone!*" Jo protested again.

"If it is," Natsuhiko said, "it's not like any we've even conceived of. But that's hardly surprising anymore, is it?"

If y'all had told me that's what you were looking for I could've saved you some time, the chat box announced.

"Been all through the system, have we?" Cynthia asked.

Been keeping busy

"So, if we were to look for anything that might've registered on satellites or RADAR?"

Feel free but you ain't gonna find anything you like. Planes and other air traffic for a few hours before it all goes to hell. Nothing else

"Something flew overhead last night," Natsuhiko said. "Near La Grange."

Ain't showed up here if it did

Again the astronauts exchanged looks.

You want to check you go right on ahead

Cynthia pushed back from the computer. "I'll take your word for now. Listen, we need to meet. In person."

HELL no

"You can't still think we're a danger to you!"

Nah. I don't think so but I don't KNOW. And even if you're not it don't mean you won't lead me to someone who is

"How long have you been alone? At least a few weeks now, right? That's got to be tough."

No response.

"Listen to me, please. We *need* you. Need your help. We're not experts on the ground control systems. You probably know the network better than we do. And you said you were in contact with others, so you've *definitely* got a better picture of what happened than we do.

"Please. We—I—need to know. It may be all we've got left."

Finally, All right. But only on my terms

"Thank you. I'm listening."

<u>Just you three and nobody comes carrying. I see anyone but you or I see a piece you're on your own</u>

"Done."

Natsuhiko leaned in. "You sure that's a wise choice?"

"We're asking for a lot of trust," she said aloud. "It's only fair we show some."

<u>Right on</u>

"When and where?"

<u>I need to</u>

"Need to?" Cynthia asked after a moment without follow-up. "You hit 'Enter' by mistake, Mr. Network Security Specialist?"

Nothing.

"Or is it Ms.? Mrs.? Something else entirely?" Cynthia's palms had gone clammy again. She wiped them dry on her pants. "Not looking to offend here." *Where the hell had—?*

<u>YOU FUCKING LIED TO ME</u>

"What? *No!* Every word I've told you is the truth! I—"

<u>You said you're not with Lamb's group!</u>

"We're not! They tried to kidnap us, for God's sake!"

<u>Well motherfuckers are HERE. If you're telling me the truth you're in some serious shit</u>

Natsuhiko was up, shotgun ready. Cynthia felt for the revolver at her waist but didn't draw it yet.

"I told you I should have a gun!" Johanna snapped.

"In the state you were in," Natsuhiko told her, "I wouldn't have trusted you with a *thermos.*"

"Can you show us?" Cynthia asked. Then, after a moment, "*Please!* Even if you don't trust us, what would it hurt?"

Her computer monitor flickered, then shifted to a feed from one of the many security cameras. A trio of vehicles had already passed through the main gate. The one in the lead looked familiar.

"They're way too close to our car," Natsuhiko said.

"Yeah, but they're going to have to spread out to search for us. We can circle around them, make for one of the other gates."

Not happening

The screen shifted to another camera, and then a third. More cars, blocking the paths to the other campus entryways.

"Shit!"

Think, Cyn! But all she could come up with was...

"We hide. Even with so many of them, it'll take hours, maybe days, to search this whole place, and we know it better than they do!"

"*That's* the plan?" Jo spat.

"You have a better one, now's *really* the time!"

She sighed. "Guess that's the plan."

I'll close down the security system so they can't try and use the cameras

"Thank you."

Much for my sake as yours. But good luck

"We need to move," Cynthia said, already making for the door. "Mission Control's one of the first places they'll look."

They darted from the building, keeping out of the campus lights that had suddenly become far more danger than comfort. Cynthia led them away from the cluster of buildings they'd occupied so far, moving instead toward the laboratories and storage facilities. An enormous number of structures, none of which they had any conceivable reason to visit and from which they could see anyone coming. With only a bit of good fortune, they could avoid a comprehensive search for at least—

"HEY, OUT THERE!"

The words boomed from a massive speaker, magnified and crackling. The sound carried clear across the campus. It must have been nearly deafening to anyone nearby.

"WE KNOW YOU'RE HERE. WE FOUND YOUR CAR, WITH ALL THE SUPPLIES."

But how did they know to come here at all? Had the hacker betrayed them? Was the talk and negotiation and fretting about Lamb's people all a delaying tactic?

"WE DON'T WANT TO HURT YOU. LAMB WANTS TO TALK TO YOU. BUT WE LOST SOME GOOD PEOPLE WHEN

YOU LED THE HUNTERS TO US AT CAMP MABRY, AND SOME OF THE GUYS, WELL, THEY'RE REAL SORE ABOUT THAT."

"When we led...?" Natsuhiko growled softly.

"Yeah," Cynthia said. "Not exactly how I remember it, either."

"SO, HERE'S THE DEAL. YOU COME OUT NOW, YOU COOPERATE, YOU HAVE MY WORD NOBODY GETS HURT. I'LL SEE TO IT PERSONALLY. BUT IF WE'VE GOT TO COME LOOKING FOR YOU, EVERYONE SPREAD OUT AND JUMPY... WELL, I CAN'T MAKE ANY GUARANTEES. SOMEONE'S MAYBE LIABLE TO GET SHOT."

"He's all heart, isn't he? I can't imagine why Ethan and Downing didn't want to go with them."

The trio crouched behind a rough hedge. "So what do we do?" Natsuhiko asked.

"Do?" Jo wrapped her arms tightly around herself. "There's only one thing to do! We hide, and if we have to, we fight! You can't be thinking of surrendering!"

Cynthia shook her head. "Of course not! There's no way we—"

"COME ON, NOW! NOBODY WANTS THIS TO GET UGLY!"

Little late for that.

"YOU NEED TO BE REASONABLE. YOUR PEOPLE NEED YOU TO BE REASONABLE, MS. HAN."

During the "constantly looking to prove herself" phase of her USAF officer training, Cynthia had once opted to be shocked by a taser. What she felt now was remarkably similar.

"MR. PAVLENKO," the speaker continued. "MR. HASHIDA. MS. KATESTON. NONE OF YOU WANT TO SEE EACH OTHER GET HURT. YOU WOULDN'T WANT TO SEE *ANY* OF YOUR FRIENDS GET HURT."

"How...?" Johanna wobbled, steadied herself against the nearest wall. "How?"

"Only one way," Cynthia said grimly, rising from her crouch. "They've got someone, maybe more than one, from the prison."

"What are you doing?" Natsuhiko asked.

"Turning myself over. Same as you two. Or did you not catch the fact that he wasn't just threatening *us*?"

"Oh. Shit."

"Yeah."

Jo opened her mouth to object, then shut it, gnawing at her lip.

"What'd Ethan say the bastard's name was?"

Natsuhiko pondered a moment. "Morales. Carlos Morales."

"*All right, Morales!*" Cynthia shouted, hoping her voice would carry far enough in the night's silence. "*Don't shoot! We're coming out!*" Humiliation warmed her cheeks as she raised her hands over her head. She forced it down and stepped out into the open. Natsuhiko, shotgun held high in both hands, followed on her heels, and Jo a moment later.

She called out again as they drew nearer, in case they hadn't heard the first time. With every step, she cataloged potential hiding spots, the distance between herself and available cover. If this was a ruse to make them easy targets, they'd better drop her with the first shot, or she meant to make them work for it.

It wasn't. Morales's people swarmed around them, weapons readied, but nobody opened fire. They collected the astronauts' guns, then marched them to their leader.

Carlos Morales stood beside a van with a police loudspeaker mounted on top. "A smart move," he told them. "But I'm not *quite* so stupid I can't count to four."

"Grigory's dead," Cynthia told him bitterly, jaw trembling in fury that she had to speak of her friend's despair to this bastard. "After what we saw today, after the lake? He couldn't take it."

"Seems like every time we meet, you've just lost someone. Not sure I'm buying it, Han."

"Fuck you. Go see for yourself. He's in one of the offices outside FCR1. I don't... don't remember the number."

"Building?"

"Thirty."

Morales reached out. Someone inside the van slapped a piece of paper into his waiting hand. "David," Morales barked. "Ashton." Two of the men broke off from the rest of the group, one taking the campus map as they went.

"How did you know we were here?" Cynthia demanded, refusing to wait for them to return and confirm what she already knew to be true.

"Frankly, we didn't think you still would be. Figured we'd have to try to and see what you'd learned, and where you'd gone next."

Cynthia waited, scowling.

Morales waited, smirking.

"You know what I mean!" she finally snapped.

Morales pointed back toward one of the cars. Cynthia struggled to make out the figure sitting, hunched and miserable, in the passenger seat.

The very *familiar* figure.

"Oh, no…"

"Yep," her captor told her. "I can't tell you what a relief it's been, how helpful it's been, to have a new doctor on board."

Chapter Three

The gate rattled shut, and Ethan watched through the chain links as his last remaining friends in the world shrank into the gray distance.

Not yet out of sight, and he missed them, wanted to wave them down, call them back.

Not yet out of sight, and he hated them, seething with a bitter resentment that would have shocked to the core all who knew him (or thought they did). Hated them for leaving him alone, for putting him in so precarious a position where everything he'd struggled with for years could so easily come crashing down, along with whatever future this messed-up world still offered.

Most of all he hated himself.

Behind him, the daily routine of the little colony that had been Travis County Prison was well underway. Several of Marcus's people walked the perimeter, checking the fence and the obelisk-blocking fabrics. Others were hard at work in the garden, tending to what food crops and medicinal herbs would deign to grow in the Central Texas winter.

The *chug-chug-chug* of the generator reverberated from its metal shed, feeding power to the kitchen, the living quarters, and the gate that had just severed Ethan from what might have been his lifeline. After a bit of tinkering on Downing's part, the machine now accepted a mixture of kitchen grease and other biodiesels with its regular fuel, dramatically stretching the prison's resources. They now ran the generator twice a day, for an hour or two each session. It kept the housing unit substantially more comfortable and was one of two major changes that had drastically heightened the quality of the food.

Major change number two would already be hard at work in the kitchen, and Ethan turned his steps that way. He had to eat something, no matter how severe his lack of appetite, but he absolutely would not and could not sit in the common area while he did so. Not this morning, especially. *I'll just pick up a plate straight from the source and disappear for a few hours...*

The kitchen was a study in artistic chaos. Hot and full of steam, with stovetops glowing orange and sinks running, people running this way and that, carrying that in thick oven mitts or stirring this as it threatened to bubble over.

In the center of it all, coordinating and controlling with a wooden spoon wielded as a conductor's baton, was Chavela Olmos, the new unquestioned sovereign of the cookhouse. For the most part, her English was good enough—augmented by emphatic gestures and occasional demonstrations—to get her orders across. When it wasn't, well, several members of the community spoke Spanish.

"*Buenos días,* Doctor Bell."

"Good morning, Mrs. Olmos. Mind if I just grab something real quick?"

She frowned at him, making many of her wrinkles frown in turn. "Of course not, but you always do this, Doctor. Is no good for you. You should sit, talk. Company, *sí*?"

"I-I'll get there."

Still frowning, Chavela redirected the ongoing dance with her spoon, so that Ethan swiftly took delivery of a cup of coffee and a plate of eggs, beans, and some sort of corn cake.

It would be better if the eggs hadn't been powdered, of course—Marcus had recently discussed sending a search party out to try and round up some chickens, if any had survived the hungry dogs and coyotes, but until then they were stuck with whatever would keep—but as post-apocalyptic cuisine went, it was amazing.

"Doc."

Ethan, who had already crossed half the kitchen on his way out, glanced down at the legs sticking out from behind the refrigerator. "Downing."

The CEO/engineer sat up, wiped away the steam that filmed

over his glasses, and stretched until his back popped.

"As a doctor," Ethan said, "I can let you in on the little-known secret that bending yourself into a paperclip for long periods of time is bad."

"Thanks. I'll file that away."

"What are you doing back there?" He didn't really much care, wanted out and away from everyone, but while general isolation and lack of socializing was one thing, this place was too small and tight-knit for overt rudeness.

"Trying to figure out if it's feasible to install some kind of battery here. If we could keep the fridge going twenty-four/seven, instead of relying on whatever cold it can store between generator runs, our food situation would be a lot better."

"And if you can? Where are you going to get a battery?"

"One thing at a time."

"Walther?" the old woman called over. "Do you need anything?"

"Just a glass of water would be great, Chavela, thanks!"

Ethan took the opportunity to move on. Downing seemed to have toned down the ethnic barbs, whether because he was actually coming around or simply realized they wouldn't be tolerated. Whatever initial conflict he'd sparked between himself and Chavela, they'd moved past it or at least put it aside.

Be nice if I had that option myself.

As he stepped back into the cold breeze, it occurred to Ethan that, for all the time they'd been forced to spend together, he didn't know all that much about the man. The CEO of Cedalion Enterprises, an engineer of no small skill, the living avatar of oblivious white privilege, and a nervous fidgeter. That was it.

Who had he lost when the world ended? A family? A spouse, a lover? Kids? Friends, though God knew how? What were his dreams? What had he still meant for Cedalion to accomplish?

How little any of us really understand each other. A fact for which Ethan remained grateful.

He passed the folks gathering in the common hall, ready to set out for the kitchen and their own breakfasts. Nodded politely at Marcus and several others clustered around a map of the yard and a list of crops, debating what to plant when the weather changed. Watched for a moment in mild fascination as Lieutenant Dukes and a couple of former guards checked over the gear in the armory, taking apart and oiling a few of the shotguns, gathering random shells to fire so they could be sure the batch hadn't gone bad.

Caught his breath, as he did every time he passed this way; clenching his fists and his gut, steeling himself.

One of the larger rooms—Ethan thought it had once been a guards' break room, though he couldn't swear to that—had been converted into a play area for the children of Travis County Prison. Tag, soccer, those were outdoor activities, but here were board games, jump ropes, a few dolls and action figures, even a hula hoop. Whatever simple entertainments could be scrounged and scavenged that didn't require ongoing power. Under the supervision of two of the parents—they rotated regularly—the kids spent large stretches of the day here, keeping out from underfoot as everyone else went about necessary chores and upkeep.

His gaze locked straight ahead, refusing even to glance toward the open door, Ethan rushed past at a swift, stiff-legged pace, struggling to tune out the giggles and jokes, the arguments and cries.

With a sharp gasp, he was through. Another turn, another hall, and he gratefully hauled the door shut behind him. He was safe, for a while.

He flicked on the lights, taking advantage of the running generators to get his tools organized and to gather the flashlights and powerful lamps he'd be using throughout the day. It wasn't much, as clinics went. Walls discolored by the wear of years, a few creaking metal-frame beds, and a bunch of shelves and cabinets containing bandages, needles, stitching, a variety of cleansers and antibiotics. Scarcely better equipped than a first aid station, really. They'd never expected to need much more. After all, in case of *real* emergency, Austin's hospitals were only a quick ambulance ride away...

The lights flickered and died as the generator shut down. Ethan leaned back in his rickety chair. The nearest lamp was only inches away, but he left it off, letting the darkness wash over him. The clinic was peaceful, a sanctuary even more so than his own cell. Here, nobody popped in to chat, knocked on the door to see if he wanted to join them for dinner. Nobody came to the infirmary unless they needed to, and on an average day, a quiet day, few needed to. He might get a quick visit from someone who'd gashed a hand on a stubborn tool or tweaked their back pulling weeds. Nothing he couldn't handle in a few minutes.

God willing, today would be a quiet—

"Doctor Bell?" The door thumped beneath a timid knock. "Are you in yet?"

Dammit.

"Yes, just a moment!" He thumbed the switch and the portable lamp glowed white, painting thick shadows on discolored walls. "Come on in!"

He knew the woman who first stepped through the door—he knew everyone here, to one extent or another—though he couldn't recall her name off the top of his head. Pale, thin, brunette, with a worn demeanor that made her look far older than her thirty-some-odd years. She'd had it rough even before everything went to hell, or so he understood, having fled an abusive bastard of a husband and worked two jobs trying to raise her...

A small figure entered behind her, limping, face puffy from crying.

...her daughter.

Ethan wanted to scream. To weep. To send them away. To rail at God Himself, *What do you want from me?!*

Instead, he smiled, imagining his teeth gleaming in the lamplight. *Like the Big Bad Wolf.*

"Well, Mandy." Funny he had no trouble remembering *her* name. "What happened?"

"She was running through the dining hall," her mother said. The *again*, though unspoken, was as loud as the rest of it.

Perhaps ten or eleven, the dark-haired girl was old enough to want to seem brave. So it was without further tears, though through constant sniffles and quavering voice, that she described how the game of tag had moved indoors, how she was looking back to see if Tishon was still behind her, how she'd thought she was farther from the tables, and the jutting seats attached to them.

Ethan had helped her up onto one of the examination tables during her recitation. His hand tingled where he'd touched her; he wanted to grab a scalpel and saw it off.

"All right." Was that his voice? How the fuck was it so steady? "Let's take a look."

The knee was badly swollen, already a mottled purple.

His attention wandered, following her leg upward to the hem of her skirt, hiked high from scooting against the exam table.

For God's sake, stop! Please stop...

"Okay, Mandy, now I need you to be brave just a little bit longer, okay? I have to see if you've broken anything, and I'm afraid it might hurt. Can you be brave for me?"

The girl's eyes went wide and her breath quickened, but she nodded. Her mother came over and took her hand.

Ethan prodded carefully at the swelling, ignoring the renewed tingling in his fingers, ignoring Mandy's whimpers of pain, ignoring what the sound did to him.

His vision clouded and for just an instant, he clearly saw his other hand reach for the nearest hypodermic to jam it in his ears, rupture his eardrums so he wouldn't have to hear anymore.

In that moment, his hand had wandered. He no longer felt the spongy flesh around the injury but the smooth skin of Mandy's thigh.

"Well." He stood abruptly, forcing his cheeks to smile until they ached. "You did very well, Mandy. I don't think anything's broken. We're going to put a brace on that anyway, to help it heal for a few days, and I'm going to prescribe some painkillers from the stores." He turned to Mandy's mother, a presence he deeply resented even as he nearly drowned in gratitude that she hadn't left. "She'll need to take it regularly, with meals. It might upset her stomach a little, so she needs to drink a lot of water, too. And keep off that leg. Bring her back in, oh, three days and we'll see how it's doing."

He sleepwalked through the thank-yous, the feel-betters,

the passing off of pills. When they were gone, he slumped back into his chair and dropped his head into his hands.

Not again. Not again. You will not give in again. You will never *give in again!*

Do no harm. Do no harm. Do no Goddamn fucking harm!

Not again.

The day crawled by in a slow-motion blur. He had other patients, the usual minor scrapes and abrasions, but he couldn't remember a thing about them. He ate a small dinner, he was sure he did, but not a taste of it registered. He couldn't even recall whether he'd gone to the kitchen again, or if he'd sat oblivious in the hall until someone brought him something.

Thinking back later, he had vague, partial memories of an unusual hour or two of socializing, of laughing voices and the slap of cards on table. He may even have laughed himself, and he must surely have spoken, but they were all of them actions performed by someone else. Whoever it was he'd thrown on over his skin while the real Ethan Bell curled up and cowered within.

A few minutes in Cynthia's cell, feeding and playing with Lombardi, who possessed the only two eyes in the entire prison that he didn't feel were peering into his soul, burning through his masks, judging and hating and promising violent retribution. Then, finally, as the evening's generator run wound down and the lights clicked off, he found himself alone in his quarters.

The door was shut, the window covered by a makeshift curtain. Again Ethan selected darkness, ignoring the flashlight that always stood by his bed. He stared at nothing, and within that nothing, all through that nothing, was Mandy, her skirt hiked high, her expression not one of pain but confused fascination and mischievous innocence.

Ethan broke into ugly, wracking sobs. Hot tears and thick ribbons of snot ran unimpeded down his face, into his mustache and beard, even as he fumbled with desperate haste at his belt, planted himself on the cold metal toilet seat, stroked himself to fearsome, shuddering, shameful climax over the span of seconds.

For long minutes he sat, limp and hollow, making no effort to clean himself up at either end.

He'd tried. For so long, he'd tried. He'd restructured his practice: adult patients only. Deliberately fallen out with Leslie's sister so they'd stop visiting—and bringing his niece with them. He'd even tried to leave the damn planet, at least for a while, worked hard to get back into the program, back on ISS rotation.

But there was no escape, not really. Even now, after the end of the world, there was no escape.

And nobody he could turn to. Nobody he could tell, dared tell.

Leslie had known something was wrong, almost from the beginning. It was why she'd worked with him, tried so hard to make the marriage a success, why she'd supported his every change in lifestyle, his every effort—and why she'd eventually drifted so far from him, why she'd finally left. Even now, Ethan didn't know how much she'd figured out, or how much she'd admitted to herself. He hoped it wasn't a lot.

He shouldn't be here. *Couldn't* be here. Damn Cynthia for guilting him into staying! For not understanding!

And damn me for not trying harder.

Decision made.

He wasn't aware at first than he *had* made it, only that he was finally cleaning himself up, washing in cold water from the sink, toweling off just enough to get dressed again.

Flashlight in hand, he carefully pushed his door open and stepped out. With his fingers mostly covering the glass, he had just enough illumination to avoid running into things without disturbing any of his neighbors who chose to sleep with windows uncovered or doors open. Once he'd crept into the first unoccupied hall, he uncovered the flashlight and broke into a rough jog.

At least, at this hour, the playroom was dark and empty. Small favors.

Once in the clinic, Ethan turned on the lamps and made for the medications. Between what he and the others had brought with them, what Marcus's people had gathered, and of course what the infirmary already possessed, the selection was substantial, but what he sought was pretty damn specific. Still, it should be here; this *was* a prison.

Drawers opened, slammed. He sorted through bottles, through large plastic bins, digging like a squirrel unearthing acorns. The irony and even hypocrisy of the situation, given the circumstances under which he'd confronted Cynthia back aboard the station, weren't lost on him. Still he searched, ever more desperate.

Nothing, nothing, come on, why the hell hadn't he finished organizing this place once he'd started, nothing…

Yes.

Medroxyprogesterone acetate. An antiandrogen with multiple uses—including chemical castration.

The place didn't have a lot of it. This was, after all, an institution intended for shorter sentences. Severe sex offenders would mostly have been sent elsewhere. It should be enough of a supply for several months, though. Enough time to come up with some other solution. Maybe a strong course of the right antidepressant, many of which were known to decrease libido…

Ethan had the first needle in hand, reaching again for his belt so he could inject the stuff deep into the muscle of his thigh, when he heard voices. The sounds were so muffled, so distant, he wasn't certain at first that they *were* voices. Certainly they'd be inaudible from most of the men's housing unit.

Somebody wanted their conversation kept secret.

The doctor gave serious thought to ignoring it. He had his own secrets, let other people have theirs. Besides, how bad could it be? An illicit affair? Maybe someone wanted to leave? So what?

When he left the infirmary, however, he headed deeper into the darkened halls, not back toward the living quarters. Maybe he'd grown paranoid over the past few weeks, maybe he was just curious, but something about what he'd heard, no matter how faintly, had felt not just secretive but furtive.

He kept his flashlight dark, feeling his way in the dark with one hand trailing against the wall.

From around a corner up ahead, a faint light glowed, and the voices grew clear.

"...have stayed one more fucking day. *One day.*"

That sounded like Vivian. The hell was she doing down here?

"Look, bitch, I don't fucking care who's here and who's gone. Just tell me it's still going down. I'm fucking sick of this cell."

And *that* was a voice Ethan had only heard a handful of times, but was unlikely to ever forget.

A careful peek around the corner confirmed it. Vivian Reed stood at the near end of the next hall, her back turned toward him. She held a shotgun braced over one shoulder, and a large canvas bag lay at her feet.

Facing her were Eugene McKinnon and most of the other inmates who'd remained locked up when the bulk of the prisoners escaped under the influence of the obelisks.

Except they weren't locked up now, were they?

"Mr. McKinnon," Vivian said, "we don't really like to use violence unless it's necessary. But call me bitch one more time, and I'll show you how flexible my definition of 'necessary' can get. There aren't so few of you that I can't do without one."

Eugene snickered, but kept any further comment to himself.

"And yes, it's still going down." She kicked the bag over to the convicts, who eagerly tore into it. The contents proved to be a selection of kitchen knives, wrenches, hammers, and other heavy tools. "I reported that most of the astronauts left, but Lamb didn't spend weeks planning this just to give up on it."

Holy shit.

"No guns?" one of Eugene's people complained.

"Not necessary, and frankly, I don't trust you enough. Once this is over and you've shown yourselves to be *reliable*..." She sneered audibly around the word. "...then you'll have more privileges."

Eugene nodded, hefting a claw hammer. "Fine. Let's do this shit."

"Don't forget. You only kill if you *have to*, McKinnon."

"How would you know?" he taunted.

"Lamb will know."

She said it with such sincerity, such conviction, one couldn't help but believe. Eugene nodded.

Ethan was already backing away. He had to wake everyone, alert Marcus...

"Howdy, Doc."

He'd barely registered the voice as another of Eugene's people—a sentry they'd been smart enough to set, and he'd been oblivious enough to miss—before a fist landed hard against his right kidney and Ethan could do nothing but scream.

Chapter Four

He hadn't entirely expected to wake up. One of the louder voices of his mind wished he hadn't.

He remembered the first spike of agony, remembered hitting the floor. He remembered Eugene's sneering "Hi, Doc!" and he remembered a hail of fists and feet. Vivian had been shouting something—maybe about not killing him? He'd honestly been beyond caring at that point—before a heel to his skull set off a final detonation and then nothingness.

Ethan pried his eyes open, wincing at the light, the nausea, a hundred different flares of pain. He couldn't have been out long. His head ached, but he didn't think he was concussed. *Of course, if I was, I might not be thinking clearly enough to recognize it, would I?*

One particular ache at his wrist, as he discovered when he tried to roll over and was jerked to a halt with a *clink*, proved to be a pair of handcuffs. He was chained to one of the tables in the main hall.

He rolled the other way, vomited across the floor, then scooted as far from the mess as the chain allowed. Perhaps the acrid fumes completed the process of waking him, but Ethan finally began to take stock of what was happening around him.

Lights were on, which meant someone had started the generator. From all around, he heard the moans and cries of others. Some, like Ethan, were cuffed or tied to the tables or, in the case of Lieutenant Dukes, the stairwell banister. Others were unrestrained but backed into the far corner under the watchful gaze of one of Eugene's compatriots.

The watchful gaze and the gaping shotgun. Apparently

Vivian's efforts at keeping firearms out of their hands hadn't lasted long. Ethan tried to summon a reassuring smile for Mandy and her mother, near the front of the pack, but he couldn't pull it off.

To judge by Duke's bloodied and swollen face, and the similar condition of several more of Marcus's people, Ethan had no doubt where the weapons had come from. He hoped nobody had died in the process.

The convicts must have caught everyone sleeping.

Shouting and loud clatters and clangs sounded throughout the building, from open cells and darkened halls, audible even beneath the wail of an alarm siren. Footsteps echoed in a growing stampede. Once or twice, a shot rang out. Surprise or no, Eugene and Vivian didn't have the numbers to take the whole building without a fight. The sounds of struggle were omnipresent, impossible to pinpoint, and Ethan felt a swell of hope. The more separate battles waged, the more likely any individual or pair of inmates could be isolated and overwhelmed. Indeed, the occasional worried glance from the man guarding the hostages confirmed that things weren't progressing nearly so smoothly as the agitators might have hoped.

A shout sounded from above, cut off by a wet thud. Ethan saw a man he'd treated for a twisted ankle four days ago—Robert, was it? He wasn't sure—come tumbling down the steps, half his face caved in by some blunt object. Several hostages screamed as the body thumped and tumbled to lie limp at the base of the stairs.

"Give it up, Marcus!" Even raw from shouting, Eugene's vicious tone was unmistakable. "You ain't winning this!"

The response was a pair of rapid shotgun blasts and loud cursing.

What are they doing? They're outnumbered, outgunned, what do they expect to…?

The last of the fog finally cleared. Without the fuzz of disorientation, Ethan's many pains redoubled, making him cringe, whimper on the verge of tears. He also, finally, remembered everything he'd heard before the beating, and thought clearly enough to understand what it meant.

"Marcus!" He tried to make himself heard over the chaos, but it hurt so much to shout, to try and catch his breath. "Marcus, it's not just them! They—!"

A shadow fell over him, and he looked up into the lone sentry's shotgun. "Wanna keep talking, Doc?"

Fuck it. Shoot me. Be easier on the both of us. He struggled to draw one more breath, utter one more shout.

The roar of an engine—no, multiple engines—drew everything to a sudden halt. Hostages and fighters on both sides stopped. Listened.

Realized the significance of the alarm they'd been hearing, that they'd ignored in the struggle, chalked up to the inmates' escape.

Perhaps two dozen people poured in through the main doors. Men and women of every ethnicity, every shape and size, all they had in common was the hardware. MP5 submachine guns, M4 carbines, and a variety of other military-grade weapons spread out to cover the entire room, the doors, the balcony above.

Behind them, under heavy guard, came the night sentries responsible for watching the gate. The poor souls had hit the sirens as soon as they saw trouble coming. Thanks to Eugene's and Vivian's uprising, nobody had responded.

His own weapon dangling from a shoulder strap and steadied in one hand, Carlos Morales stepped to the front of the new arrivals.

"You've looked better, Doc."

"I'd imagine so," Ethan said.

As though that had been some deep exchange, Carlos nodded, his face solemn. Then he raised his weapon and fired a barrage into the ceiling.

The lingering sounds of struggle faded.

"Have I got your attention?" he shouted. "Captain Olmos, I don't know if you remember, but we shouted at each other a lot a few weeks ago across the fence! Before we tried to shoot each other!

"Well, I'm not one to hold a grudge, you know? So I got no desire to see you or any of your people die here. But that's up to you! There's more of us outside, we've got a *lot* more guns, we're inside the walls, and, well, not to get ugly about it, but you've got a lot of people down here who don't wanna get shot even more than I don't wanna shoot them! So how about you put down the hardware and come on out, and we can chat like reasonable guys!"

Fearful panting, occasional sobs, and impatient shifting formed the only response.

For a moment.

"If we give up," Marcus called back from one of the adjoining halls, "you won't hurt anyone else?"

"Got my word, Captain! I know you won't believe it, but we're not your enemies here."

Ethan could just imagine the soft scoff, but Marcus proved wise enough to swallow it. Instead, after a few shouted orders and metallic clanks, he and others slowly filtered into the hall from the side and from above. Many were still dressed in their night clothes, robes or pajamas or underwear, and all were disheveled. Walther Downing, hair still matted flat on one side by his pillow, appeared as dazed as any of them, but the half-dried blood around his knuckles suggested he'd put up a fight. Ethan, despite himself, was impressed. And maybe just a bit ashamed.

Even Downing made a better show of it than I did.

At a quick estimate, Ethan figured that maybe fourteen or fifteen people of the entire Travis County Prison colony remained unaccounted for. With any luck, most were hiding, not dead.

Eugene and five of his convicts followed behind the surrendering group, expressions an ugly mix of gloating and fury. Ethan had no doubt at all what had become of the rest of *them.*

And finally, her hair disheveled but otherwise as composed as ever, came Vivian Reed.

The traitor.

Carlos waved a hand, summoning three of his people forward. "Go and find anyone who's still missing," he ordered. "Give them every chance to cooperate." Two nods and a grunt, and they were gone.

"Captain," he continued, stepping toward Marcus. "I'm real sorry it had to go down this way, but you didn't leave us any..."

He trailed off. The captain wasn't even looking his way.

"Vivian?" Marcus demanded through a cage of teeth tougher than any cell.

"Did what I had to," she said. "You'll understand soon."

Only the bristling array of guns retrained him. "Don't fucking count on that!"

If his anger, his betrayal, touched Vivian at all, she gave no sign. "Even if not, I'm sure you'll agree this was better than us blasting our way in. For you and us both."

You and us. Originally, Ethan had wondered if Vivian had been recruited only lately, via whatever secret method of communication Lamb's people had established. Now, it sounded like she'd been a deliberate plant, on Lamb's side since before she ever "took shelter" here. This was their plan from the get-go.

Just another reason to regret, to resent, not having gone with Cyn and the others.

Eugene appeared behind Marcus, lips peeled back like an enraged ape. He spun the guard captain around, drove a fist into his gut, kneed him in the face as he doubled over. Marcus hit the floor gasping, strings of blood wobbling from lips and nose, one tooth dangling loose in its socket.

Several of Eugene's surviving toadies closed in to watch as the convict passed a thick steak knife from left hand to right and raised it high.

Carlos's own fist closed around his wrist and Vivian stepped between him and the captain. "Back off, McKinnon."

"What?! Fuck you, bitch! This motherfucker's gotta pay for—!"

"You were promised freedom and maybe the chance to join us," Vivian said. "Settling petty grudges wasn't part of the deal."

Eugene yanked himself free of Carlos's grip. "If you think I'm just gonna—"

"Lamb prefers us not to spill blood unless we have to," the other man told him. "Vivian should've made that clear to you."

Vivian frowned at that. "I did. More than once."

"Gotcha. Give me the knife and step off, Mr. McKinnon."

The convict was shaking, near purple with frustrated rage. "And if I don't?"

A dozen gun barrels pivoted his way. Vivian smirked, while Carlos's smile remained friendly and genuine.

"Any more questions?" he asked.

Spitting obscenities, Eugene tossed the knife to the floor and stormed from the room, a couple of his friends following after.

"Please help Captain Olmos to a seat," Carolos ordered. "And someone uncuff the doc to look him over."

Grateful to be free of the painful clamp—and to get away from the mess he'd puked up earlier—Ethan moved over to prod carefully for a couple of minutes at Marcus's battered face.

"You got lucky," he said softly. "Somehow your nose isn't broken."

"Yeah, that's how I feel all right. Lucky." Marcus's jaw barely moved as he spoke. With every word, Ethan could see the man's toes clench against the pain, even through his boot.

Ethan stood. "I need bandages," he told Carlos. "Saline, antibiotic ointment, gauze, and tape. And some painkillers." He glanced around at the others who'd been brought into the hall, then poked at a few of his own lacerations. "A lot of all of them, not just for Marcus."

Carlos barked orders. Four of his soldiers—along with two of the locals, to lead them to the infirmary and help carry supplies—headed out.

Only then did Ethan feel a sudden surge of panic. Odds were they wouldn't even notice the syringe lying on the desk in the clinic, or the various other meds he'd left strewn around. Even if they did, they most probably wouldn't recognize the names, know what they were used for.

That wasn't comforting. His secret, his struggle, wasn't anything he wanted to leave to "odds" and "probably." It was, however, far too late to do anything about it now.

Two more of the invaders returned as the first group left, prodding three more of the missing ahead of them at gunpoint.

"Still not everyone," Vivian reported after a quick head count. "But almost."

"Good." Carlos slipped his MP5 off his shoulder and handed it to Vivian. "We are the New Covenant. My name is Carlos Morales." He politely directed the new arrivals to sit with everyone else. "And you see? We're not looking to hurt any of you. We're not your enemy."

"The fuck was that attitude a few minutes ago?" Lieutenant Dukes growled from the stairway, followed by mutters of agreement from one side of the room, murmurs of anger from the other.

Hands raised, the leader of the invaders moved to the center of the hall. "Look, I get it. Tonight was ugly. We're violent, when we need to be. And we don't take no for an answer.

"But this is a new world, with new rules and new enemies, and there just ain't that many of us. The other bands out there? They're aimless. Out for themselves, and way too eager to pull the trigger. Some of you've seen that for yourselves."

Ethan's thoughts flew back to the firefight outside the hospital.

"We have to be united," Carlos continued. "Someone has to call the shots. And Lamb's the man for it. He knows better'n anyone what was wrong with the old order, and what needs to happen in the new one. How to bring us together and make sure we not just survive, but *thrive*. Rebuild!"

Oh, good. Ethan heard Cynthia's voice in his head so clearly he almost looked for her. *For a minute I was afraid these guys were fanatics or something.*

"But more than that, he understands the Obelisk-Bringers and the Hunters far better than you or me! He protects all of us in the New Covenant, and he can show us how to fight back, in ways you don't even know enough to imagine yet! You'll understand once you've gotten to know him, once you see what he's capable—"

"Hey! Marcus!"

The call came from the second-floor balcony. Ethan didn't know when Eugene had returned to the main hall, but he stood there now, so determined to be noticed he was willing to interrupt Carlos's speech.

The man radiated smugness, a cruel gloating far more

frightening than his earlier murderous rage. Ethan felt the return of his earlier nausea.

"I have good news," Eugene continued, "and I wanted to make sure you were the first to know! Looky what I found!"

He stepped back from the chain link restraining wall and briefly out of view.

He returned dragging Chavela Olmos along with him.

"Marcus?" Fearful and quavering, barely audible from above.

"Mama?" His words quivered through battered jaw and battered emotion.

Sporting a gruesome jack-o'-lantern grin, Eugene hauled her around and drove a piston-like fist into the old woman's face.

Shouts filled the room from wall to wall, shouts of horror, of fury, so thick they threatened to cut off the air. Marcus thrashed, screamed wordless, incomprehensible sounds. It took Ethan and four others to hold him back for his own sake, terrified he might get himself shot in his unthinking rage. Carlos, too, shouted, pointing, and half a dozen of his soldiers charged up the stairs, footsteps shaking the balcony.

And Eugene kept pounding, punching, over and over, though his knuckles grew split and inflamed, though Chavela's face was a misshapen mass of blood and broken angles, her twitching body held upright only by his grip on her collar.

One of the New Covenant grabbed the old woman about the waist while the other drove the butt of his assault rifle into Eugene's side. The convict staggered, gasping, dropping to one knee, and the remaining four soldiers gathered around him, guns leveled.

"Doc!" Carlos spun, now pointing at Ethan. "Get up there!"

Given his own injuries, the stairs were a struggle, but he moved as swiftly as he could. A single glance told him he needn't have rushed.

Chavela's only movement was the spasming of a single finger and the bursting bubbles as a ragged breath passed through a mouth full of blood.

Bubbles that ceased even as Ethan knelt at her side.

He went through the motions. He checked her pulse, forced

swollen eyelids open to examine her pupils. All for show, to be sure of what he already knew.

Numb, Ethan moved to the top of the stairs. Everyone stared up at him, many weeping openly. He was a bit startled to note that Downing, twisting his glasses in his hands, was among them, his face soaked with tears.

Ethan could only muster a worn, "I'm sorry."

More sobs, more shouts, from below. Those who had held Marcus back now held him upright, helping him to sit before he collapsed.

Behind his mustache and scruff, Carlos's cheeks were mottled red, his jaw clenched until it bulged. "Bring him the fuck down here. Now!"

Eugene didn't fight the men holding him, but neither did he move to cooperate, forcing them to manhandle him down the stairs. Several of his own people followed, expressions pugnacious but wary of the guns.

"You did this," Eugene said upon reaching the ground floor. "You and Reed. Marcus was *ours*! If you hadn't—"

Carlos drove a fist deep into the convict's gut, and the man clearly knew how to throw a punch. Eugene wasn't a fragile, brittle-boned old woman, but he dropped to the floor, wracked with dry heaves.

"I don't know if I'd rather put a round in the back of your fucking head," he growled, "or just put you in a room with Captain Olmos and a few of his friends for half an hour."

"That..." Eugene coughed, spat a gobbet of phlegm and bile at Carlos's feet. "That'd... really put the lie... to your... 'don't like violence' pussy bullshit."

Vivian moved closer, though whether for moral support or to intervene was unclear. "Carlos..."

Whether Carlos would have carried through with either threat, whether Vivian might have talked him down, they would never know. Before either could speak another word, the main doorway once more flew wide.

A sense of calm settled over the room like a light, comforting quilt. Ethan felt his fears, his revulsion, his grief, diminish. Not *much*—he still felt all of it—but muffled enough to take the edge off. Among the prisoners and the convicts and the New Covenant, shoulders untensed and breathing grew less frantic. Ethan had never felt anything quite like it, even under the influence of medication.

The first into the hall were eight more New Covenant soldiers, as heavily armed as the first batch. What drew Ethan's attention, however, what drew *everyone's* attention, was the man who followed just behind. A man who seemed, though Ethan couldn't explain *how*, to be the source of that unnatural calm.

"My name," the stranger said, to Ethan's complete and utter lack of surprise, "is Joshua Lamb."

Chapter Five

He looked, if anything, like a small-town preacher or politician. Hair and goatee in blended shades of blond and gray framed a face naturally fair but weathered and reddened by the elements. He wore the trousers and vest—but not the coat, despite the outside chill—of an ash-colored three-piece suit.

Something hung about his neck on a cord of braided leather, but Ethan couldn't tell what it might be. The end of the thong, and the object it held, sat tucked in Lamb's vest pocket.

"I'd be very much obliged," he continued from his introduction in a voice that might have carried across a running factory or a battlefield as easily as it did the hall, "if someone could tell me what all the shouting's about."

Every member of the New Covenant straightened and turned his way. To Ethan, it appeared somewhere between a military "falling in" and a congregation rising for their priest.

Carlos cleared his throat. "We've had a bit of upset, Mr. Lamb."

Lamb waited, unmoving save to look where Ethan stood beside Chavela's body, as his lieutenant reiterated all that had happened. The doctor couldn't help but notice, and shiver at, Lamb's wide and unblinking gaze.

"I see," the New Covenant leader said as Carlos wound down. "Vivian?"

"I explained our policies when we recruited them, Joshua. And again tonight."

"I see," he repeated. Then, with a deep sigh, "Please rise, Mr. McKinnon."

When he proved slow to do so—out of orneriness or because

he hadn't recovered from Carlos's gut punch—two of the New Covenant hauled him up by his shoulders.

"While your assistance in our endeavor is appreciated, Mr. McKinnon, it's quite clear that your time in prison taught you nothing. You cannot be trusted to abide by society's rules."

"Man, fuck you! You ain't 'society'! Society's *gone*! It's—"

Lamb raised a hand, halting Carlos as he moved to throw another punch. "You have no place," Lamb continued, "in the New Covenant. You have until dawn to gather any possessions you might have, tend your injuries, and make whatever preparations you require. Then you will leave."

"Fine by me." Eugene shrugged off the hands still holding him. "I don't want any part of your fucking freakshow!"

"No!" Marcus, too, struggled free of those who'd been helping him, wobbling to his feet. "You're just going to let him go? After he... after..."

"Captain Olmos, is it?" Lamb moved to his side, clasped him by the shoulder. "I'm sorry for what happened. I truly am. But if we throw aside our own rules on whim, what sort of society are we building? We shed blood only when we must, and we haven't the resources to keep prisoners long term."

"He murdered my mother," Marcus rasped, tears falling once more.

Eugene smirked, gloating. Somehow, without looking, Lamb knew it, too. He shifted to one side, blocking Marcus's view.

"I know. Think of it this way, Captain. What has Mr. McKinnon to look forward to? A life of scrounging and want, without protection from the Hunters, the obelisks, or any remaining survivors we haven't yet dealt with. It will be a life without comfort—and almost certainly not a long one."

Ethan felt a touch of satisfaction watching the convict's expression fall. He was surprised, however, that Marcus seemed, though still distraught, more composed after hearing it. *That same unnatural calm, maybe?*

Lamb turned back toward the convict. "Any of your friends are, of course, welcome to leave with you, if you can talk them into it. I wouldn't recommend it, of course, but I won't stop them. Those who choose to stay will be given the same treatment and the same options as everyone else."

Not that you've explained what that treatment and those options are yet, Ethan couldn't help but think.

As if he heard the thought, Lamb looked upward and smiled at him. "Doctor Bell, I presume?"

"Uh, yes. That's right."

"Please continue treating the injured." Then, to Carlos, "Have everyone untied and uncuffed. We're all going to be friends, and I don't believe anybody here's foolish enough to try anything untoward."

A few of the locals—Marcus, Dukes, three or four others—still looked resentful enough for Ethan to doubt Lamb's optimism. Where the rest were concerned, however, the man was spot on. They seemed more frightened or resigned than defiant, though that peculiar, almost alien sense of calm kept them from being overwhelmed.

As Ethan returned to work and those prisoners who'd been restrained were released, Lamb moved through the crowd, addressing them as whole, yes, but also as individuals, pausing briefly before each and every one of them.

"For those who haven't heard of me, I am the architect of the New Covenant—of the foundation of the new world. As those who have been with me for a while will tell you, I am no despot. Although our introduction has been a violent one, I have no interest in conquering you, enslaving you.

"Nor is it arrogance when I say only I can guide you, protect you from the threats that would see us all dead or subjugated to the will of the obelisk-bringers. I know them, and I have been granted gifts to battle them."

He smiled, pausing in his rounds. Ethan realized that, as he passed each person by, Lamb had on occasion frowned or nodded ever so slightly, as if he'd subjected them to some test only he understood.

"Many of you are thinking that I'm full of it, full of *myself,* maybe even delusional. That's okay. I'm not deaf to how this sounds.

"We'll be staying here a few days, taking the opportunity provided by your prison to rest. You'll all have the chance to talk to my people, hear what they have to say, and maybe even to see for yourselves what it is I have to offer. What God-given gifts I have to share.

"When we move on, unless you've proven yourself unsuitable, each of you will be welcome to come with us, as part of the New Covenant."

"And what," Marcus asked, "if we don't *want* to sign up?"

"Then you'll be free to make your own way, as Mr. McKinnon must. I really don't think you'll want to, though. It's rare that anyone chooses to leave after seeing how much better life with us can be.

"Besides," and here Ethan swore Lamb focused on him specifically, "I might even be able to help some of you with your own demons as well.

"For now, unless you still need first aid, please try to get to sleep. You all have so very much to see in the morning."

When Ethan finally woke up, having already missed most of the morning, his first conscious thought was that he might just stay in bed and give the rest of the day a pass as well.

Everything hurt. He'd treated his wounds, downed a handful of painkillers, but nobody took a beating like he'd suffered the night before without the aches to show for it. For some time he tossed and turned beneath the blanket, trying to fall back asleep, or at least to find a position that didn't hurt.

Only when all such efforts failed, and he found himself beginning to stiffen, did he rise from the bed with a grumbled but heartfelt "Fuck it."

The hall below was deafening, louder than he'd ever heard it except in the midst of battle. Hardly a surprise, given the sudden population surge. The New Covenant occupied the bulk of it, with Marcus's people keeping mostly to themselves—also hardly a surprise. If Lamb really meant for the locals to join up, he had an uphill journey ahead of him.

Ethan reached Cynthia's quarters and nearly had a heart attack. *The door was open!*

A quick peek inside showed nothing missing, little disturbed—and most importantly, Lombardi hiding under the bed, doubtless spooked by the strangers and the excess noise. Relief swiftly giving way to irritation, he refilled the cat's food and water, decided the litter box could go a while yet, and stormed out, carefully shutting the door behind him.

A moment's indecision about where to go next, then he jogged downstairs and headed for the outer doors.

"Hey, Doc!" One of Marcus's people waved him over to a table. Ethan allowed himself to be coaxed off course.

"What's up, Robbie?"

"You heard?"

"Um. I haven't actually been awake that long. Heard what?"

A few moments later, when he finally hit the door, Ethan was even more irate, determined to find Vivian or Carlos or Lamb himself and give them a piece of his—

For long moments he could only gawp at all that had changed.

The prison grounds, and the lot outside the gate, were packed with vehicles and brimming with activity. Dozens of cars, SUVs, and vans sat within, but it was the trucks that snagged his attention.

Two fully refrigerated sixteen-wheelers stood beside the kitchen, people toting foodstuffs in and out like a parade of ants. A full-sized tanker truck was currently exiting through the gates to take its place back in the outer lot; Ethan would learn later that it had been refueling the generator.

Or rather, one of the generators. A second one sat on a trailer, ready to be used as needed. Several more people worked on it, Downing included, doing Ethan couldn't guess what.

Two other tanker trucks—one propane, one water—sat outside, waiting for the third to join them. Alongside those was a pair of flatbeds with *a military helicopter* on each: one in the camouflage patterns of the Army or Marines, the other sporting the orange and white of the Coast Guard.

And speaking of camouflage, a small fleet of military trucks stood at the far end of the campus. The whole operation was under heavy guard, but those in particular were tightly surrounded by men and women with very big guns.

Struggling not to trip over his own feet as he stared, Ethan moved into the yard. He pushed through several clumps of people, several lines of folks carrying supplies, and around several trailers before he finally found one of the trio he'd been searching for.

"Vivian."

She'd seen him coming, yet she appeared almost startled when he spoke to her. "Doctor Bell."

"Something wrong?"

"No, it's just…"

"Just," he picked up as she trailed off, "you're surprised I'm speaking to you."

"Nobody else from the prison colony will. And before you ask, no, I don't blame them."

"You *did* spend weeks lying to them, pretending to be one of them, so you could set them up."

"Had to be done. Trust me, it was a lot less bloody this way."

Ethan grunted. "How did you get the inmates out of their cells without power?"

"The doors *do* have backup keys, Doctor. They were a pain in the ass to get to, but I had time. Is that really what you came to ask me?"

"No." Ethan began walking, trusting that Vivian would follow, out of curiosity, if nothing else.

"This is incredible," he said, waving at pretty much everything. "How big *is* the New Covenant?"

"Several hundred of us, now."

"Christ."

"And you can already see how people are better off with us, can't you? We have supplies, goods, amenities nobody else has. Food, medicine, fuel, and more than enough firepower to protect it all.

"We have mechanics. Engineers. Doctors, though not nearly enough. Teachers, to educate the children."

Ethan tripped, then made a show of looking around as if to see what he'd stumbled over. "Children?" he asked, struggling to sound curious, casual, not panicked.

"Hundreds of us, Doctor. Of course that includes kids. We've got a full curriculum going, daily classes. We've already offered to let the children who live here start participating."

He wanted to run, though after the rumors Robbie had repeated to him, he wasn't sure how far he'd get if he tried.

Instead, deliberately changing the subject, he said, "Even your fuel isn't going to last indefinitely. And there's only so long you can scavenge what's out there before it goes bad."

"We've got our people—and Mr. Downing, now—working on that. Not just biodiesel, either. We've picked up some hybrid cars on the way, collected some solar panels. We should have alternatives by the time we're out of gas."

"You're really trying to build a new society here, aren't you?"

"That's what we told you. Are you surprised?"

"I, uh, don't necessarily trust the word of people who have captured me at gunpoint, Vivian."

She actually laughed at that. "I suppose that's fair."

"So what's in those?" he asked as they moved around the kitchen and the military trucks once more came into view.

The answer didn't come from Vivian. "More supplies."

They both turned, Vivian straightening, as Joshua Lamb approached with a friendly smile.

"What kind?" Ethan pressed.

"Important."

"I thought you were being honest with us."

"Not lying, Doctor Bell, is not the same as keeping secrets. We don't know that we can trust *you* yet, after all.

"Vivian, please go see to the preparations for this evening. I'll take over the good doctor's little tour."

She nodded sharply and left.

"Preparations?" Ethan asked.

"A service. For Mrs. Olmos and the others who didn't make it."

And whose fault is that?!

Ethan allowed himself a moment to examine this man whose name he'd heard from so many, who seemed to hold such ambition. Lamb's expression was more relaxed, but otherwise he looked unchanged from last night, even wearing the same suit—sans jacket—or else one just like it. Ethan wasn't sure the man had even slept, though he showed no signs of fatigue.

Plus he wore that same...

Lamb smiled wider still. "Curious about this?" he patted his vest pocket, then removed the object on the end of the leather cord.

Whatever Ethan had expected, a small glass vial full of what appeared to be gravel and sand wasn't on the list.

"A reminder of past setbacks," Lamb told him. "And a token of hope for victory." He slid it back into the pocket and seemed disinclined to explain further.

As he was already planning to challenge the man's authority on other matters, Ethan didn't press.

Before he could say anything, however, Lamb spoke again. "Come. Walk with me."

So they did, and this time the sea of people, however busy they were, however caught up in their own tasks, parted for them as though Lamb was Moses striding before the Israelites.

For a few moments, Ethan allowed him to speak, pointing out more of the features and supplies and advantages Vivian had alluded to.

Until, finally, "Mr. Lamb?"

"Only if you're more comfortable with it. 'Joshua' is also fine. Whichever you prefer."

"So noted. Mr. Lamb, I understand that McKinnon left early this morning. Took a couple of his guys with him."

"As he was supposed to, yes."

Ethan steeled himself. So far, Lamb had been nothing but polite, but that could readily change. "I'm also given to understand that several of Marcus's people tried to leave and were turned back from the gate at gunpoint."

"Ah. I see. You've come to protest, have you?"

"You did say we'd be allowed to go our own way if we decided not to join."

"Doctor." Lamb led them into the lee of a small storage shack and out of the cold wind. "Have you ever had a patient check himself out of the hospital against medical advice?"

"Well, yes, but—"

"And would you have prevented that, if you could?"

"The law says—"

"But *if* you could?"

Ethan didn't care for where this was going, gave some thought to lying, but, "Yes, if I felt they didn't understand the significance of their decision."

"There you go, then. *When* everyone has seen what we can offer, has truly been made to understand the protection I can provide against the Hunters, against the Heretics of the Cathedral, *then* they will know enough to make an informed choice. Not before."

Heretics? Cathedral? The hell? Lamb wasn't making Ethan any more comfortable with all this.

Perhaps spotting that doubt on Ethan's face, Lamb continued, "I've also got to consider the good of the community as a whole, Doctor. I can't protect people once they've left. Not reliably, at any rate. McKinnon and his deviants, they know they'll find no sanctuary here. But if I were to let others depart before we do? Suppose they run into the Hunters and, by some miracle, escape? Where do you suppose they'll run?"

"Ah. Back here. And just maybe bring the Hunters with them."

"I'm glad we understand each other."

"I suppose so." Ethan started to turn away, stopped himself. "Listen, I realize things were chaotic last night, but in the future, if any of your people are going to search the living quarters, please have them close the doors. My friend's cat almost escaped."

"We wouldn't want *that*. I'll pass it along." Then, as Ethan once more made to leave, "Is there nothing more you'd like to see, Doctor Bell?"

"I'm sure you must have more important things to do than playing tour guide."

"Oh, I think you'd be surprised." They walked again, side by side, though Ethan didn't quite recall when they'd resumed. "You're a special fellow."

"Yeah, yeah, I know. Not enough doctors." The constant walking and talking was starting to make the ache in his ribs, his back, and his jaw flare up again.

"True enough, but not what I'm talking about. Many of my people were drawn to me because I could help them. And you, Ethan, are one of the most in need of my gifts."

It's "Ethan" now, is it? Though it wasn't the use of his given name that set him simmering with offended ire. "Look, Mr. Lamb, if you really want to help people, it's appreciated, but you have to realize all this talk of 'gifts' is a little—"

"Off-putting?" If Lamb was offended, he did a remarkable job of concealing it. If anything, he sounded mildly amused. "Foolish? Perhaps even delusional?"

"Well..."

"Of course it does. You're an educated man, a man of science and medicine. You don't believe the human mind capable of oracular insight or extrasensory perception. You're not certain you believe in God, and you definitely don't believe in 'psychics.'"

Ethan could all but hear the quotation marks. "Exactly."

"Of course, you don't believe we've been visited by aliens, either."

He found himself unable to formulate a reply.

"Ethan, you've seen people enraptured by the Scripture on the obelisks. Given the limitations of the English language, what would you call writing that can rewire the mind, if not psychic?"

"Um."

"Most of humanity, well, they're gone now because of it. You're happier not knowing exactly how." He offered Ethan no opportunity to argue that pronouncement. "But some weren't affected in quite the same way. A few were instead driven mad. Some only moderately—paranoia, hostility, mania, that sort of thing. Troubled but fully functional. I've taken them in where I could, made them part of my New Covenant. Others became catatonic or bestial, even downright murderous. All I could do for them was end it quickly. We haven't the means to treat them, care for them."

Ethan sputtered in horror, revulsion.

"An even smaller group seem unaffected by the obelisks at all," Lamb continued. "Immune, or at least resistant. And then... Then there's me."

"You."

"Yes. Perhaps others as well, but if so, I've yet to meet one. I found a new understanding of the universe in that writing, Ethan. A new *faith*. But it also granted me its blessings. It's how I keep my people shielded from the Hunters, from the Cathedral. It's how I can do things like this."

He made no motion, his expression didn't change, but Ethan's aches and pains faded until they were barely noticeable, a residual twinge he felt only if he focused on it. He gawped like a fish, unable to believe what had just happened.

"There are a few people I can't protect," Lamb admitted. "People whose minds, for whatever reason, whatever quirk of the brain, won't allow me to shield them. I *think* they're the same who would be driven mad by the obelisks, if they were exposed to the writing, but haven't been yet. That's just a theory, though."

Ethan practically choked. The man was talking as though he hadn't just performed a minor miracle. "You... You just... How..."

"I'm sure you have questions, but now's not the time. I'll tell you more, much more, once you're one of us, once I'm certain I can trust you."

"I'm still not entirely certain *we* can trust *you*," Ethan retorted, getting hold of himself.

"But that's why we're here! So I can help you, and prove my friendship to you." He sat himself on the chair beside the bed.

Bed? My bed?

It was. Ethan couldn't comprehend when, even how, but their steps had carried them back into the housing unit, upstairs to his cell. He didn't even remember moving back indoors!

"It must have been hell, Ethan. I'm so sorry."

"It... What are you talking about?"

"You've been so very desperate to escape it. Isolating yourself from family, altering your practice. You even tried to leave Earth itself. And why? Because society would judge you, shame you, punish you for being who you are."

Ethan didn't so much sit on the edge of the bed as fall onto it. "How...?"

"You still have to ask?" Lamb's smile gleamed, positively

angelic. "Besides, what matters isn't how I know. It's that you don't ever need to feel like that again. Dana?"

At his call, a slender figure entered the room. She wore jeans and a tee-shirt, and her hair in cornrows that were just starting to fray. Ethan, his breath catching, would have guessed her to be around twelve or thirteen.

"Dana's actually a little bit older than you prefer, I believe," Lamb said, "but she's small for her age. I think you'll be quite happy. I admit, I find it distasteful personally, but it's not about my preference, is it? It's about me ensuring my new world has a place where you can be yourself. Truly, finally, yourself."

You're no protector, you bastard! You're Satan! You're the fucking Devil! But he couldn't force the words out.

He did, however, manage to mutter something else, something under his breath. He'd no idea he was doing it, let alone what he was saying, until Lamb leaned in to hear it.

"'Do no harm.' Commendable, Ethan. But I assure you, you won't be." He cocked his head, tapped a finger against his temple. "I can ensure that Dana won't recall any details of your time together. Even if your affections *were* harmful, she won't suffer any."

"How... how can you do this? How is this any different than drugging her? How can you think that makes it better?!"

"But Dana wants this, don't you dear? She knows I would never ask her—never *permit* her—to do anything that wasn't in the best interests of all we're trying to build. Isn't that right?"

"Yes, Joshua." She knelt, resting her hands on Ethan's knee, her chin on her hands, and gazed up at him. He wanted to scream, but it wasn't remotely *all* he wanted.

"It is, of course, your decision, Ethan. Just know that, whatever you choose, I'll never judge you. Never let you suffer for being who you are." He rose, and a couple of long strides carried him from the cell. "I'll leave you two to talk it over."

The slamming door echoed in what remained of Ethan's thoughts long after Lamb was gone.

Chapter Six

He'd awoken only a minute or two ago from inescapable, almost feverish dreams that crumbled from warm and comforting into soul-flensing nightmares and back again. Now, arms crossed behind his head, Ethan lay back and watched, through eyes still narrowed against the overhead light, as Dana dressed herself in the clothes she'd left lying on the chair.

It took her three attempts to button her jeans for shaking fingers, and she sniffled constantly as though fighting a cold. Deliberately or not, she would not meet his gaze.

That the girl was upset was obvious. In his near-drowsing mind, exulting in his newfound freedom despite his bouts, Ethan felt that he probably ought to have a better idea of *why* she was upset. Honestly, though, it wouldn't quite come to him. Still...

"You're going straight to Mr. Lamb, right?"

"Wh-what?"

"Mr. Lamb? He's supposed to help you?"

"Oh. R-right."

He found himself frowning, concerned and resenting that concern for impinging on his newfound contentment. *I'm going to have to speak to Mr. Lamb myself, find a better way to handle this. I don't like the idea of her hurting even for as long as it takes to track him down.*

Dana reached the door, shoved it with both hands.

And was nearly bowled over as someone took the opening door as license to come in.

"Doc—oh!" Downing swerved just in time to avoid said potential bowling. "Excuse me. Doc, we've got to talk. I'm *really* not sure about this whole Lamb-Covenant business, and I want to know what..."

He jerked to an abrupt halt, his mind presumably catching up to what he'd just seen. Slowly, pushing his taped and mangled glasses back up the bridge of his nose, Downing craned his neck to look behind him.

He and Dana locked eyes for an instant, and then she vanished into the hall.

Just as slowly, he turned back, staring down at Ethan, who was obviously half undressed if not more so, based on the shoulders and upper chest showing above the edge of the blanket.

Ethan felt little of the absolute panic he'd have felt only a day earlier, but this still wasn't a conversation he wanted to have, wasn't information he wanted to spread. "Walther..."

"You... sick... *fuck!*"

He'd seen the CEO of Cedalion Enterprises belligerent, irritated, put out, even fighting for his life. But until this moment, Ethan had never seen the man *enraged*. He actually found himself scooting back on the bed, sitting up against the wall in a futile attempt to avoid Downing's advance.

"You bastard!" His fists rose, white-knuckled, trembling. "What the fuck is *wrong* with you?!"

"Walther, it's okay. It's—"

"Okay? *Okay?* What is she, twelve? Thirteen?"

Somehow, *I'm not sure*, while honest, didn't feel like Ethan's best bet.

Nor did Downing apparently expect an answer. "I was actually starting to like you! Do the others know?"

"No. You think I'd still have worked for NASA if they did?" He'd expected the words to emerge plaintive, self-pitying, and was surprised to realize that he sounded more angry than anything. *Who the hell were they to judge?*

And for that matter...

"Who are *you* to judge me, Downing? Why would I *want* you to like me?" Ethan shot upright, standing beside the bed, unconcerned with his own nakedness. "You're pretty well a dyed-in-the-wool bastard in your own right, aren't you?"

Ethan honestly expected Downing to take a swing at him,

but the other man controlled himself. "Yeah, *Doctor*. I'm an asshole. I'm selfish and opportunistic."

"And fucking racist."

Downing's scowl grew sharper still, but whether because he acknowledged the truth of it or just wasn't willing to argue, he ignored the comment. "But I am *not* a child molester!"

"It doesn't matter! You're talking about the old world, old laws! And Lamb's making sure this doesn't cause any harm!"

"What the fuck are you *talking* about?"

"His gifts!" Ethan poked a finger at the side of his head. "I've seen them, felt them. They're real. And he's going to make sure Dana doesn't suffer any psychological damage. Don't you see? I can be who I am, *without hurting anyone*! After all the horrors we've seen, I've finally found something good!"

"Something..." Downing staggered back, fingers reaching for his glasses in his habitual fidget, then dropping to his sides. "You're insane. And if Lamb knew about this, he's fucking insane, too!"

Still shaking, he stormed from the room. Ethan thought about following, then shrugged.

He couldn't entirely blame the man, still stuck in old ways of thinking. This *would* have been horrific, not that long ago. The guy just needed to accept that the world had changed.

And he would. There was a man with his own demons, certainly. One of these days, Lamb would find a way to help him, as he had Ethan.

Then Downing would understand.

For most of the day, the confrontation with Downing was the furthest thing from Ethan's mind.

The arrival of the New Covenant meant his skills were in demand as never before. He showed Lamb's other doctors around the infirmary, how he'd organized about half the medicine supply and would like the other half arranged as well, and they in turn provided access to drugs and equipment he'd previously lacked. The ongoing work kept them busy with a veritable conveyer belt of cuts, gashes, scrapes, bruises, strains, sprains, and the occasional break.

Ethan worked on it all, cheerfully. Even more than after he'd readjusted to Earth's gravity, he felt as though he could move again, as though he weren't fighting the atmosphere and his own body. Even when one of Mandy's classmates came in with a piece of broken glass in her foot, he found himself only moderately distracted. He could do anything, deal with anything, knowing that Dana awaited him.

And when she got older, well, no reason Lamb couldn't provide the same mental and emotional protections for one of the other girls, was there?

It was a bit past sunset, after most of the inhabitants had already eaten. Ethan and the others were just closing up, tired and more than eager to go grab a bite for themselves, when Carlos appeared in the infirmary door.

"Hey, Doctor Bell? Mr. Lamb would like to see you."

"That's fine, but can it wait until I've had dinner? I'm—"

"Afraid the man said *now*, Doc. Seems there's an, uh, incident he'd like your input on."

Grumbling, Ethan waved in a "lead on" gesture. He paid little attention to where they were headed at first, assuming Carlos was taking him to the guards' operations center, which Lamb had transformed into his business office/audience hall.

Only when they turned instead toward the door did Ethan start to wonder, and that wondering turned to surprise as they marched across the grounds, the grass already trampled into a smooth carpet by the constant back-and-forth of the past two days.

Their destination turned out to be the frontmost structure, the one that stood both within and without the gated perimeter, where prison visitors had once signed in and office workers had gone about their daily routines.

Where pockmarks in the outer wall and a couple of broken windows still showed the evidence of the New Covenant's *first* attempted takeover.

Several lights glowed within. Having brought more than enough fuel, Lamb had ordered power restored to several buildings beyond the housing unit and the kitchen. Ethan wasn't entirely sure what this place was being used for, but right now it played host to a nerve-wracking tableau.

Lamb half-sat on a desk at one side of the room, his attentions distant. Five of his New Covenant soldiers stood clustered halfway between him and the door, brandishing automatic weapons.

And in the midst of them waited Marcus and Downing, expressions defiant, heavily laden backpacks lying at their feet.

"Ah, good." Lamb rose, nodded to Carlos, smiled at Ethan. "Thanks for coming."

Ethan absently shook the offered hand, but his focus was on the two... prisoners? "What happened?"

"I'm afraid Mr. Olmos and Mr. Downing have rather abused my hospitality."

"*Your* hospitality?" Marcus snapped. "This was *our* place! You—"

Either Lamb's upraised hand, or the rather more numerous upraised barrels, silenced him.

"They tried to leave?" Ethan asked. It wasn't all that much of a guess, what with the packs.

"Indeed they did."

Downing was no surprise, but Marcus? Ethan would have thought Marcus would rather die than abandon his people.

But then, they weren't really his people anymore, were they? He'd been beaten and betrayed, watched his mother brutally murdered, seen his authority usurped and his home conquered all in the span of one night. Maybe the surprise wasn't that he'd tried to leave, but that it had taken him two days to make the attempt.

"So what's the problem? You've already turned them back, like the earlier group."

"That's just it. 'Like the earlier group.'" Lamb sighed, leaning against the doorframe. "Discipline, Ethan. Rules. They're all that make society function, especially a burgeoning, struggling society like ours. Warnings are all well and good when people don't know any better, but once they do, that discipline has to be enforced."

"Wait, wait a minute." He closed, got in Lamb's face as much as he dared. Several of the armed disciples shifted, fidgeted, but nobody actually aimed a weapon his way.

Yet.

"How do you even know they knew?" he demanded. "Maybe this was just another misunder—"

"They knew. Word spread quickly that morning. Besides, they snuck out through the gate as part of a work group, then hid until everyone else came in for dinner. Are those the actions of men who don't know they're transgressing?"

"Um."

"And where do you think they got their supplies? The New Covenant has a lot, but not so much that we can afford to let people steal from us."

"Mr. Lamb…"

"You know how much I prefer to avoid violence, but—"

"Then avoid it, for God's sake!" He nearly smacked Lamb, waiving his hands about for emphasis, took a step back to avoid even the appearance of a threat.

"I have to make an example, Ethan! My own people know the importance I place on discipline, on the rule of law. What sort of message am I sending if I treat newcomers any differently?"

Ethan fell silent, mind racing. The faint whistle of the wind through the broken windows a few rooms over filled the building.

"So make an example," he said finally, "but a mild one. Downing's far too useful a resource to throw away after one infraction. And Marcus? You do anything too nasty to Marcus, you can forget *any* of his people joining your New Covenant."

Was it Ethan's imagination, or did the corners of Lamb's lips quirk in the faintest hint of a smile?

"Both valid points. All right." He turned toward the two condemned men. "Both of you will be placed under guard until you've regained my trust. You'll be allowed out of your cells only to work, and you'll be supervised at all times. You're also on short rations for, oh, let's say three days. And gentlemen, I need you to understand, I'm not being a hard-ass for the thrill of it. My rules are for everyone's benefit, your own included. Once I believe you *can* be trusted, I'll be more than happy to explain.

"Please return them to their rooms."

Neither appeared entirely convinced, but they went along without prodding. Ethan smiled at Downing, hoping his advocacy might partially make up for their misunderstanding that morning, but the CEO's face remained stone. Ethan would've had more luck trying to get a giggle from his own reflection by scratching it under the chin.

Once everyone else had gone, Lamb said, "I want to thank you for your input."

Ethan grunted. More and more, he was starting to feel like he'd just been part of an elaborate stage play for which they'd neglected to give him a script.

Why had Lamb even called for him? Vivian knew Marcus much better than he did. And yes, he knew Downing better than anyone else present, but so what? Lamb hardly struck him as the sort to be so easily talked out of a course he'd already chosen, and he was *certainly* smart enough to have already considered all pros and cons of treating the would-be escapees gently.

No, this had been a performance. But had it been for the New Covenant's benefit—to prevent grumbling when Marcus and Drowning got off lightly—or was it for Ethan's own, an opportunity for Lamb to prove himself reasonable, merciful? If so, why? Ethan would already have followed the man into hell, for freeing him.

"I know what you're thinking, Ethan," Lamb said, then laughed at the sudden stricken expression. "No, I don't mean literally. I'm not reading your mind. I just mean it's obvious.

"And maybe you're right. If the New Covenant is going to grow, to birth a new humanity, it needs to be controlled, but perhaps I've gotten into the habit of being too strict. It's an easy enough to trap to fall into at the best of times."

He clasped Ethan's shoulder. "But I want the New Covenant to be a refuge. A collaboration people *want* to join, without force. It's so much safer than being by yourself in this new world, but people need to *feel* that to believe it."

His hand dropped abruptly, as did his expression. "Come to think of it, you have friends wandering alone out there right now, don't you?"

Ethan stepped back out of reach. "If this has all been about getting me to help you find Cynthia and Grigory…"

For the first time, Lamb's scowl looked offended, perhaps even hurt. "Is that what you think?"

"I… No, I'm sorry. It's a sensitive topic. I'd wanted to go with them, and I worry about them."

"Of course. I understand." Lamb paced most of the room's length before continuing. "Obviously, yes, I believe your friends would be better off here. They're in even more danger than they could possibly understand. If they knew half of what I do, they'd never have gone."

Ethan shivered.

"But it's entirely your call. I won't try to make you reveal anything you don't want to."

"Couldn't you just, you know…" Again Ethan poked a finger at his temple. The gesture felt silly—hell, the whole *notion* still felt silly—but he'd seen too much to disbelieve. "*Take* what I know about where they've gone?"

"Even if I could," Lamb replied, once more beaming that beatific smile, "what sort of trust could *that* possibly build?"

With a polite goodnight he was gone, leaving Ethan alone to ponder.

Still picking bits of breakfast from his teeth with his tongue—bacon, mostly—Ethan wandered down the hall beneath the overhanging balcony until he reached a particular room. The man leaning against the wall beside the door grunted what might, eventually, have grown up to be the word "Morning."

"Morning," Ethan replied. "Is it okay if I see him?"

The guard mulled it over. "Hmm. I guess Mr. Lamb just said he couldn't leave outside work detail, not that he couldn't see anybody, so sure. Give a yell when you're done." He turned, pounded on the door, then hauled it open.

They weren't keeping it locked. Guess they figured Downing knew better than to try anything else.

Other than the bedsheets, which were wadded up against the wall, the cell was meticulous. Downing himself sat at the small desk, working—surprise, surprise—on his glasses with that tiny screwdriver. He didn't pause, didn't look up, as Ethan entered and the door clanged shut.

"Those frames aren't going to hold up too much longer. You should probably try something more than tape and new screws."

"Good to know," Downing said. "Nice chat. Fuck off."

Why am I even here? Why do I care what he thinks? He'd never liked Downing, not from the moment they'd met, with plenty good reason, and he'd only been given ever more reasons as time went by. No, he hadn't wanted to see the man shot or caught by Hunters, but other than that, who gave a rat's ass?

Yet here he was.

"Look, Walther—"

"That sounds like you speaking, *Doc*. Not like you fucking off."

Ethan felt his throat giving slow birth to a growl. "Okay, you don't like me. Fine. You don't have to approve of me. But—"

"Approve? *Approve?*"

"*But*," he repeated, refusing to be interrupted, "you really need to start trusting Lamb. He's got his rough edges, but he's trying to build something good here. Something worthwhile. And I know there's a lot you can do to help! They need you here. For everyone's sake, and your own, you need—"

Downing finally turned from the desk, hatred radiating from stooped shoulders and clenched jaw. "Let me tell you something," he said, scarcely above a whisper, "about your trustworthy, child-peddling dear friend Lamb."

"He's a liar, Doc. A fraud."

"What? No, I've seen his—"

"His whole 'We're only violent when we have to be' spiel? Crock. Of. Shit."

Ethan began to sit down on the edge of the bed, then thought better of it as Downing's face purpled. "What are you talking about?"

"His people didn't catch up to Marcus and me for a good half hour or so after we snuck out, did you know that? We played a bunch of hide-and-go-seek in the woods out behind the neighborhoods."

"Okay?"

"You want to take a guess what we found out there?" His voice remained low, so that Ethan practically had to lean in. It only belatedly occurred to him that Downing was trying to ensure the guard heard nothing through the door.

"I really have no idea."

"Eugene McKinnon and his two friends. They'd been covered by a heap of dried leaves until something dug them up and snacked on them."

"I-I don't understand."

"The other two? They'd been shot once each in the back of the head. But McKinnon? They took their time and spared no bullet, Doc. Kneecaps. Shoulders. If he was real lucky, he passed out at the cock shot."

"You don't know that was Lamb's people!"

Downing's glare took on a tinge of pity. "Are you that stupid or just that desperate? Who the fuck else is out here? It was Lamb, all right. Well, probably Carlos and a few others. They waited until McKinnon was far enough away that nobody would hear anything, wouldn't spoil any of Lamb's 'reluctant bloodshed' bullshit for the masses, and took them out."

"They deserved it," Ethan insisted, feeling just a touch queasy.

"Didn't say they didn't. Marcus was elated, and I don't blame him. But what do you think would happen to us if Lamb knew we knew?"

"Nothing would happen, because Lamb's not what you think he is! He probably just realized McKinnon was a threat and didn't want to upset anyone."

"You're an idiot." Downing went back to work. "But if you're so sure, tell him what I told you. See what happens to me. That'll make things easier on you anyway, right?"

He was wrong, Ethan knew that much—or, if not wrong per se, then at least misunderstanding. Lamb knew what he was doing. If he'd ordered McKinnon and his companions killed, if he'd hidden that fact from most of the New Covenant, he had his reasons.

The man was trying to build a whole new society, for Christ's sake! "Don't kill unless you have to" was a damn important part of that foundation, and if he couldn't always afford to practice what he preached, it remained worthwhile—vital, even—to preach it!

Lamb just hoped Downing would come around sooner than later. The guy was just smart enough and just petulant enough to cause more trouble, even to his own detriment.

In the interim, though, Ethan decided to say nothing about the grisly discovery. Not that he was afraid Downing was right about Lamb's reaction—there was no reason to be afraid—he just didn't feel it would be helpful to sow any further distrust.

There was no reason to be afraid.

There wasn't.

He was just dozing off that night, sated and warm beneath the covers, his back pressed up against Dana's, when the walls trembled.

He bolted upright, placing a hand on the cement. It vibrated, as though with distant thunder, but constant, unending. From the sounds of stirring and the flickering lights he could see through the gaps in the curtain; others in the unit stirred as well.

Ethan yanked his pants on, pulled a shirt over his head. "Dana?"

"You go." She still faced the wall, curled up tight, knees to her chest.

He started to say something, then just tugged his shoes on and went. If he didn't know better, he'd wonder if Lamb's "treatments" were even working. As it was, he'd begun to grow impatient with her general sullenness. It made her hesitant, reluctant, even in the midst of her best moods, and that had begun to damage his own.

Something to worry about later.

The main hall was already close to full with bleary people, but while Ethan recognized the signs of concern, even fear, he saw only a few expressions as confused as he felt. Ignoring all of them, he made his way outside.

The sound was louder out here and, though still distant,

seemed to make the air itself harder, heavier. The night smelled of something almost, but not quite, ozone. Lamb, Vivian, Carlos, and a dozen others stood in the yards, gazing to the southeast. Ethan followed suit.

There. In the dark of the moonless overcast, he swore he spotted a faint trace of motion, high and far, as though some great hand stirred the clouds themselves.

"What—?"

"*Shh!*" The hissed admonition came from half-a-dozen mouths, Carlos's and Vivian's included. Ethan obeyed, swallowing his questions.

The peculiar rumble went on, and on… and finally faded. Lamb stumbled as if he'd been shoved, gasping through clenched teeth. Hands reached to steady him, but he waved them away.

They, in turn, tried to wave Ethan off as he approached, until Lamb said, "No, it's okay." Then, when he drew closer, "Thanks, Ethan, but I'm fine. Just need to catch my breath."

The doctor, however, hadn't been thinking entirely about Lamb's health. "What *was* that?"

"The Cathedral," he said, then clarified as Ethan continued gawping. "The Heretics, my friend. The obelisk-bringers."

"Good God. Did… Are we in danger?"

"No. Well, no more than usual, anyway. They couldn't sense us."

Ethan began to ask why, until the reason for Lamb's exhaustion dawned on him. He could only repeat, "Good God," this time in awe.

Lamb chuckled. "I told you, I protect my people. It was… difficult, tonight, with so many relative strangers here. The better I've come to know someone, the easier it is to shield them, and the farther away I can do it. If Captain Olmos's followers weren't all concentrated in one spot, I don't know that I could have helped them all."

"I'm definitely starting to understand," Ethan began, "why you don't want people wandering off on their…" The words clung suddenly to his throat.

"You're worried about your friends."

Ethan said nothing, but… Southeast. The thing was moving southeast.

"Yes," he finally admitted.

"I can certainly understand that. It seems it's not only the Hunters they've got to avoid."

Chewing his lower lip, Ethan pressed his head to the chain link fence. He'd made Cynthia a promise!

But would he have, if he'd known then what he knew now? Was it worth keeping at the cost of her life, their friends' lives?

Lamb's hand came to rest once more on his shoulder. "You know I'll treat them fairly. The Heretics, the Hunters, won't."

"I…" Ethan swallowed, hard. His teeth still ached from the shape's passing. In the dark, he saw JD's body, shriveling, collapsing.

"I go along," he insisted. "To make sure there aren't any 'misunderstandings.'"

"Of course, Ethan."

One more second of hesitation, of uncertainty.

But only one.

"Johnson Space Center. I don't know if they'll still be there, but they were headed to Johnson Space Center."

Chapter Seven

The van bumped and rattled across Houston, first some pothole-ridden neighborhood roads, then one of the city's many freeways. Neither those bumps and rattles, however, nor the wheezing chug of the worn vehicle's engine, had been audible over the past few minutes.

Not over Cynthia's infuriated, profanity-laden ranting.

Her tirade ultimately ground to a halt only because she'd run dry of epithets and curses, not because her anger had faded.

The driver and his passenger largely ignored the three "guests" in back, though Cynthia felt certain she'd heard them snickering at her at least twice. Jo continued to stare vacantly at the opposite wall. Only Natsuhiko seemed to pay her any attention, and his expression made her feel like a specimen in a glass cage.

"What?" she snapped.

"You might," he said gently, "want to actually hear Ethan's side of things first. Before calling him any of those admittedly creative names and titles to his face. We don't know any of what's happened since we left, why he's with Morales. Or—"

"He broke his promise! He—!"

"*Or* what they said, or *did*, to make him talk."

Cynthia waved her hands helplessly, then fell back in the seat, letting her head thump lightly against the wall of the van. "Augh! Stop being right, God dammit!"

"Okay. I'll work on that."

Bump. Rattle.

"You *are* right," she admitted. "We don't have a clue what's going on. I just..."

"Yeah. I'm worried, too."

"I should know better, shouldn't I? I mean, it's Ethan, for crying out loud. If there's anybody we *know* we can trust to do the right thing..."

She twisted her neck to watch out the rear window—the *only* window, here in the back of the van—at the highway rolling away behind them. The bench seats, built along the side walls like an old-fashioned police van, made the view uncomfortable but not impossible.

Not that she could see much. Only the headlights of following cars provided any illumination. Other than the occasional reflection of a building when the highway turned, Houston was invisible to her.

Cynthia, who had spent enough time traveling to and from Johnson to have a vague sense of the city's layout, was pretty sure they were on the southern stretch of Loop 610, coming up on the various NRG sporting and show venues, and the partly refurbished Astrodome.

Guess it's never gonna get to "completely refurbished" now, is it?

The shortwave radio crackled, announcing something or other she couldn't make out. The man in the passenger seat said "Acknowledged" into his own transmitter.

Scintillating conversation.

"We were lied to, you know."

It took a moment for the comment to register—in part because Natsuhiko had pitched his voice down, presumably so their captors wouldn't overhear, and partly because she hadn't the slightest idea what he was talking about.

"I haven't," she told him, "the slightest idea what you're talking about."

"Our hacker friend, back at Johnson. He lied to us about how he accessed NASA's systems."

Also speaking softly, "I'd gotten that impression myself, but you seem pretty sure."

"I am. It took days before the interference in the atmosphere cleared enough for us to penetrate, remember? Until then, he'd have had no satellite access. So he hasn't had nearly as long to work on penetrating security as he implied."

"Okay, but—"

"Even if he has equipment to access the satellites, he has no control over them, and the planet-side networks are all down. They'd be moving in and out of position, requiring him to constantly reconnect, and there wouldn't always be one in place to link up with his location and Johnson both. You think he had long enough to penetrate the firewalls and infiltrate the security subsystem under those circumstances? And he just *happened* to have connection, to be in the system, and to be watching the camera feeds, at the precise time we arrived?"

Huh.

"Put that way," she acknowledged, "it doesn't sound likely, does it? I—"

She nearly bit through her tongue, startled and on the abrupt edge of panic, as the side of her head went numb.

They're here! Oh, fuck, they're here!

"Cynthia?" Natsuhiko leaned forward as far as the seatbelt— which they'd been told in no uncertain terms not to remove— would allow. "Cynthia, what's wrong?"

Even as she began to speak, however, the sensation was gone, fading as swiftly as it had arisen.

"The Crooked Men are in Houston!" she whispered.

Natsuhiko paled to the gums. "What should we—?"

"I don't think we're in immediate danger. The numbness went away fast. We probably just passed through their, I don't know, their 'range' or whatever. But they're definitely here."

"Do we warn Lamb's people?"

Now *that* was a question. "Probably," she said. "But not yet. Let's try to get a feel for things first."

"Your call."

"He *did* have access," she said a few seconds later.

Natsuhiko's turn not to follow, now. "Uh, what?"

"The hacker. Whatever lies he told us, he *was* in the system."

"Definitely." He chuckled. "With all your government's budget cuts and bureaucracy, is there any possibility Johnson still had a landline modem somewhere? If he was near enough, he might be able to dial in without going through a connecting server or switching station."

Cynthia snorted. "I doubt it. And even if they did, I don't think he was watching live video feed on a 56K connection."

They'd turned northbound, now, and even in the feeble illumination, Cynthia recognized the massive shape of the Williams Tower skyscraper reflecting the headlights of the following vehicles. *So, okay, that puts us not far from the Galleria and...*

The van rocked slightly as it turned. They were exiting the freeway.

Another turn, another, and another, until Cynthia couldn't even guess which way they were headed. With the final change in direction came a *thump* and the tilt of another ramp, before darkness subsumed everything outside the window.

When the following cars caught up, their headlights returning some reality to the world, Cynthia saw only empty space and the occasional cement column.

A parking garage?

Sporadic abandoned cars, glinting dully in the headlights, confirmed it. The van climbed up several stories before finally coming to a stop.

The engine died. Neither driver nor passenger spoke.

"Um. So, are we supposed to wait," Cynthia asked, "or...?"

The rear doors opened, revealing Carlos and a handful of his people.

"Oh."

Carlos stepped aside. "I hope the ride wasn't too uncomfortable, Ms. Han."

"Drivers were uncommunicative and didn't take direction at all well. Two stars."

"Funny. Please step out of the van now."

She had no desire to do any such thing, but stalling wouldn't serve much purpose. Tense almost to the point of muscle cramps, she obeyed, with Natsuhiko and, after a moment, Johanna following.

Headlights and flashlights provided only a few pools of illumination, but a variety of running motors, slamming doors, and mingling conversations suggested more vehicles, and a *lot* more people, than she could see—or had been part of the convoy that brought them here.

Louder rumbles from beyond the walls suggested engines outside as well. Trucks, she guessed, too large to fit inside. She panicked briefly at the group making itself so visible, at the thought of Crooked Men even now converging across rooftops and skittering along the sides of nearby buildings. She forced it down. No numbness in her head, as yet, and Lamb's people had been operating long enough to know what they were doing.

Presumably.

All thoughts of which fled screaming from the garage and out into the empty city when Cynthia turned and finally saw the second band of people who'd assembled behind Carlos while she'd been distracted. Or rather at one such person in particular.

"Ethan."

Although she couldn't see it in the feeble lighting, she *felt* the flush that came over him. "Cyn, look, I—"

Carlos stepped on whatever explanation or excuse the doctor meant to offer. "Don't mean to be rude, here, but the salutations will have to wait. Lamb wants to see you all, pronto."

He marched ahead, pulling Ethan with him, leaving those who came after to ensure Cynthia and her friends followed suit. She'd have to sit on any questions, demands, or profanities she had in mind for her friend a while longer.

The skyway from parking garage to main building was dark enough to allow a faint view of the outside. Below, on the street, a massive truck was illuminated by an array of portable lights. People swarmed it like ants, adjusting this and hooking that up to the other, and the whole thing vibrated with an inner rumble she heard even from this distance. More vehicles, some even larger, were just visible at the edges of the light, too indistinct for Cynthia to make out any details.

Then they were through.

First, she realized that the structure into which they'd been taken was a fancy hotel, though she'd overlooked any signs or logos that might have told her which one. The halls were broad, nicely carpeted, and this one in particular wound past a bank of elevators to open up into a wide lobby below, full of customer service counters, sofas, and a dining room to one side.

The second realization, of course, was that the place was sufficiently illuminated for her to make out the first.

She nearly walked into Carlos, who had stopped several paces ahead. "Eric and Katherine will take you to a suite where you can get cleaned up," he said. "I'm afraid most of the group only got here an hour or so before we did, so the generator hasn't been up and running long enough to heat the water. I figure you're used to cold showers by now, though."

"Um, okay, but—"

"Hold the questions for later, please, Ms. Han. I'm sure Lamb will be happy to answer them. Dinner's in an hour."

He was off, leaving his new guests in the hands of a small group led, Cynthia assumed, by Eric and Katherine.

"This way." It wasn't a request.

The halls and stairwell were all filled, either by people moving goods and equipment, or by the sounds of conversation behind closed doors. Lamb's "New Covenant"—Cynthia had overheard the name more than once already—was a *lot* bigger than she'd anticipated. She couldn't imagine how they'd managed to keep from attracting the Crooked Men or that colossal ship.

Her shower was, indeed, pretty close to frigid, but she still felt better with the scents and sweats of the past thirty-six hours sluiced away. (Although there was something deeply surreal about making use of the hotel's own complimentary soaps and shampoos, under the circumstances.) While she'd showered, someone had laid out a small pile of clothing for her to choose from, more or less properly sized. She selected a pair of jeans and a light sweater—formality was not, apparently, a prerequisite for dinner with the mysterious Mr. Lamb—but decided on her own shoes. Filthy as they were, she wanted to be comfortable if she had to run.

Though God only knows where the hell I could go.

Cleaned and dressed, she, Natsuhiko, and Johanna found themselves escorted back downstairs by the same group of guards.

Somebody had been busy while they were cleaning up. The dining area was now covered in multiple dishes, heaped with food that, though not exactly fancy, was far more appetizing than what Cynthia had grown accustomed to. Only Chavela Olmos had produced anything comparable, and the scents of steaks and roast vegetables, while appealing, didn't smell like her work.

Several dozen people were gathered around the smaller tables, another sixteen or so about the longest. In the center, Ethan stood arguing with...

Cynthia tripped over her own foot and only Natsuhiko's quick grab saved her from an embarrassing stumble.

For an instant she wasn't in the hotel dining room, but back on the plains of Central Texas, lying flat, coming out of the barrage of imagery and hallucination thrust upon her by her first prolonged look at an obelisk.

This was the face she'd seen in her hallucination.

Slightly less exaggerated, perhaps. The eyes not quite so wide, not quite so blue. But it was him.

Cynthia's mind reeled, trying to explain how this was even possible, when he turned her way.

It was all she could do to swallow a scream.

She could never have described precisely *why* she reacted that way, what had terrified her so badly. She could liken it only to that moment in a nightmare, or a horror movie, when who you thought was a friend or loved one turns around to reveal someone else entirely.

It wasn't a perfect analogy; she didn't know this man at all. She knew only that something was very wrong with whatever watched her from behind the mask that was Lamb's face.

And nobody else seemed to notice.

He smiled, waved them over to join him at his table, but said nothing to them, instead turning his attention back to the doctor.

"...just think," Ethan was saying, "you should have told us earlier."

"How?" Lamb asked. He sounded, to Cynthia's ear, perfectly normal, perfectly rational. She wasn't buying it. "How do you think that would have gone over, Ethan? 'Oh, by the way, I'm going to leave a few of you behind, on your own, because something about your brain makes you impossible for me to hide from the Hunters.' How much trust would *that* have engendered?"

Ethan waved his hands helplessly, carelessly setting a water glass to teetering. Lamb caught it before it could topple. "I mean, I get it. But Lieutenant Dukes? No way Marcus is okay with that!"

"He's not. In fact, I have him under guard until he calms down." Lamb sighed, poured the glass full from a small pitcher, and handed it to Ethan. "I understand you're upset. I do. I've had to abandon friends, too. We do what we must for the group.

"Welcome, Ms. Han, Mr. Hashida, Ms. Kateston. I'm Joshua Lamb. Please, sit. Eat."

Cynthia sat slowly, never tearing her gaze from the man. He looked normal enough, now. Whatever she'd seen in him earlier was gone, hiding behind its mask of flesh.

Or you imagined it, Cyn. Let's not forget the whole "You're gradually losing your mind" possibility, here.

Apparently deciding Cynthia wasn't going to speak first, Natsuhiko said, "I have to admit, this isn't precisely the greeting we were expecting."

"Yes, well." Lamb took a sip of his drink, waved for someone to pass the serving dishes around the table. "I'm sorry about how you were brought here, but I didn't think you'd come willingly. I think you'll find it was in your best interests, though, as well as ours."

"Really," Cynthia said, tone flatter than the table.

"Oh, very much so. Do you think Ethan would have told us where to look for you if he didn't believe it was for your own good?"

"I don't know *what* to think."

Ethan shrank, and for a moment the only sounds at the main table was the clatter of dishware.

"Grigory?" he asked finally.

Cynthia deliberately looked down at her plate. "Didn't make it."

"I... I know, I mean..."

He clearly wanted to know what had happened. Cynthia

wasn't yet prepared to be civil enough to tell him.

The food was good. She barely tasted it.

"What about Downing?" she asked.

"Mr. Downing has gone to bed early," Lamb told her. "He worked very hard, helping us get the generator connected and running so quickly, and he was tired."

She and Natsuhiko exchanged suspicious glances— apparently not so subtly as they thought.

"No, it's true," Ethan insisted. "He's fine."

"Coming from you, that means less than it used to," Cynthia said.

For the first time, Lamb frowned. "Now, Ms. Han, I really must insist—"

"What's this about you leaving people behind?"

His frown sharpened until it threatened to chip the glass next time he took a drink, and several others at the table ceased eating long enough to snarl. Lamb was, apparently, not a man accustomed to interruption.

Which was precisely why she'd done it.

"I take my responsibility to protect my people very seriously," he explained, expression softening as he spoke. "My gifts include the ability to conceal our presence from the Hunters and the Heretics, both."

"Gifts?"

"An unfortunate few, however," he pressed on, ignoring the question, "have proved impossible for me to conceal. And obviously, I cannot risk everyone's safety for them. So when we left the prison to come here, they—as well as any who chose not to join us—stayed behind."

"Well, that's awfully convenient." Had Cynthia's doubt run any thicker, she might have poured it over her plate as a sauce. "A perfect excuse to ditch anyone you don't like or won't go along with your agenda. I assume nobody but you can confirm these people aren't 'safe'?"

"Cyn," Ethan warned, "maybe you should—"

Lamb waved him off. "It's all right, Ethan. As I recall, you had your misgivings to start with, too. I'm not deaf to how this sounds, Ms. Han, and your disbelief is quite understandable.

But I assure you, I'm quite serious and quite sane."

I'm willing to believe exactly half of that.

"And if I weren't able to do what I claim, how would you explain the fact that we haven't been found yet?"

To that, Cynthia had no answer.

"Speaking of which," Lamb rose and leaned over the table. The vial of gravel slipped from his vest pocket to dangle on its leather cord, giving Cynthia her first good look at it. She started to ask...

And rocked back in her chair, her body locked taut, at the burst of agony in her head.

"Ah." Lamb looked away, and the pain faded to a dull roar. "My apologies, Ms. Han. I thought it might be you, but I didn't anticipate quite so dramatic a reaction. We'll discuss it later."

It might be me? What might be me? She couldn't yet catch her breath enough to ask.

Their host went on to study Natsuhiko, who appeared vaguely puzzled, and Jo, who scarcely noticed. Lamb's frown returned for an instant before he, too, sat back again.

For a time he remained mum, allowing them to eat. Only as they were winding down did he speak again, explaining—as he had to Ethan and the inhabitants of Travis County Prison—the significance of the New Covenant. He extolled the virtues and necessities of cooperation, of unity and discipline, of a nascent society capable of protecting itself from threats both mundane and otherworldly, from without and from within. He explained, too, the gifts he'd been granted by the obelisks and by God, not just in terms of what he could do, but of understanding, of *faith*. That his was not merely the voice of one man, but of the divine, a higher power who sought to see mankind rise from the ashes of the old world to be better than it had been.

Cynthia, her skull still pounding, found the entire sermon to be further evidence that Lamb had not only lost his marbles, but possessed zero interest in looking for them.

A situation made worse by how completely most of the room, Ethan included, seemed to buy into it all.

"I knew you were coming, you know."

Cynthia blinked. "What?"

"I knew you were coming." Lamb poked at the roasted vegetables on his plate. A single column of steam rose past his face, a dancing, transparent serpent. "As soon as your vessels hit the atmosphere, the Cathedral picked you up..."

The who?

"...and sometimes, if my thoughts and theirs line up just right, I learn what they know. Then, when you first saw the obelisks, when the Scriptures first collided with your mind as they have no one else's, I felt that, too. Although I didn't know it was you, specifically, at the time. I've been waiting and working a long while for this meeting, Ms. Han."

"I'm... flattered?"

"I only wish it wasn't surrounded by so much unpleasantness." Lamb crooked a finger and one of his people approached the table, carrying a heavily laden backpack. He politely laid it on the floor beside Johanna's chair.

For the first time, she seemed more than half present. "What's this?"

"Supplies," Lamb told her. "I wouldn't turn you out empty handed."

The meal she'd just eaten began trying to work its way back up Cynthia's gullet. She could only imagine how Jo felt. "What?"

"I'm sorry. I truly am. But your mind is one of those I referred to earlier, Ms. Kateston. I cannot protect you."

The obelisks... Jo had been immune to the obelisks...

"No." Jo rose to her feet, trembling violently enough to shake the chair as she pushed it back. "No, you can't leave me alone out there with those... those things! You *can't!*"

"I have no choice." Either Lamb felt genuinely distressed, or he did a remarkable job of faking it. "I'm *deeply* sor—"

"No!"

Jo drove the heel of her palm into the face of the man who'd brought her the pack. He fell back, spitting blood, and she followed, yanking the large chrome pistol from his belt.

Johanna, don't!

Around the table, napkins drifted and plates clattered to the floor, men and women jolting upright, grasping for weapons.

Jo's own pistol twisted back, leveled across the table...

Shock and the disorientation of the screaming headache conspired to dull Cynthia's reactions. She could only stare, slack-jawed, until Natsuhiko tackled her from her seat, dragging her downward…

Was it her imagination? A byproduct of the sudden chaos? Cynthia could have sworn that Jo had Lamb dead to rights, yet the woman froze for a few extra breaths, just long enough…

Half-a-dozen guns fired. A single body fell. And Cynthia, Natsuhiko on top of her, stared through the legs of the chair into Jo's empty, lifeless eyes.

Chapter Eight

The rest had been shouting.

The shouting of Jo's friends from the prison, horrified at seeing her cut down. The shouting of New Covenant soldiers charging in from adjoining halls, weapons at the ready, drawn by the sounds of gunfire. The shouting of Lamb himself as he worked to restore order to the dining room.

And Cynthia, shouting at Lamb for putting Jo in the position to do something so desperate, so foolish, for threatening to turn her out on her own; and at all the others, Ethan especially, for going along with it all, for buying into Lamb's excuses.

This can't be what it takes to survive! This can't be what we've become!

Now she sat in her own private room, to which she'd been firmly escorted. All her possessions were here except her weapons, and the small refrigerator had been stocked with bottled drinks and a few snacks. It would have been quite comfortable, under different circumstances.

She was, she'd been told, free to wander any of the occupied floors on her own. Any visits to the kitchen, the supply rooms, or the hotel's exercise facilities would require an escort—any one of the various guards stationed throughout the building would do—and she was not, under any circumstances, to attempt to return to the garage or otherwise leave the hotel. They didn't threaten any specific consequences if she violated those rules, but Cynthia had no doubt they'd prove severe.

Maybe not "gunned down in the dining hall"-severe—unless

she, too, was crazy enough to pull a weapon on Lamb in front of his people, however much she sympathized with the urge—but bad enough.

So she sat, until the pounding in her head grew intolerable, and then dug into her ever-present pack of medication. It was when deciding between various treatments that her mind finally caught up with recent events and screamed a question she should have asked hours ago.

Yanking her door open, she stomped into the hall on bare feet, pain temporarily forgotten, until she found one of Lamb's sentries standing near the elevators.

"Hey! You!"

The other woman, a short-haired and pale-complexioned Texas blonde, crossed her arms and raised an eyebrow. "Yeah?"

"Where's my cat?"

"Your what, now?"

"Cat? You know? Small, furry animal? Says 'meow'?"

"Cute. The hell should I know?"

"Find out."

The woman straightened. Even figuring that some of her height came from the cowboy boots she wore, she had a couple of inches, and probably several dozen pounds, on Cynthia.

"You givin' me orders, hon?"

I can take her.

Yeah, okay. And what then?

Cynthia choked down pain and pride both until she shook. "I'm sorry. I'm just... I haven't seen him since I got back. I had to leave him at the prison when I left. Please. Please find out?"

The guard remained motionless for long enough that Cynthia was starting to reconsider physical violence, and then dropped a hand to the radio at her belt.

"Hey, Eric? Han's here asking about a cat from the prison. Any idea what she's talking about?"

Static crackled, and then, "*Oh, yeah. I thought he was the doc's. He's with the others.*"

"Roger that. Thanks."

"Others?" Cynthia asked as the radio clicked off.

"Yeah. What, you think you're the only one who managed

to save a pet? The cats live in a room off the kitchen. We figure they'll keep it free of mice and shit."

Not optimal—Lombardi had never struck her as much of a hunter—but at least he was okay. He could stay there until she figured out what to do next.

"Thanks."

"Sure."

Back in the room, Cynthia decided "Fuck it" and went for the Dilaudid. The current headache probably wasn't enough to justify the big guns, but she found it hard to care, and the notion of knocking herself out for the night way too tempting. A quick injection, and then she lay back and waited for the room, the hotel, and everything to do with Lamb and his damn "Covenant" and Jo's death to fade away.

It did, but when she blearily pried her eyelids open to see her window still ink-black, she realized she hadn't been out the whole night like she'd hoped. It might have been only a couple of hours.

She yanked the blanket over her head, buried her face in the pillow, all to no avail. Her options were either *awake* or *more drugs*, and she wasn't quite desperate enough for escape to go mixing Vicodin with hydromorphone just as a sleep aid.

Cursing, she rolled out of bed and grabbed something wet to wash the fuzzy taste of poor sleep from her tongue. That was enough to bring full wakefulness. With wakefulness came thought, and with thought, anger.

She thought about stepping across the hall and pounding on Natsuhiko's door, but why shouldn't he get to sleep just because she couldn't? More to the point, it wasn't just conversation she needed, it was information.

Again she got dressed—shoes and all, this time—and left her room. Either she'd guessed correctly that she'd only been out a couple of hours, or else the guards here worked really long shifts, because the same woman was meandering the same section of hall.

"What now? You lose a dog, too?"

"More like a pig," Cynthia said. "You know where Walther Downing's room is?"

The blonde leered. "Didn't realize you two were so close."

"You make me vomit on this carpet, I'm not helping you clean it up."

"Hmm." The woman flipped open a notepad and ran a finger down the page.

"I see Lamb keeps you all well organized."

"We need to be ready for anything, and that means being able to find anyone. Here he is. Five-seventeen."

"Thanks." Cynthia made for the stairs.

Another guard, this one a broad-shouldered Latino, leaned against the wall near room 517. Cynthia wasn't sure if he was guarding these rooms specifically, or why Downing would warrant such treatment. Since he made no move to stop her, however, she decided not to ask.

For an instant, she paused, fist raised. Was it any more fair to wake him than it would've been Natsuhiko?

Ah, screw it. He could spare a bit of sleep. She knocked.

I can't believe things have gone so completely off the rails that I actually want to speak with Walther fucking Downing.

"It's open!" The response came swiftly enough, clearly enough, that he'd obviously been awake. One less worry, at least, however minor. She opened the door and went in.

He sat at the desk, doodling on hotel stationery. When he turned, she saw that his glasses were, at this point, made more of tape than anything else.

He looked as though he could use some tape himself. Walther Downing looked so worn down he was on the verge of falling completely apart.

"Hey, Cyn! I'd heard they found you. I'm glad you're okay."

"Cyn"? I'm Cyn to him, now? She decided it wasn't worth fussing over.

"I'm okay. Natsuhiko's okay. Grigory and Jo, not so much."

"I heard about what went down at dinner. It's all over the hotel."

"Yeah, and everyone seems just fine with it. Are you?"

"I'm... I don't know. Shit's gotten complicated since you left."

Cynthia sat on the corner of the bed. "Damn. It was all so easy up 'til then."

Downing snorted. Then, "What... what happened to Grigory?"

She told him—and she told him *why*, told him the waking nightmare they'd stumbled into on the shore of Clear Lake. By the end of it, they were both in tears.

"Oh, God." Downing held his glasses in one hand, wiped futilely at his cheeks with the other. "I mean, I... I knew they had to be gone, I guess, but... Oh, God..."

Cynthia stepped into the bathroom, returned with two handfuls of tissue and passed one his way. Downing blew his nose, loudly—it sounded rather like a duck call, and under other circumstances Cynthia might well have laughed—and forcefully pulled himself together.

"I guess the point," Cynthia said when she, too, had gotten hold of her emotions, "is that there's too few of us left. We can't afford to turn people out to die because they don't buy into Lamb's bullshit!"

Downing twisted his glasses, dug around in his pockets for a moment and then—spotting the keychain screwdriver over on the nightstand, well out of reach—gave up. "It's not quite that simple. I mean, I agree with you, to a point. Whole reason I'm under guard is that Marcus and I already tried to take off once. But, uh, Lamb's not entirely wrong, either. Like I said..."

"Shit's complicated. Yeah. How did you all even end up with him?"

So now it was Downing's turn to spin a tale. Cynthia found it, to say the least, less than reassuring.

"How can you even think of going along with this?" she demanded. "If he's willing to work with people like McKinnon, if you're right that he's killing the people he says he's letting go... Jesus, what about Dukes and the others?! And after what happened to Chavela..."

"I haven't forgotten any of it! But look at what else he's done. In a matter of weeks, he's built a group of hundreds of survivors, with supplies, laws, education. They've got a real shot at rebuilding, Cyn. That's not nothing."

"And I guess they'd find someone with your skills pretty

valuable, huh?" It might have been an accusation, or a simple observation.

Downing straightened, put his glasses back on. "They do. As an engineer and a manager, both. I've already accomplished a lot. There's a good chance I could make a real difference. Be someone important."

"Even if it means working for someone like Lamb?"

"I'm not saying I trust him, and I'm not saying I'm okay with his methods, but maybe if I can make myself important *enough*, I can help mitigate some of what he does. Kind of steer things, you know?"

"Uh-huh. The man's a delusional narcissist, Downing. You can't 'steer' someone like that. You fall in line or get walked over."

"That's just it, though. Whatever else he may be, he's *not* delusional."

Cynthia only realized she'd been twisting and fidgeting with the edge of the blanket now that she stopped. "What are you talking about?"

"I don't know he does it, but those 'gifts' he goes on about? They're real."

"Oh, come on—"

"I'm serious! He knows things he shouldn't. He can walk into a room and change the entire mood with a look. And he *has* kept his people safe from the Hunters, though I couldn't tell you exactly how."

Much as she wanted to, Cynthia couldn't dismiss it outright. She'd felt the writings on the obelisks dig into her own head, knew that the Crooked Men were somehow "psychic," much as she still hated using the word. And she'd experienced *something* when the man had examined her at dinner.

To say nothing of that image of Lamb's face, during her first contact with the obelisks.

Some element of truth, though, didn't mean she had to accept every last detail as gospel.

"Even if all that's true, I refuse to believe that abandoning people, or executing them, is the only option!"

Downing nodded. "And it's awfully convenient for Lamb.

Believe me, I know. I haven't made any final—"

"If Lamb has all these abilities," Cynthia interrupted, the thought abruptly sprouting, "how do we know he didn't somehow *make* Ethan tell him where we went?" She felt foolish even saying it, but the more she spoke, the more the idea appealed. It would explain so much, justify so much! "Maybe even more than that! I mean, I can't believe Ethan would go along with *any* of this, with someone like Lamb..."

Downing's expression had soured the instant the doctor's name passed her lips. "Cyn..."

"...if he had a choice! He—"

"Cynthia!"

"*What?*"

The chair squeaked as Downing leaned forward. "That fucking... Your *friend's* not under any damn 'influence.' He's been keeping secrets from you, and he fucking sold himself as soon as Lamb made him an offer."

"The hell are you talking about?"

"Bell's a goddamn pedo, Cyn."

This time it was Downing himself who squeaked. Cynthia was off the bed and looming over him, fists tight and jaw twisted. The chair scooted back as far as he could push it, only to thump into the desk and roll no farther.

"Ethan is my friend, and a better man than *you will ever be!*" She didn't speak so much as roar, unconcerned with who in the hall or the neighboring rooms might overhear.

"Okay! Fine! Sorry!"

"Whatever your fucking problem is, I am officially over your horseshit. Leave him *out* of it!"

She hesitated, wanting desperately to knock his teeth down his throat, then forced herself to turn away.

The door was within reach, her hand hovering above the knob, when the questions she absolutely did not welcome squirmed through her mind, maggots in rotting meat.

Why would he choose now, of all times, to lie to her? It wasn't any of his little bigotries; Bell was as white as he was.

And of all the accusations he might have leveled, why *that* one?

Cynthia watched the reflection of her fingers in the dull brass. It trembled.

"*Fuck!*"

One long stride back toward him, and then she leaned against the narrow length of wall separating bedroom from bathroom. "All right, tell me. What's going on?"

"Nothing." He refused even to look her way.

"Downing…" She pinched the bridge of her nose between thumb and forefinger. "I'm sorry, okay? But we don't have time for sulking."

He glared, which was better than a sullen pout. "Her name's Dana."

It was about the worst thing he could have said. A name made it real. A name made it feel possible.

She sagged, until only the wall held her upright. "No."

"Lamb…" Downing cleared his throat, tried again. "Lamb *gave* her to him."

"He wouldn't! He… He's a good man, he's a doctor…" How pathetic did she sound? How desperate? How many other friends and family had ever said the same about someone they loved? Still, Cynthia couldn't seem to stop herself. "He'd never hurt anyone! Certainly not a child!"

"He doesn't think he *is*." She wasn't sure she'd ever heard such revulsion in Downing's voice. "He told me, when I first caught them together. Said Lamb can make it so she doesn't remember details, so he's not *really* causing any harm. Like that somehow makes it fucking okay."

A sharp rap on the door saved Cynthia from having to reply.

Downing, puzzled, called out, "Come in?" And then, as the door drifted open, "Well, speak of the fucking devil."

Ethan indeed stood, framed by the light of the hall, but he wasn't alone. It was Vivian who spoke. "Sorry for the interruption, Cynthia, but Joshua wants to see you."

"Now? It's… What is it? About four in the morning?"

"After five. But it's not like you're sleeping, right?"

One of the guards must have reported that she was out and about, visiting Downing. Or maybe it was Lamb's so-called mind-reading. Who the hell knew?

"Okay. What's *he* here for?"

Ethan visibly recoiled. "We thought you might be more comfortable if I was here. To assure you that Lamb doesn't mean any—"

"It doesn't." She pushed between the two of them.

Vivian turned to follow. Ethan didn't.

"What the hell did you tell her?" he demanded.

Downing rose from his chair. "The truth."

"You don't *understand* the truth, how could you possibly...? Cynthia?"

He must have just noticed that she wasn't waiting, was already halfway down the hall. Nor did she stop when he called her name.

"Cynthia, I... We should talk later, okay?"

Still she didn't look back. "You have nothing to say that I want to hear, Doctor Bell."

Only after she'd turned the corner did she slow down to let Vivian catch up, and said nothing more on the walk to Lamb's office.

Ethan followed for a few paces, shuffled really, one hand outstretched—and then drifted to a halt. What was the point? This was Cynthia Han. If she'd decided not to speak with him, nothing would change her mind until she *chose* to change it. He should just—

"Hold up a minute, Doc."

It was just as well that Downing had only come as far as the doorway. If he'd come out into the hall, if he'd been anywhere within reach, Ethan would already have started swinging.

"What the *fuck*," he snarled, "could possibly make you think I want to hear a word from you?"

"Pretty sure you don't, any more than I want to be talking to you."

"Good." Ethan moved to go.

"I don't know why you care what I told her, anyway. She'll probably be dead before too long."

Ethan froze near the intersection, teetering in indecision. Then, growling out loud, he stormed back to the open door and stepped inside as Downing cleared the way.

"What are you talking about?"

"That tumor." Downing sniffed and returned to his chair. "Or whatever it is going on in her head."

"There's no reason to think it's going to prove terminal any time soon."

"I don't mean it's going to kill her, I mean it's going to *get* her killed." He sighed, then, at Ethan's uncomprehending stare. "Look, whatever else you are, you're not an idiot."

"How magnanimous of you to—"

"Shut up and listen. You know she doesn't react to the obelisks like anyone else does."

"True."

"Not to the Crooked Men, either."

A blink, then two. "What?"

Downing once again poked at his glasses. "Yeah, I guess you wouldn't know. She told me tonight about what happened while they were away. Turns out she can feel it when those things are nearby.

"So," he continued before Ethan could reply, "how do you think that's going to mesh with Lamb's precious 'gifts'? What if she's one of the ones he can't shield?"

"He'd have said so at dinner, when he told Jo to leave."

"Would he? And even if she's not, what if she's immune to his influence? Or he just decides to use it as an excuse?"

"Why would he—?"

"You think Cynthia's going to just fall in line, like we did? I'd say between the thing in her head and the *hardness* of her head, there's a pretty damn good chance Lamb's not going to want her around for long."

"You're paranoid. Lamb isn't that kind of person. He cares about people."

"Like Jo? Like Dukes?"

"He had no choice!"

"Like Dana?"

The entire floor shook with the sound of the door Ethan slammed on his way out. Nearly blind with fury, he stormed headlong toward the stairwell.

The kitchen. They kept a reasonable stock of booze among the other foodstuffs. A good, stiff drink ought to calm him down, if not enough to sleep then at least enough that he didn't desperately want to break something. How dare he? *How fucking dare he?!* Slimy, manipulative, paranoid son of a...

He stopped at the base of the stairs, wavering. Downing *was* paranoid. The man had never liked Lamb, had never forgiven him for what happened the night they'd taken the prison. Cynthia was in no danger.

But now that the weaselly bastard had put the thought in his head, he wouldn't feel better—drink or no—until he'd proved Downing wrong. With an irritated sigh and a silent promise to make the man pay for this, Ethan turned, not toward the kitchen, but toward the front office.

Chapter Nine

"Are you sure I can't interest you in a drink? Perhaps a light breakfast?"

Lamb had taken the hotel manager's office for his own, and the sheer mundanity of it felt surreal, even dreamlike, compared to the apocalypse surrounding them. A desk, a filing cabinet, an array of chairs and a small sofa, various inoffensive paintings, an obsolete computer... If Cynthia hadn't known better, this might have felt like a job interview.

"No." She'd chosen a chair near the desk, rather than the sofa. Less comfortable, but easier to jump out of. And it somehow felt less submissive. "I'm fine."

His lips quirked. "What you are is suspicious. Do you suppose I'd resort to poisoning you, Ms. Han?"

"Well, you sent Vivian and the others away." She'd been surprised at that; still was, really. "So it's not like you can just have me shot."

Lamb sighed and poured himself a glass of orange juice from one of the hotel's decanters. "I miss the fresh kind. So many other luxuries I've learned to do without, but I just can't get used to stuff from concentrate." A sip, and then, "Ms. Han, I don't enjoy killing people. If Ms. Kateston hadn't gone for a gun—"

"She was still dead, and you know it! Turning her loose out there, on her own? That's still an execution, just a slower one!"

And that's if you weren't going to have her murdered anyway, after putting on a show of "merciful exile" for your peons! She pressed her lips shut before the words could escape. It wouldn't be good for her—or her friends—letting him know what they knew, what they suspected.

"I have to watch out for the community first. We are the seed of a new civilization, Ms. Han! I'm responsible for seeing that it sprouts!"

"Why you? Because of your 'gifts'? Because God speaks through you?"

"Yes."

"Do you even realize how you sound?"

"Of course I do. That doesn't make it any less true."

Cynthia snorted. "That's where 'Joshua Lamb' comes from, right?"

Her host chuckled, took another drink. "You know, surprisingly few of my people have actually made that connection."

"You're kidding."

"I'm not."

"Maybe it just hasn't occurred to them that anyone would be so arrogant as to take the name and title of Christ?"

"Are you normally this rude, Ms. Han?"

"No, this is a special occasion." It might, however, be wise to dial it back. She forced her fists to relax. "So, what's your *real* name? If you don't," she added grudgingly, "mind me asking."

"Joshua Lamb is my real name. If you mean my *original* name, it was Jerold Cabot."

"Ah." Then it sank in. "Your initials were JC?"

"Indeed." His grin had returned, with reinforcements. "So you see, one could argue that I was destined for this, one way or the other. Perhaps it was even... ordained."

Oh, for... "Do you *really* believe that?" She kept her tone as courteous as she could, but the incredulity dripped from each word. "That you've been chosen by a higher power?"

"I do." Lamb turned his gaze to his glass, tracing patterns in the condensation with a finger. "Several, in fact, not just the 'higher power' you *think* I'm talking about.

"Tell me, Ms. Han... What do you make of the writing on the obelisks?"

She blinked at the apparent non-sequitur, then flinched at the memories. "I try not to think about it, honestly."

"Given the pain they cause you, I can't blame you. But I'm

asking you to, now. What do you imagine they're for?"

"I mean, it's some sort of mind control." She scowled at her own phrasing. "Hypnotic suggestion or, um, psychic, or what have you. If there were more of the... the aliens, I'd wonder if it was some sort of invasion tactic, or maybe—"

"They are scripture. The holy text of a faith older than life on Earth."

"Holy?!" The chair creaked with the effort she poured into keeping herself in it, into not lunging across the desk. "You call what they've done to us *holy*?"

"People have killed in the name of the Bible and the Quran. Does that make the words unholy, or those who misinterpret them?"

Cynthia's voice shook. "The human race did not drown itself by the billions over a *Goddamn misinterpretation!* The obelisks *did this to us!*"

"True. Still, perhaps it is we who need to grow stronger, purer. In either case, we can fight them. The Heretics who brought the obelisks, I mean. That's why I carry this." He held out the glass vial she'd noticed earlier.

Again Cynthia felt the abrupt twists in this conversation might give her whiplash. It almost felt...

Nervous? Is the great Joshua Lamb avoiding something?

"What do you mean?" she asked, going along for now.

"The first thing we did, when I'd gathered enough people who were immune or already affected to get close to one of the obelisks, was to try to destroy one of them. We used a few dozen pounds of C4 and several *hundred* of ANFO.

"The result was, we blasted free a wide swathe of the surface—with only a few inches of penetration. Nothing we did harmed it any deeper than that. And when we went back the next day, to consider our options, the stone was *healing*, Ms. Han."

She stared in silence. It never even crossed her mind to doubt the truth of his words.

"I kept some of that loose rock. As a reminder."

"A reminder of *what*? You didn't accomplish anything!"

"Didn't we? The damage was minimal, unnaturally so. And

it didn't last. But it *was* damage. The obelisks aren't invulnerable. Neither are the Hunters. I believe it was Arnold who once said, 'If it bleeds, we can kill it.'"

"Mr. Lamb…" Cynthia finally relented, waved a question at the decanter. He poured her a glass, passed it over the desk. Only after taking a sizable slug did she ask, "Why am I here?"

"Ah. And if I told you it was because I wanted your help developing strategies against our mutual enemy?"

"I would say I'm flattered, but I don't believe it. You went through a lot of trouble to find me, and you're not having this discussion with any of the others."

"No." Lamb leaned back and tented his fingertips together. "In part, from the moment I sensed you were different, I wanted to know if you might be like me. If the obelisks had *changed* you at all. I know now that's not the case." He sounded wistful, as if part of him wished it were otherwise. "And in all candor, I don't know what I'd have done if you had been. But either way, I needed to know."

"Nope, no 'gifts.' Just your friendly neighborhood tumor." She wondered briefly if she should be showing such bitterness to him, so much of her emotional truth. *Fuck it. Isn't he supposed to be a mind-reader anyway?* "And the other part?" she pressed.

"I may not have been entirely honest earlier, Ms. Han."

You don't say? "You want to be a little more specific?"

"When I said my real name is Joshua Lamb. You see, I'm not entirely certain I'm Lamb *or* Jerold Cabot any longer."

"If you're about to tell me you think you really are Jesus—"

"Sometimes I know what they know. The Hunters. The Cathedral. Feel, in a very general way, what they feel, sense what they're doing, what they're planning. I am even granted, on occasion, a sporadic glimpse into the future, Ms. Han. What will be, or at least what very well *may* be."

You really are insane!

"But I know more than them. I *understand* more. I have knowledge of their own faith, their own truth, that the obelisk-bringers don't. I have… memories. Of other times, other places, other states of being.

"Of walls formed of sacred texts. An existence of pure

thought, imprinted on the fabric of the universe and bound in holy scripture, and of an endless, dream-filled sleep."

The whites of his eyes shone, a feverish gleam, and widened until he scarcely looked human. Cynthia felt pinned to the chair, a specimen ripe for dissection. Since the start of this tirade, she couldn't recall him blinking once.

"I believe something survived the eons, Ms. Han. Something from the dawn of this religion, caught up in the telepathic energies of the obelisks' Scriptures, slumbering in the very thoughts that were carved in ancient stone. A remnant, a being of thought, of psyche. Something that, due to a peculiarity of the human mind, has finally awakened.

"And I believe that entity, disoriented and dazed, has confused itself with the man—call him Jerold Cabot or Joshua Lamb or whatever you prefer—whom it currently wears as a tailored suit."

Finally, he did blink, and in that instant the madness, the inhumanity, were gone. He was again, for better or worse, the man he'd been when she first entered the office.

"Or at least," he said, "that's how it feels, sometimes. It's just a theory, but I haven't been able to shake the idea. What do you think? Is it possible? And as long as I still have the best interests of the New Covenant at heart, does it really matter?"

Cynthia's mouth was dry as Mars. She had to take a drink before she could possibly form a single word, and the juice nearly sloshed over the rim of the glass with her shaking. "How in God's name," she rasped, "could I *possibly* know?"

"I just figured—"

"Why are you asking me this? Why are you telling me *any* of this?"

"I told you, I've sensed since long before we met that you were different."

"*So?*" She needed to keep it together, but this was too far beyond anything she'd anticipated.

Lamb sighed and stood, pacing behind his desk. He didn't have a great deal of space: three steps one way, three steps back the other.

"I still don't entirely understand all the gifts I've been

granted, Ms. Han. One of them allows me to influence the emotions of those around me. Not too dramatically, enough to lessen pain, increase joy, reduce suspicion. I am not entirely certain, however, that it only happens when I will it to. That I'm not constantly influencing everyone near me, if only by degrees.

"Except you. Just as the obelisks cannot influence you on that level, neither can I. Which makes you the only person from whom I can expect a truly *honest* answer, unswayed by any hopes or fears of my own."

However shaken, it took Cynthia no time at all to follow that thread to its logical conclusion.

"Then I'm dead."

"Excuse me?"

"If your 'gifts' don't work on me, that means you can't hide me, right?"

"I honestly don't know yet. But I'm not sure it works that way. You could be *easier* to conceal, too."

She, too, stood up, ready to bolt—or attack. "Even so. If you can't read my mind, erase my memories, control my thoughts? You're not going to tolerate that for long, my 'honesty' notwithstanding."

Lamb's jaw dropped, and then he laughed. "Ms. Han, please sit down." Then, when she reluctantly obeyed, "For a doubter, you give me far too much credit. If I could do everything you think I can, and relied on it, then perhaps you'd have more of a point. But I can't.

"I've told you much of what I can do. I can sense people's emotions and desires, as well as influencing them. I can, with effort, sometimes read a belief or even a thought, if it's a very deep, powerful one. And the better I've come to know someone, the more easily and more distantly I can perform these feats, hide from the Hunters, all of that.

"But that's more or less the extent of it. I can't read minds at whim, and whatever rumors my people may believe of me, I cannot control or manipulate their thoughts. Your value to me as an impartial observer outweighs any threat you might pose."

Assuming one word of what you're telling me is true... Nonetheless, Cynthia found herself relaxing, if only slightly.

"So," Lamb continued, taking his own seat once more. "Can we put aside the suspicions for a few minutes and actually talk?"

Cynthia probably answered in the affirmative, but Ethan never heard it.

He rocked back on his heels, away from the door to which his ear had been pressed for several minutes. Truth be told, he hadn't expected to get close enough to hear much, and certainly not for long, but apparently when Lamb had dismissed Vivian and the others, he'd meant it. The hall beside the office was empty.

Presumably because he hadn't wanted any of them to overhear, either. Given some of what he'd said to Cynthia, that was understandable—but just now, Ethan dearly wished they'd stayed, that he'd been interrupted before overhearing.

Because either Lamb had just lied to Cynthia about the extent of his gifts—*or...*

Ethan was pounding up the stairs before his thoughts caught up with him, before he'd fully considered what that "Or" meant. Bile burned the back of his tongue, and he tripped on the steps, sending a near paralyzing jolt of agony up his shin, before he could blink his vision clear.

He reached his destination, pounded on the door until his hand tingled and threatened to go numb. Sunup wasn't for a little while yet. He'd probably awoken not just the inhabitants of this room, but most of the floor.

He couldn't be bothered to care.

"Doctor Bell?" The door creaked open, revealing a bleary middle-aged woman in a worn robe. "What are you...?" She clutched at the robe, suddenly alert. Her jaw twitched in fear. "What's wrong? Have you learned something? Is my baby okay?"

"Coretta..."

"What's wrong?"

"I'm sorry for frightening you." He wanted to scream in her face, toss her aside, but he kept *just* enough control. *Maintain the façade. Protect the lie.* "There's nothing new for you to worry about. I'm in a hurry because..."

Think, man!

"...a sample was spilled, and if I don't get it replaced quickly, we'll have to start a whole battery of tests over. It'll cost us supplies we can't afford to lose, and possibly add days, even weeks, of delay."

It made no sense, he was blathering, but Coretta didn't know the first thing about medicine. Nor, given her sag of relief against the doorframe, was she apt to question.

"If I could see her for just a few minutes?"

The woman nodded, smiling through her tears. "Of course. Do you want me to—?"

"No, I should see her privately, I think. You know how sensitive she is about all of this."

"Of course," Coretta repeated. "Doctor Bell, thank you so much. You've put in so much of your personal time into taking care of her, letting her come to you personally instead of the clinic, I can't tell you—"

Smiling, nodding, making all the right noises, he brushed past her into the suite. It was larger than his own quarters, but then, he lived alone.

He knocked, this time on the door to the smaller bedroom. "It's Doctor Bell. I'm coming in, okay?"

Dana sat pressed against the headboard, knees tucked to her chest, quilt pulled protectively to her shoulders. "What do you want? Why are you here? It's not supposed to be here."

Ethan made certain the door latched firmly behind him. When he spoke, deep and low so they wouldn't carry to the rest of the suite, the sounds seemed to rise from the floor beneath him. "Do you remember?"

"Huh? What are you—?"

He was at her side, one knee on the bed, so close they shared breath. He yanked her head back, hard, fingers entangled in her hair. The tears in her eyes, the whimper in her throat, barely registered. In that moment, all his protestations and flimsy ideals about causing no harm fell away, though he'd never admit it even to himself. He needed only to know, and damn anything else.

"Lamb!" Spittle flecked his lips, spattered Dana's cheeks.

"Did he actually take any memories from you?" Then, when no answer emerged from quivering lips, *"Do you remember?"*

She cringed, so far as his grip on her hair would permit, wracked through with heaving sobs. It could have been in response solely to Ethan's fury, a product of adolescent fear.

But he knew, somehow, that it wasn't.

His hand went slack and he fell back from her, wobbling precariously on the edge of the mattress.

"Yes," she squeaked between ragged, tearful gasps. "I remember! Mr. Lamb told me..." The words barely came. "Told me it... was for all of us, the New... New Covenant. God want... wanted me to... But you had to think...

"Why?!" A broken, despairing wail, that Ethan could only hope nobody else heard. "Why does God want you to hurt me? What did I do? What did I do?"

Ethan turned away, doubled over, and vomited a broad, acrid swathe across the hotel's fancy carpet.

"Is it truly so awful, though? Surely being able to sense the needs and desires of my people, to take the edge off their suffering, can only be a boon?"

Cynthia nearly shouted in frustration. Lamb sounded genuine in asking for her opinions, and gave every impression of listening as she spoke, but thus far he'd proven either unwilling or unable to absorb her words.

Still, she tried again. "In the short term, sure. It's an effective way to get people to follow you, and to go where you point. Maybe even to get them to worship you, if that's your goal.

"But it's not *sustainable*, Lamb! It's not sustainable, and it's not stable. It's ripe for abuse, whatever your intentions right now. It's just a nicer form of authoritarianism. And *even if* you never misuse it—" *Which you already have, frankly,* "—you're not immortal. You're trying to build a lasting society with yourself as a foundation, and that *can't* last."

Lamb raised his glass, realized it was empty, and apparently decided not to bother with a refill. "And what do you suggest as the better alternative?"

"Trust," she said immediately. "You need to earn your

people's trust—genuinely, personally, without manipulation or shortcuts. And you need to offer that trust in return."

"You think I don't trust my people?"

Cynthia had been waiting for that question, and pounced. "You keep going on about your 'insights' into the obelisks and the aliens. What are they here for, really? What do they want? What are the Hunters trying to accomplish? And the, uh, Cathedral? What about them? Why do you call them heretics?"

He tapped a nail on his empty glass, frowned, and said nothing.

"Okay, maybe you don't trust *me* enough to answer that yet, but what about the people who've been with you since the start? Or your lieutenants? Have you told *them*? Because I certainly haven't gotten the impression they understand much more than I do."

"There are... risks involved, Ms. Han. Truths they're not yet ready for, or that might drive them to make unwise choices."

"See? There you go. If you won't trust your people, if you won't even give them the information they need to make their own decisions, how can you ever expect them to trust you?"

"I don't, really. You're the one who keeps harping on trust. What I need from them—from *everyone*—is *faith*."

"Um."

"Faith is what drives our enemy. Deep, unwavering, unshakable. It makes them strong. It makes them focused. It makes them *powerful*, in ways you cannot fathom and I have only just begun to comprehend. We need that strength for ourselves, if we're to have any hope of countering them. And to be blunt, that's not something I can afford to wait for."

Part of her wanted to ask him to expand on that. Another, larger part was shrieking a warning that his man had once again become dangerous, that whatever grace period he'd offered had ended.

"I really do appreciate the conversation, though, Ms. Lamb. You've given me insights I couldn't have gotten anywhere else."

"Such as?" *Keep him talking, keep him distracted.*

"You've shown me that I cannot count on people to understand how essential it is that they put their faith in me.

That I can't worry about *convincing* them. This is simply too important to permit people to make the wrong decision."

And since I'm the only one he for sure can't manipulate...

Cynthia launched herself from the chair, hand landing on the desk. She knew she could be over it in a fraction of a second, could almost certainly take Lamb one-on-one, especially with the element of—

Agony. White, hot, blinding, it ripped the strength from her body, washed all but the flimsiest strand of conscious thought from her mind. Her arm went limp and she crashed first to the desk, then to the floor, in a tangle of loose limbs. She might have screamed; she didn't know. The wetness on her face might be tears or blood or spittle or anything else.

Her skull felt as though it must surely crack from the pressure, and she'd have welcomed it. This was already beyond anything the obelisks had inflicted upon her, and still it grew worse.

"My gifts are of the obelisks." Lamb's voice echoed from far above, *worlds* above. "Or of one who dwelt within them. I figured I could do this to you, as they did, even though I couldn't read you, couldn't touch your thoughts.

"I can only imagine the pain, and for what it's worth, Ms. Han, I'm sorry. I have no idea how long this will take, but I hope it's quick. I promise you, we'll win. We'll survive. And you will be remembered, in the world to come."

Chapter Ten

Still. Silent. Wrong.

From a beach of scintillating whites and somber grays, tiny flecks of what could only barely be called sand, the endless waters stretched. The surface sat motionless, unbroken, without tide or ripple, glinting in the stark light of an ancient, shrunken sun. It was cold, all of it— that light, that water, the unmoving air that smelled of ammonia and the sickening under-scent of car exhaust. Cold in temperature, cold in demeanor, contemptuously indifferent.

The horizon was invisible, for the placid sea perfectly reflected a sky nearly as white as the aberrant sun. Far from the beach, great stone daggers pierced the water's surface, stretching like grasping fingers for that cloudless, empty expanse. Much as the obelisks they were, but far greater; tens or even hundreds of thousands of feet, the sacred scriptures legible for scores of miles.

Finally the waters moved, as something stirred in the tenebrous deep...

Furious, incomprehensible shouting. A loud crash, followed by softer impacts, grunts, and cries. The vision disappeared. The pain did not, though it began to subside, slowly receding.

Like an ocean tide.

Cynthia struggled to sit as her head screamed in protest and the room spun. Hot vomit caked her lips, the side of her face where she'd lain helpless. When she wiped a sleeve across the mess in revulsion, it came away stained not merely with puke and bile, but crimson smears of blood.

Ethan kept screaming, knuckles bruised and splitting, as he landed blow after blow on Lamb's face, his chest, his gut. The New Covenant leader hung partly limp, bent backward over the desk, lips and cheeks already swelling, mouth full of yet more blood.

Awful as he looked, however, he was starting to rise, arms coming up to ward off the worst of the doctor's wild swings.

For a few pounding heartbeats, Cynthia froze, undecided. Help Ethan? She knew Lamb was her enemy, but she wasn't sure who her friend was anymore, if they *were* still friends. Didn't know how swiftly or how easily Lamb could turn her mind, her illness, against her again, or whether she could take another second of it without going mad. Didn't know how soon anyone might hear the struggle, or what would become of her once they did.

Gripping the nearest chair, she dragged herself to her feet and stumbled, swaying and nearly toppling, to the door.

Those few steps cleared her head a bit, and the pain continued to fade. Steadier now, she broke into a slow run along the hallway. Never once was she even tempted to look back.

Natsuhiko? Downing?

No. Whatever else he might be, Lamb was pragmatic. Both men were too useful for him to take out his anger on them—*if* they remained innocent of "wrongdoing." Going to them would only drag them down with her.

And even if, by some miracle, they escaped with her, they'd probably all die out there together. No, despite everything, her friends were safer, were better off, here.

She was so very near the lobby and the main entrance, close enough she felt almost a physical yearning. But there, too, she would find a group of New Covenant soldiers, and even if they had no idea anything was wrong inside, she knew they had orders to prevent the newcomers from leaving.

Though it pained her, she turned away from the false salvation those doors offered and made for the stairs.

Which floor did we come in on? Third? Fourth? Remembering wrong would cost time she didn't have.

She burst from the stairwell, leaving the thudding echoes of her footsteps behind. Every nerve shrieked at her to keep running, until she felt as though she were being electrocuted. Nevertheless, she held herself to a brisk, stiff-muscled walk.

Lamb might sound the alert any time, but until he did, the last thing she needed was to raise suspicions on her own. *Keep it casual, Cyn!*

Although, with any luck, she wouldn't run into anyone.

She turned a corner and had no luck at all.

"Cynthia," Vivian greeted her, only barely glancing back from her conversation with another of Lamb's patrolling sentries. "You and Joshua done?"

"Yep." Cynthia gave a single nod and kept walking, hoping to bull through with sheer nonchalance.

Keep it casual, keep it casual, keep it—

"What the *hell*? What happened?"

Only as she followed two stupefied stares down to her own arm and shoulder did it occur to Cynthia that she probably still wore large splotches of everything she'd thrown up under the influence of Lamb's psychic assault.

Well, shit.

The man, being on guard duty, was armed. Vivian, deep in the heart of the New Covenant sanctuary, was not.

Vivian was closer.

Shoving aside the lingering traces of pain and disorientation, Cynthia lunged.

The guard was fast. Where most of Lamb's people carried American military weaponry, this guy wielded an Uzi; God knew where he'd acquired it, but he looked to Cynthia like a villain from an '80s action movie. He'd already raised it before she'd covered half the distance, but Cynthia threw herself to the left as she closed, putting Vivian between her and the gleaming black barrel.

He'd just reached out to push Vivian aside, clearing his line of fire, when Cynthia hit them. Literally.

Leading with a shoulder, she plowed into the other woman, sending her flailing into the gunman, who staggered in turn. Again he reached out, shoving Vivian aside, but now Cynthia was near enough to smack his arm down just before he fired.

She'd meant to disarm him, but she wasn't at her best, wasn't quite strong enough to break his grip. Instead, when the weapon roared, cycling through about ten rounds in the split second before the guard could release the trigger, it sprayed downward rather than out.

At least half those rounds went through what had been his own left foot.

No sound but an abortive squeak emerged as he collapsed, his whole body wrapped tight around the mutilated limb—and around the Uzi, which hit the carpet with him.

Cynthia had no time to dig for it and try to pry it loose.

Vivian came at her, fast and snarling. First a thrust kick that would have broken ribs had it connected, which Cynthia sidestepped, and then a quick jab.

She knew how to throw a punch, certainly. Tae Kwon Do or Karate, Cynthia guessed. She'd had training, back before the world ended.

But only casually.

Cynthia caught the punch, yanked and twisted. Vivian's cry of pain ended with a sharp cough as she landed on her back, hard.

The arm probably wasn't dislocated—thanks again to Cynthia's weakness, her exhaustion—but she wouldn't be comfortable using it for a day or two.

More voices down the hall, questioning and angry. No chance, now, for stealth or deception. Cynthia broke into a run and prayed she had enough of a head start to find something she could hotwire before everyone realized that the parking garage was her only real option.

She almost changed her mind.

The sky had brightened from black to a diffuse charcoal, the ubiquitous dust set aglow by the pre-dawn light. Insufficient to make out much at any distance, it still allowed Cynthia, as she dashed across the skywalk between hotel and garage, a fuzzy glimpse at the trucks parked on the street below.

She skidded to a halt and stared in unabashed longing, face and hands pressed to the glass.

Helicopters. Two flatbed trucks carried *Goddamn helicopters!* Military at that, if she wasn't imagining the camo patterns she could just barely make out on the nearest.

It'd be perfect. Sabotage one, take the other, and they'd have no possible means of either pursuing or finding her. Even if time proved too short for sabotage, she had no doubt she could evade anyone who gave chase. Helicopters hadn't been her thing in the Air Force, but she'd bet on even her base-level training and experience against whatever civilian pilots the New Covenant might produce.

Cynthia swayed with indecision, costing herself time she absolutely could not afford.

And then, with a sigh and a few bitter curses, she tore herself from the window and continued.

Every exit was guarded. The trucks were guarded. And who knew if the choppers were even ready to go? They could be unfueled, they could be undergoing maintenance. The chains and straps holding them in place might have locks.

Too many unknowns. Too risky.

God, it was frustrating, though!

The garage, too, had its guards—on the exit, around some of the more important vehicles and supplies, but not at every car, not on every level, and not, thankfully, on the entrance from the skywalk. Ducking low, she slipped from door to column, from van to car.

Her shirt reeked, making her nostrils itch. She ignored it.

Great, you're here. What now, Cyn?

She knew enough about cars to hotwire one, or thought she did. What she lacked, however, was any guarantee she could do it *quickly*. Though her gut churned with every extra second, she had to look around, had to make sure nobody was near enough to interrupt her while she worked.

Voices, hollow and echoing from half a level below, told her otherwise. She dropped to her stomach and wormed forward, peering over the concrete lip.

One ramp down, half-a-dozen Army trucks sat in a row, guarded by an equal number of armed sentries. Even as she watched, one of the men lifted the radio from his belt, responding to a call she hadn't heard. He began barking orders, and the entirety of the group charged up the slope, heading for the skywalk.

Ready to intercept the fugitive Cynthia Han, should she make a run for the garage. Except, of course, they were about two seconds from discovering that she was already here—at which point, the *best* she might hope for was being shot dead on the spot.

She held her breath and rolled, forcing herself under a nearby Camry.

The footsteps and their echoes grew louder, louder—and then faded. Not much, as she wasn't as far from the skywalk as she now wished, but enough. She forced the breath that tried to emerge as a relieved gasp into a slow hiss, instead.

Save the celebrations; not clear yet. The slope made it impossible for them to see her from where they'd gathered, but the Toyota itself was in plain view if they so much as turned around. And that meant getting out from under remained a problem.

Unless...

Slowly, wincing at every scrape no matter how quiet, Cynthia inched forward and peered over the lip separating this stretch of ramp from the one half a level below. This near to the bottom of the one slope and the top of the other, the drop between them looked to be only about ten to fifteen feet. Doable enough.

The clearance beneath the car wouldn't allow her to squeeze out over the concrete. Again retraining herself to a turtle's pace, she slipped out from underneath the Toyota on the side opposite the guards. With toes, elbows, and fingertips she advanced. Lengths of steel wire formed a safety fence above that concrete edge, but though she snagged skin and hair, jaw clenched hard to keep from responding to the pain, she managed to slip beneath it and even turn herself around, dangling by her hands.

Careful as she was, she couldn't entirely muffle the sound of her drop to the next floor, and while the guards would *probably* attribute it to the regular shifting and other random sounds of the garage, she wasn't about to chance it. Making for the closest concealment, she hauled herself up into one of the military trucks, slipping between edges of the tarp.

Darkness descended on her, and all she could do was listen. Thirty seconds was enough to tell her that nobody had come running. Nobody had heard her.

Now that she wasn't so focused on the possibility of discovery, however, Cynthia noticed the smells. Various acrid chemicals. Something like dirt or soil. And motor oil? Was the truck leaking?

The sky beyond the garage lightened further, Cynthia's vision began to adjust, and slowly shapes emerged from shadow.

Most of the truck contained barrels, both metal and plastic, and massive plastic sacks. Near the door, right beside her, were stacked numerous blocks, wrapped in blue polymer.

Oh. Fuck. Me.

C4. The bricks were C4, over a hundred pounds if it was an ounce. And if the barrels contained what she thought...

Cynthia shifted, even risked lifting a tiny flap of the tarp to let in more light, and stared at the bags. Yep. Fertilizer. The barrels probably contained more of it, or else the results if the New Covenant had already processed it. ANFO, or at least the materials to make ANFO.

And there were, at a quick guess, *thousands* of pounds of it.

In this one truck alone, she was sitting on enough explosive to significantly outdo McVeigh and Nichols. If the others held similar cargo?

Jesus Christ, Lamb, are you planning to level a small town?!

Very, *very* carefully, she backed out of the truck.

Her feet had just settled on pavement when multiple roaring engines reverberated from below. After a jump so violent she worried about setting off the plastique, she realized she was hearing a pair of motorcycles entering the garage.

Made sense. Lamb almost certainly had people patrolling the streets around his refuge. He'd probably called everyone in to search for her.

Too bad for them they'd just given her a way out. Cynthia grinned, wide and more than a little wild. She just needed to pop back into the truck for a second...

The first of the new arrivals, riding the larger motorcycle, probably never knew what hit him. The massive tire iron took him off the bike and laid him flat out on the pavement, likely cracking a number of ribs in the process.

Unfortunately, none of Cynthia's training included knocking

a man off a running motorcycle with any degree of stealth or subtlety. The second rider slammed on the breaks, skidding sideways before halting and fumbling for the MP5 slung over his shoulder, and the confused shouts from above announced that the sentries were on their way.

She leapt over the fallen motorcycle, bringing the tire iron down on the man's left hand, still wrapped around the handlebar. Cracking bone faded into a piercing scream, and in that flash of agony, the gun was briefly forgotten. He clutched at his injured hand with the other—and Cynthia smashed *that* hand with the tire iron, too.

Sorry about that. But he wouldn't be firing at her, and she hadn't had to kill anyone. Two big plusses.

In seconds, albeit it difficult, muscle-straining seconds, Cynthia had the first man's gun off his shoulder and his motorcycle—a late-model Triumph Bonneville in British racing green—standing upright. She swung her leg over and gunned it down the ramp, whipping around the corner *just* before the guards charging from above could open fire.

She rode the brakes all the way down, barely squealing through turns without embedding herself in concrete pylons. Ahead, on the ground level, more guards waited at the exit to the garage.

A violent shrug dropped the strap from her shoulder. Controlling the motorcycle with one hand, she spun through the final turn and opened fire.

Bullet slammed into cement or flew into the street beyond. She'd deliberately aimed high, firing over the heads of the sentinels. They, of course, didn't know that, and dived for cover the moment the MP5 opened up.

The weapon ran dry in two seconds, but it kept their heads down long enough. She tossed it aside, braced herself against the grips with both hands, and drove through the flimsy wooden barrier ubiquitous to all parking garages.

She wobbled, nearly knocked aside, and she heard shattering glass as her headlight disintegrated, but she was out. Praying her course remained free of obelisks for at least a few blocks, she redlined the engine, shooting past the parked trucks and startled New Covenant soldiers. The wind bit at her skin and narrowed eyes, tore at her loose hair and soiled shirt. Between her speed and the morning chill she was already shivering. If she could get away, she'd have to stop somewhere, find some heavier clothes, some supplies. Hell, she'd have to figure out where the hell she was even going!

It took a minute for Cynthia to realize, over the howling of the wind, that the wind wasn't all she heard.

Chapter Eleven

The right mirror had been knocked askew in the collision with the barrier, but the left stood just fine. A glance revealed a gray Mustang and the other motorcycle—albeit with a different rider—coming up fast from behind. Way back, beyond them, a large sedan and a larger pickup had come late to the chase but worked to make up lost ground.

Cynthia pushed herself to dangerous speeds, fishtailing through turns, flinching every time she faced a new street for fear of those vile stone-carved letters worming into her brain. Despite the cold, the sweat on her palms made her grip slick, unreliable.

She couldn't outrun them indefinitely. Even if she managed to lose them briefly, the thunder of the motor carried for miles in the empty city. Cut that engine and try to hide, though, and they'd know roughly where she was. They could box her in, block her escape, and then hunt her down at leisure. What options did she really have?

Oh. Oh, no.

Madness. Absolute madness. She'd lost it. No way. No.

So what's the alternative, genius?

Lips pressed in a tight line only because she was too winded to curse, she took a few extra turns and made a mad dash back toward the freeway.

The circuitous route, past empty strip malls and restaurants and a park that might be quite nice in warmer weather, put her on the northbound side of 610. Well, it wasn't as though she had any oncoming traffic to deal with, right? She raced up the exit ramp and southward, ignoring the vague sense of vertigo from traveling on the wrong side of the road, gaze fixed as wholly on the cement in front of her as she could manage at these speeds.

Was this the way she'd come? She thought so, thought she knew Houston well enough, but she wasn't sure. Even if it were, how far did she have to go? How fast had the convoy been traveling yesterday?

And what if they aren't even there anymore?

Her pursuers were still behind her, all four, spread out across half a mile and slowly gaining. Unconcerned about the obelisks, apparently, they could afford to look farther ahead, drive faster, than she could. This was the *only* trick she had to pull; if it didn't work...

She felt it, however faintly, squirming through her head, and gasped her relief.

Not done yet, though. Still had to pinpoint them. Still had to *survive* them.

Barely keeping the bike upright, Cynthia twisted sharply and slewed across the grass, off the freeway, back onto the side streets.

In search of the last thing she ever wanted to see again, and the only thing that might save her.

If she was wrong, she was dead.

If she was right, she still might be dead.

Cynthia would have preferred more time, would have preferred to feel her way around, measure the outer limits of the peculiar sensation in her head, pinpoint its center. Her pursuers, the city, even nature seemed disinclined to allow it.

The sleet started falling just as she left the freeway, grimy and sullen. Not heavy, but sufficient to coat the roads in a thin slush that, with a bit of added color, might have been the lifeblood of a dying 7-Eleven. Enough to make tires slip, enough to set her shivering violently atop the Triumph without even a coat to protect her. She'd all but lain the bike down in the middle of the street when a bad turn brought a distant obelisk into view. She'd flinched, hard, skewing sideways, and it was only thanks to the slickening road that her momentum kept her upright long enough to regain control.

Behind her, the second motorcycle had fallen back, but the other vehicles, far more stable, drew nearer, ravenously chewing through whatever time she might have had.

Shops and offices flashing past behind thickening curtains of gray, fighting the bike with fingers that could no longer feel, Cynthia ran as far as she could, until just maybe the numbness within her head, now nearly impossible to distinguish from the numbness without, had begun to fade. Praying she felt what she thought she felt, that her best guess was accurate enough, that she could stay ahead of the New Covenant just a little longer, she pointed the bike toward what had damn well better be the heart of the alien sensation.

At the far end of a large parking lot hunkered a Home Depot, with wings of smaller stores spread to either side as though ready to take flight once the weather cleared. More chain link fencing isolated an array of gardening tools, potted plants, and Christmas trees. She screeched the motorcycle to a halt beside it, hoping it would block her pursuers' view for just a few seconds, buy her just that much more time.

No power to the sliding doors, of course, and her fingers were dead weights, unwilling to obey, so trying to pry them open would be a fool's errand. She wasted close to half a minute, casting around for a tool or a board she could hopefully grip well enough to break the glass before she realized they were *already open*.

Either someone else had sheltered here, at some point, or she'd found exactly what she was looking for.

She stared into the darkness, through the gap like an open abscess, and wondered what the hell she'd been thinking. This had to be the stupidest idea she'd ever—

Engines roared and tires sloshed in the parking lot. She dashed through the opening.

The floor and checkout lanes nearest the entrance wore a layer of dust and muck, now accumulating bits of sleet as well. As she fled into the cavernous warehouse beyond, however, it grew drier and warmer, replete with the familiar atmosphere of wood and oils. Cynthia snatched a cheap flashlight from the impulse buys hanging beside the register and ripped it open as she jogged into the first of the massive aisles, nearly colliding with the metal framework shelving. The notion of flicking the thing on, of making herself so readily visible in the dark, nauseated her, but if she couldn't see what the hell she was doing...

Voices and footsteps echoed behind her, and she decided she could stand the darkness for a minute or two more. She ran a hand along the various bits and pieces hanging beside her.

Bristles and wood. Paintbrushes. Useless.

"Come on, Ms. Han! This is foolish!"

Carlos. Of course it would be Carlos.

"Whatever happened, I'm sure it's not too late to talk it out with Lamb! Don't make this harder on yourself!"

Just step on out where we can shoot you. Right, that's *gonna happen.*

Next row. She placed her palm over the glass and switched the flashlight on just long enough to get her bearings. Storage materials, God dammit. She was on the wrong side of the store.

"You make us look for you, I can't promise nobody gets hurt, Han!"

Neither can I. Keeping to a low crouch, she backed farther into the massive warehouse and cut across the first open walkway.

No sign of anyone but the Covenant. Were they even here? Were they watching? Waiting? Did she hope they were, or they weren't?

Someone near the front of the store turned on their own flashlight, the beam serving as a perfect target, if she'd only had a weapon.

She wasn't the only one to have that thought. Carlos barked a quick order and the light went away.

Another order, and the searchers spread out, two by two, advancing down multiple aisles. Eight to twelve of them, she figured. Even in the dark, it wouldn't take them *that* long to find her.

She ducked into another aisle, banging her wrist on the shelving. Still numb enough that it didn't hurt too badly, but she could only hope they'd mistake the sound for one of their own.

Hand over the flashlight again, creating a pinkish light that spread for only a few inches. It was enough.

Now we're talking!

"Over there!"

Cynthia cut the light, grabbed what she needed, and scrambled for the next aisle.

It was occupied.

Barely visible as thicker shadows against the gloom, two of Carlos's people proceeded slowly, weapons raised. Nigh invisible as they were, she still saw the strain in their posture, the nervousness in each step.

She could also see, if only just, what hung in rows and lay on shelves where they passed.

Cynthia tucked the flashlight into her waistband, carefully lifted a three-pound drilling hammer from its bracket, and crept forward on the balls of her feet.

At the last second, she couldn't quite make herself aim for the head. She'd killed before, but always either from the cockpit or under fire. She'd do it again if she had to—it might, given her half-assed and desperate plan, even be kinder—but only when no choice remained. Right now, it still did.

The first New Covenant soldier screamed as the hammer slammed into his right knee. Cynthia let the weapon fall as he did, grabbing instead for his M4 and swiftly putting two rounds into his partner's leg. A second scream, a second collapse, and a variety of shouts and running feet from all around her. Cynthia scooped up the second gun as well, slinging both over her left shoulder by the straps, and climbed.

By the time Carlos and several others converged on their wounded companions, she was crouched above them atop the metal-frame shelving. She gave them all a good few seconds to gather, to check on the injured, to desperately cast about in the dark to see where she might have gone.

Then she opened fire.

Only for a second, long enough to make them dive for cover, and then she was gone, leaping across the gap to an adjoining aisle and then scrabbling down.

She'd shown them she was armed and prepared to lie in wait for them. Slowly as they'd searched before, it was a mad sprint compared to the crawl they'd move at now.

A pair of MP5s roared and bullets sparked off nearby shelving, forcing Cynthia, too, to drop to her stomach. They'd fired blind, guided at best by the sound of her descent, but she got the message clearly enough.

Carlos was done pretending to be polite.

A few quick sprints, and she had the rest of what she needed. Armed now with several bottles of lighter fluid and a bit of tape, along with the soldering torch she'd grabbed earlier, she crept back toward the entrance.

Fuck!

She'd hoped Carlos had set every one of his people to searching, but nope. A pair of New Covenant soldiers crouched near the door, waiting in case she doubled back.

A pretty obvious precaution, frankly. If she hadn't been freezing and exhausted when she'd come up with her plan— such as it was—she'd not have been even a bit surprised.

Instead she returned the way she'd come, dashed across the open dark, and took shelter behind a row of washing machines.

Okay, so grabbing a propane tank from the rack outside and blowing up one of the cars was out. The lumber, then? With the lighter fluid and a bit of tape over the torch's trigger, she could probably ignite the pile pretty quickly, but so what? The wood was farther from the front windows than she'd have liked, harder to see from outside. Even if *they* were nearby, would they even take notice if she set the pile ablaze? Would it grab their attention where the racing engines and the gunfire hadn't? Certainly not as well as an exploding car would have.

They were supposed to have been here, dammit! Or at least close! Now...

Fuck it. Even if the fire didn't attract their attention, it should draw some of Carlos's people. Get them in one spot, backlit. They'd be good... She swallowed, steeled herself for what had to happen. Good targets.

Not that she expected for one second she was getting out of this, with the odds so stacked. But she was damn well going to give it everything she had.

Gun in one hand, torch and bottles tucked tight in the crook of her other arm, she tensed to run, stretched her neck in a futile attempt to loosen up, left, right, back, a deep breath.

Overhead, barely visible, several of the ceiling fans rotated, so slow as to be nearly silent.

It was such a mundane sight, Cynthia had already looked away and taken her first step before it truly registered. *But the power's out!*

Nor was she the only one to notice. In a hissed whisper, from several aisles away, "Carlos! Look!"

"It's another distraction! Check around you!"

"But how'd she even get up—?"

"I don't care!"

It wasn't me! She nearly shouted it aloud, biting her tongue only at the last second. This what she'd needed. What she'd counted on.

That didn't mean it was what she *wanted*. Not even for Carlos and his people.

One of the door sentries screamed, high-pitched and broken. A single piercing note that swiftly fell apart, rolling and burbling as if smothered in oatmeal—and then that, too, had faded. Cynthia cringed, clutching violently at the steel in her hands.

Running footsteps in the shadows. "Report!" Carlos shouted.

"Greg's gone!"

"What'd the bitch do to him?"

"No, I mean he's *gone!*"

Carlos, no idiot, finally understood. "It's not her."

Another of the ceiling fans began to turn. This one sat heavy in its socket, metal against metal. *Screech. Screech. Screech.*

Multiple flashlights clicked on, the desperate need to see outweighing the need to remain unseen. Half-a-dozen beams converged on the slowly rotating blades.

The blades, and the desiccated load draped over each. Individual bits of the missing Greg.

Leg. Arm. Arm. Leg.

"Jesus Christ!" Not Carlos, that, but one of his people.

And then, from the ceiling, from three different spots within the thick cobweb of shadow, amidst the sudden ear-splitting, soupy keening, it came back at them. *"Jesus Christ! Jesus Christ! Jesus Christ!"*

A dozen weapons fired, punching countless holes in the tiles; a dozen throats cried out in fury and fear. Three figures plummeted from on high, still shrieking, limbs outstretched at impossible angles. In the dark, lit only by the strobe of gunfire, Cynthia could have sworn that *even their freefall* skipped and stuttered.

She saw only the vaguest details of the closest of them: the checkered pattern of a flannel shirt that even now maintained its perfect vertical alignment. That one dropped from the fan bedecked with body parts, and Cynthia found herself not remotely surprised that of all the Hunters, the Flannel Man would prove the most twisted, the most sadistic.

It knew she was here. It never so much as turned its head, looked her way with that blank and featureless face, but she knew. She knew, and she ran, before it could finish with the larger threat.

Before she could stop and think about the men and women she'd just, for all intents and purposes, *fed* to the unholy things.

No stealth, now. She sprinted, dropping the torch and the bottles, firing two three-round bursts at the storefront window. A few more shots pinged off the shelving and the tubing as she darted by, but whether they were meant for her or wild shots aimed at the Crooked Men, they never came too near. Cynthia turned her shoulder forward and hit the bullet-pocked window, flying from the store in a shower of shards.

She felt several lines open up and down her arms, begin to bleed, but the wind and the sleet cut worse than the glass.

A few more shots took out two tires on the Mustang and mangled the whole front wheel of the other motorcycle. Carlos's people could still pile into the other two vehicles, if some were willing to cram themselves into the bed of the truck. It wouldn't be optimal for chasing her any further, but it should get them back to the hotel.

If any survived to *try* getting back to the hotel.

Protected by lingering adrenaline from the worst of the cold and the worst mental images of the people dying horribly inside, Cynthia kickstarted the Triumph and roared away from the Home Depot, and the monsters within, as fast as the whipping sleet and fear of the alien writings allowed.

Chapter Twelve

"Step aside, please, my friends. Make room."

Ethan peeled his right eye open—the left was far too swollen—and watched the Joshua Lamb-shaped blur approaching amidst the other, similarly shaped blurs.

He didn't bother trying to sit up. Even if the beating hadn't left him too sore to move, lying on this poorly padded bench, legs draped to each side and left arm cuffed to the machinery above his head, had stiffened him up quite nicely.

"How are we doing?" Lamb asked, crouching beside him.

"Not sure about your friends' choice of location," Ethan mumbled around a split, puffy lip. "Really not feeling up to a workout just now."

Snarls and mutters from the people surrounding them, the people who'd happily pounded on him when they found him brawling with their beloved leader, suggested that they didn't appreciate his humor. Their voices echoed faintly in the hotel's exercise room, bouncing from the mirrored wall off to one side and around the various machines and contraptions—such as the leg press to which he was currently chained. A mélange of iron, oil, and old sweat permeating the bench's plastic covering helpfully diluted the scent of his own blood currently clogging his sinuses.

Holding his head still, Ethan tried to focus on Lamb. This close, his vision was still relatively clear.

"You're looking surprisingly good," he said to the man's only mildly bruised, faintly swollen face. "I must be getting old."

"Let me teach him a few more manners, Mr. Lamb," one of

the men growled, rubbing a thumb over the split and battered knuckles of his other fist.

Ethan tried to shake his head, decided it was a bad idea. "I wouldn't suggest that," he said. "You should probably ice that hand first."

Another growl, but Lamb lifted his own hand between them. "That won't be necessary, Michael. Why don't you, all of you, wait outside? I'd like a few words in private with Doctor Bell."

"Uh." The big guy—Michael, apparently—shifted foot to foot like an anxious schoolboy. "Mr. Lamb, I don't know if…"

"It's quite all right. The good doctor won't be assaulting me again. Even if he wasn't restrained, he's not in much shape to throw a punch, is he? And besides…" He gestured toward the glass-panel wall separating exercise room from hallway. "You'll be able to see us quite clearly, if he *does* try anything."

Michael still wanted to argue. Ethan could see that much even in his current state. Still, this was Lamb talking, and disobedience wasn't really an option. With a lingering sigh, he departed, the others following in his wake.

"You did bring this on yourself, you know," Lamb said once they were alone.

"Fuck you. I should have hit you harder."

"You hit hard enough. I don't bruise easily."

"I'll use something heavier next time. Like a truck."

The New Covenant leader *tsked*, twisting the vial that hung around his neck between thumb and forefinger. "You've made things quite awkward, Ethan. I've done nothing but talk you up to my people. You were to be an important part of our society."

"You lied to me!" Ethan yanked against the chain, accomplishing nothing but to add a sharp pain in his wrist to his many other aches and agonies. "You tricked me into… into…"

"I tricked you into nothing. I told you what you needed to hear to give yourself permission. I gave you leave to be Ethan Bell, nothing more."

"Damn you!" His cheeks, his whole face, still hurt too much for him to tell if he was crying.

"Fine," Ethan continued, collecting himself. "Call them back in, then. Have them finish the job."

"I'd rather not." Lamb rose, pacing beside the leg press. "I'd rather we fix this. You can still have a place with us. We still need people like you."

Ethan snorted, then winced at the bubbling pain in his nose. "Just like that?"

"We'll chalk it all up to a misunderstanding. My people won't be thrilled about it, you'll have to regain their trust, but with a little time and the right prodding..."

"There's no way Dana would—"

"Dana will say what I tell her to say."

If not for the cuffs, if he'd had anywhere near the strength, Ethan might have thrown himself at Lamb once more. Instead, he could only manage—after substantial groaning and several failed attempts—to swing one leg over the bench and slowly sit up.

"And just what is it that I'd have to do to regain my state of grace?" Any more caustic and his words might have eaten into the iron weights.

"Nothing you haven't done before."

Despite the pain, Ethan grinned. His lip opened anew, and a trickle of warmth ran down his chin. "She got away from you, didn't she?"

A tiny downturn at the corner of his mouth marred Lamb's avuncular façade. "Probably not. Carlos has had a team after her for some time, now." That much, Ethan already knew. It was all his captors had talked about among themselves while he was slowly waking up. "If she *should* elude them, however, then yes, we'll be counting on your help to figure out where she'll go."

"I wouldn't be so quick to count on—"

"Mr. Lamb?"

Both turned to see someone pushing his way through the small crowd assembled in the hall.

"Well," Ethan said as the new arrival stepped through the door into the weight room, "speak of the devil. And the devil doesn't look happy."

Carlos looked a damn sight more than unhappy. His

winter-chapped face was a mask of rage, and his jacket was covered in scratches, rents, and spatters of blood.

Lamb frowned. "I take it things didn't go well?"

"Bitch led us right into a fucking nest of Hunters!"

"I see." Lamb resumed pacing, while Carlos tried his damnedest to glare Ethan to death. "How many of you made it?" he finally asked, halting once more.

"Me, Mara, and Kody got out through the windows." He poked a finger at one of the larger tears in his jacket. "Far as I know, that's it."

Even Ethan winced at that. From what he'd overheard, the group had numbered fourteen or fifteen to begin with. Lamb's frown was now an open scowl.

"Did Cynthia make it?" The question escaped before Ethan could properly consider just how unwelcome it might be.

"Did *Cynthia*...?!" Carlos advanced on him, and only a sharp shake of Lamb's head saved Ethan from another beating, at best. "Fuck you! She *gave* us to them! Bitch's probably been working with them this whole fucking time!"

"That's ridiculous! I was with her when we discovered those things, she's not—"

"The hell should I believe anything *you've* got to say about it? You—"

"Gentlemen, enough!" Lamb stepped between them. "I had a long chat with Ms. Han last night. No, Carlos, I don't believe she's somehow been in league with the Hunters. But that doesn't mean she didn't lead you to them deliberately, and I... do not approve of that.

"Ethan? I believe it's time for you to prove your loyalty, once and for all."

Loyalty to whom? But of course, that was Lamb's entire point, wasn't it?

It also wasn't the only question to flash across the doctor's mind.

"How did you get away?"

"What?" Carlos's sneer weighed more than the nearby barbells. "I just fucking told you, through the window. That beating make you deaf?"

"I mean after that, you jackass! You know how Goddamn quick those things are! No way you were driving *that* fast, not in this weather, and this 'ambush' couldn't have been too far from here, so how'd you lose them?"

It was a question Carlos had clearly never considered in his panic. Panic that settled, refreshed and renewed, across his features as he turned a headlight-wide stare from Ethan back toward Lamb.

Gunfire and shouting erupted from somewhere in the depths of the hotel, shouting that swiftly transformed into screams.

"Get on your radios!" Lamb called through the glass. "Tell everyone the Hunters are here! You know what to do! You—"

The fiberboard tiles of the drop ceiling exploded downward, bursting into shards and showers of powder as the Flannel Man dropped from the hollow spaces above. Ears ached and gorges rose at its bubbling, ululating shriek.

Carlos Morales's last seconds in this world, in a perverse sort of way, were among his most fortunate. The sheer weight of the Hunter, denser by far than the human it only vaguely resembled, crushed half the man's bones to splinters on impact, pulping organs and shredding flesh. Carlos was dead before what was left of him, a punctured balloon of meat and skin, flopped limply to the gore-stained carpet—a far swifter and gentler fate than the creature's usual murder.

The faithful out in the hall poured into the room, charging the Hunter with bare fists and bared teeth. They swarmed it over, pounding and tearing, and barely staggered it a step or two before they began to die.

"We need to go." Ethan, gaze fixed to the writhing pile as though stapled there, scarcely understood the words, only realized Lamb was unlocking his restraints when the steel cuff fell away. He let himself be dragged to his feet, aches and pains forgotten, and toward the gaping door.

It made no sense, even in the midst of everything else in this world gone mad. No faith, no fealty, could have driven the whole lot of them forward on their leader's behalf, not in the face of such horror, not without hesitation. It wasn't human, wasn't natural, wasn't—

And then he felt it in his head, caught just the edges of the emotion—the loyalty, the bravery, the love—radiating from the not-quite-human mind of the man beside him.

"You bastard!" Even as they fled into the hall, Ethan yanked his wrist free of his host and captor's grip.

Lamb didn't even pretend not to know what he meant. "Their devotion to me was real. They just needed a nudge to overcome their fear."

"You *sacrificed* them so you could escape!"

"So *we* could. If you feel that badly about it, you're welcome to go back and wait your turn."

The Flannel Man screamed. A hundred-pound barbell weight shattered the glass, whirling like a frisbee until it punched through the wall across the walkway. It left a trail of tattered, bloody skin and half a jawbone in its wake.

Ethan kept cursing—and kept running.

The hotel around them, already on high alert following Cynthia's escape, had become a warzone. Men and women, some still in their nightclothes, dashed every which way, lugging heavy weaponry or cases of supplies. More than a few, the doctor saw, wore tanks on their backs. Many had hoses connected to spray nozzles, while others, he realized with a start, were flamethrowers, some military and some homemade.

"They're not going to find *us* wanting!" Lamb insisted as he jogged. His eyes were wide, too wide, and unblinking; his face tight and clammy. "No, sir!" Ignoring the shouts and the distant gunfire, he headed for the stairs.

Another hallway led off to the right, a hallway they had to pass on their way. Ethan glanced that way, measuring his chances.

"Don't think it, Doctor Bell. I still need you."

He stopped thinking it.

Ethan had assumed they were making a break for the garage, that the guns and the flamethrowers and all the rest were a delaying tactic while the New Covenant evacuated. He was a bit startled, then, when they hit the stairs and Lamb turned his feet downward rather than up. He must have meant to take the main exit, then climb into one of the waiting trucks on the street.

When Lamb instead made a beeline back toward his office, with its desk still in disarray from Ethan's attack and the carpet still crusty with Cynthia's vomit, Ethan's disbelief finally boiled over.

"Oh, we're not running." Again Lamb spoke without even looking his way. If the man couldn't easily read Ethan's every thought, as he'd implied when speaking to Cyn, he was certainly doing a fair job of faking it. "I just need a few moments' privacy to gather myself, to concentrate, in case my people can't stop them."

Casually and intrusively as if he were guiding a reticent child, Lamb dragged Ethan behind the desk and pushed him back into the corner by a filing cabinet, then sat himself in the chair. From here, he did nothing Ethan could see save for studying patterns in the wood.

"Apologies," he said suddenly, "but I'm going to need complete focus."

Before Ethan could ask what he meant, the countless deep aches and sharp pains of his beating, all but forgotten in the commotion and desperation, roared back with a vengeance. He shuddered, doubling over and slouching against the wall to keep himself upright.

Only then did he realize it hadn't been adrenaline holding that pain at bay after all.

More gunfire. The roar of what Ethan could only assume was a flamethrower, a suspicion confirmed by the *Reee! Reee! Reee!* of the hotel's fire alarm and what might have been the hiss of ceiling-mounted sprinklers. And a keening howl, the voice of a Hunter at a pitch he'd never heard before. He could only hope it was a cry of torment, perhaps even a death scream, that the flames did their job.

Through it all, minute after minute, Lamb remained motionless. Even his breathing had faded to almost nothing.

The office door folded back, peeling from the frame and snapping in half, accompanied by more of the all-too-familiar shrieking. The Flannel Man and another of the Hunters from

Camp Mabry, the one with its face concealed by—formed of—a cowboy hat and an old-school bandana, loomed through the gap. Jagged, broken-edged, they continually switched places, one crossing in front of the other—even, it appeared, within the narrow confines of the doorway itself. Before Ethan could absorb what he'd seen, fight through the vertigo and the nausea it inflicted, they had already crossed the office, come within feet of the desk.

"No closer!" Lamb rose, leaning aggressively forward, fists on the wood. Even from behind him, Ethan felt the heat of his gaze, the sheer energies radiating from the man as he'd never seen before.

And the Hunters froze.

The Cowboy halted in mid-lurch, shoulders forward and arms angled back as though pressing into a headlong gale, while the Flannel Man... Ethan could scarcely stand even to look at the Flannel Man. It canted impossibly to one side in defiance of anatomy, even gravity, leg at a horrid, broken angle, featureless face jutting toward them as though its neck had not only folded forward but begun hideously to stretch.

That prickly, metallic taste that the doctor hadn't consciously noticed seemed somehow to pool on the tip of his tongue, leaving the rest of his mouth dry almost to the point of cracking.

"You see now?" Lamb straightened as he shouted, gesturing wildly. "You understand what I am? How I've hidden my people from you, how much more I can do? You are nothing, *nothing*! Fools and idiots, from any world!"

Spittle landed in tiny constellations on the desktop, and Ethan was suddenly unsure that the Hunters were the scariest figures in the office.

Nor was he entirely certain it was Lamb's "gifts" that had stopped the creatures in their tracks. In unison, in blurred jolts, both heads cocked to one side. It was unwise, Ethan knew, even dangerous, to ascribe human emotion or motivation to these vile things. Yet he could not shake the sense that the Hunters appeared neither overwhelmed nor frightened so much as... puzzled.

It was a distinction Lamb failed to appreciate, if he noticed it at all. "My power is greater than yours, *older* than yours! I understand truths you couldn't begin to dream of! I—"

The Flannel Man and the Cowboy *burbled*, a sound akin to the glutinous undertones of their earlier howling but far softer. And as with those howls, that liquid sound was accompanied by vocalizations both more familiar and more disturbing.

"Greater than yours, older than yours... Fools and idiots... Truths you couldn't begin, couldn't begin, couldn't begin..."

The words themselves held no meaning and Ethan heard no obvious patterns in the revolting spatters and pops, but he would have sworn that the damned things were somehow *talking* to one another.

And then they were gone, lurching backward and out past the shattered door between one blink and the next. Only then did Ethan hear the drumbeat of multiple approaching footsteps, the angry shouts and the metallic clatter of countless weapons.

Lamb smiled angelically at his followers as they poured into the office, already assuring them that the danger had passed.

Ethan wished he could believe a word of it.

Seventeen. Seventeen men and women dead, and little shy of a miracle that the body count was so low.

Lamb had ordered them assembled and laid out in one of the conference rooms. Some of the bodies remained intact enough to be carried. Others—falling apart due to the Hunters' terrible means of desiccation or, like Carlos, mangled in other ways—required more effort. Some had to be collected with shovels and wheeled in on the hotel's room service carts.

Over those corpses, and for the sake of the dozens of other New Covenant members who had gathered, Lamb uttered a winding eulogy, veering from Bible passages to personal reminiscence to proclamations of victory over the wicked, heretical obelisk-bringers.

To Ethan, it sounded like the ramblings of a mind coming unhinged, and at first, it almost appeared that the congregation, such as it were, might agree with him. Mourning, frightened, they took only moderate solace in Lamb's insistence that his powers had proven greater than the Hunters', seemed unconvinced that today had proven any sort of victory.

As he continued, however, and though he merely rephrased and repeated himself several times over, the mood in the chamber shifted. Tearful sniffles and doubtful muttering gave way to murmurs of assent and emphatic nods. Shoulders straightened, heads lifted. A few of Lamb's pronouncements were met by shouted *yeahs* and restrained cheers.

Ethan felt his own doubts wavering, had to force himself to maintain them, and seethed at Lamb's psychic manipulation of his own people.

Still, he hadn't planned to speak out, especially given the anger most of the New Covenant already felt for him. Lamb finally got around to something in his diatribe, however, that Ethan—in his shock, in his fear—couldn't ignore.

"You want us to *stay*?!"

Lamb halted in mid-sentence, examining the doctor as though he were some new form of mildew the man had only just noticed in his house. Angry rumbles floated through the crowd at the interruption.

"I believe I made that clear, yes."

"But..." Even after Lamb had insisted on staying and fighting, Ethan had been *sure* it was only long enough to fend off this first attack, that evacuation must certainly follow. "Mr. Lamb," he tried again, fighting to maintain his calm, "surely it's safest for everyone to keep moving. They know you're here, but if we find somewhere else to go, you can hide everyone from them again, you can—"

"And how long will we keep running, Doctor Bell? How will we begin to rebuild without a home? How long will we allow ourselves to remain victims?"

Again individual voices in the throng shouted their assent.

"You—"

"We can fight them, and we can win. We know that now. We have weapons they fear. Fire."

"But it takes so much to—"

"We can build better defenses. Dig in. And above all else, we know now what I've always suspected—that the gifts I was given to guide humanity into a new age are greater than theirs! They have reason to fear us now!"

More cheers.

"It was three of them this time, Lamb! *Three!* What happens if next time it's six? A dozen? More?"

"Let them come! As single spies or in battalions, let them come!"

Ethan raised a hand, pleading, even as he lowered his voice. "I was there in the room with you, remember? I don't think you stopped them. You *confused* them, that's all! Next time—"

"Would you play the serpent, then?" Lamb asked, just as softly. "Are you trying to shake my followers' faith?"

"I'm trying to keep them alive!"

"But you can't. *I* can." He turned, smiled to the crowd who had begun to whisper and complain over the conversation they couldn't hear, but still didn't raise his voice. "It's time, Ethan. I foresaw it, even as I summoned my power to rebuke the Hunters. We're nearing the final confrontation with the Heretics who invaded our world, killed our people, and your friend Ms. Han still has her own part to play. Even if I had no other reason to keep the New Covenant here, I'd have to so she might find us again, when she finally decides she can't leave her friends behind."

"You think she's ever coming back? *Here?* She's not that stupid."

"She's absolutely coming back, sooner or later. I can wait. Unless, of course, we can find her first and don't *have* to wait. So I ask you one last time, will you help me figure out where she's gone?"

"You're insane. No way."

"I see. And I suppose you're not willing to recant your doubts, either? Stop trying to sow doubt in my faithful?"

"You're going to get them killed."

Lamb nodded—and then slammed a fist into Ethan's chest, near his heart. A shock of cold roared through him, overwhelming all the earlier aches and pains. He found himself on his hands and knees, gasping, staring dizzily at the carpet's faded patterns.

"The doctor's absolutely right about one thing," Lamb said, once again addressing the room at large. "My gifts are not infallible. *I* am not infallible. I'm still human, I can still..." His voice cracked and he swallowed once, hard. "Make mistakes. Mistakes that, I'm sorry to say, others have suffered for."

Utter silence, now, as the assembly hung on his every word.

"I thought he'd been sent to help us. Another healer, to help build the new world. I thought... I'm so sorry. I thought Dana was sick, that Doctor Bell was tending to her. And instead..."

An enraged hiss, a horrified gasp, as the quickest among the congregation leapt ahead of Lamb's halting speech.

"Instead he preyed on the insecurities and the naivete of a young girl. A girl who trusted him, trusted *me*. She was going to tell me the truth, you see. That's why he attacked me. I failed her, and I am truly sorry."

Ethan couldn't stand, couldn't even look up, paralyzed twice over by pain and now by panic. He didn't *have* to look up. The shouts, the cries, the sobs, and the terrible thud of approaching steps told him all he needed to know.

And it was, he knew, nothing worse than he deserved.

Just make it quick.

But even in that, he was to be denied.

"The New Covenant *does not kill* unless we must," Lamb reminded them, his voice carrying over the swirling mob, every syllable slathered in a coating of sorrow and compassion to conceal the rot within. "There are too few of us left. And we will need doctors in the days to come. We can *make* him useful to us, make him atone. Your fury is righteous, but we need him alive and able to work.

"But anything beyond that is fair game. We take care of our own, my friends, and it is time Doctor Bell learned that lesson for good and all."

Chapter Thirteen

She knew where to go, where she *had* to go. She wasn't sure *when*.

For a time she'd done nothing but run, putting as much distance between herself and the latest atrocity as she could until, shaking with more than just the cold, she found keeping control of the Triumph almost more than she could manage. Only then did she slow, casting about for shelter and supplies.

She'd lost sensation in her fingertips and suffered through two obelisk-inflicted headaches before she succeeded, but it was very nearly worth it.

The Walmart was unlocked and, despite the lack of power, warmer and certainly drier than the outdoors. Here she'd collected several changes of clothes, heavy coat and gloves, a helmet, canned foods, batteries, lights, flares, even some painkillers—Vicodin, nothing so strong as Dilaudid—from the in-store pharmacy. The clothes, other than what she changed into, and most of the supplies went into a backpack she acquired from the camping department; a set of tools, some tubing, and a gas can she'd strapped to the bike with bungee cord.

Her immediate needs taken care of, she'd finally had the wherewithal to think, to consider where she might lay low.

She'd first decided on Galveston. Less than an hour from here, the smaller city would have everything she might need and the New Covenant wouldn't have the first clue where to look for her.

That idea had lasted for a cold, miserable half-hour on the freeway until she'd drawn near enough to smell Galveston's beaches—and the nightmarish carrion fields she only now remembered would be found at the ocean's edge. No way, no Goddamn way, was she camping herself within sight, within scent, of another mass grave, no matter how safe the place might be. No.

Instead she'd randomly chosen a chipped blue one-story house on Houston's outskirts, near one of the fire-ravaged neighborhoods. After breaking in, Cynthia had done a quick search for corpses, either homeowner or pet. Finding neither, she'd dropped her supplies in the bedroom doorway and passed out face-down on the mattress.

And that—not even the whole house, as she'd refused to so much as enter the room with the Pokemon stickers on the door—had been her home for going on five days now.

Five wretched, paranoid, pain-wracked days.

Whether from exhaustion, because the tumor was worsening, because of what Lamb had done to her, or simply bad luck, her head throbbed more often than not. The Vicodin dulled the worst of it, but it didn't help near enough.

In all that time, she left the house on only four occasions. Once to search for ammunition—she found none to fit either of the weapons she'd taken from the New Covenant, but a pawnshop provided her with a few pistols and bullets that actually matched—and for something in the morphine family, of which she found only a few doses in any nearby pharmacies.

Once in search of more food.

And twice when she thought she heard movement around the house. In both cases, whether it had been some animal that had moved on or sheer imagination, she encountered nothing.

On the fourth day, after a surge of pain so bad she wound up with her cheek in the gritty, sawdust-colored carpet, she broke down and took an extra-large dose of morphine. Doing so pretty well erased the following afternoon and much of the night, but she felt steadier the next morning than she had in days, able to put two thoughts together without the pressure threatening to shatter her skull from within.

It was then she decided she'd waited long enough. Even if Lamb foresaw that she might go back there, anyone looking for her would have come and gone by now.

So she packed it all up, started the motor—wincing at how loudly the sound carried through the empty city—and pointed the Triumph back toward Johnson Space Center.

Between the rough vibration of the ride, her constant wariness for obelisks or signs of the enemy, and the stench from Clear Lake that she couldn't entirely avoid, the pounding in her head returned by the time she got there. Leaving most of her gear by the motorcycle—everything but a flashlight, the 9mm Ruger in her fist, and the .38 Taurus revolver at her back under the leather jacket—she shoved the pain aside as best she could and marched straight toward flight control in FCR1.

"Me again," she announced, throwing the door open and heading for the front of the room. There she planted herself before the main screens and stared at the nearest camera. "I'm tired, I hurt, and I'm fucking terrified, and I'm in no mood for any more shit.

"I know you're here. Not 'tapped in' here, I mean *here* here. Somewhere on campus. If you want, I can go through all the little details that tipped us off, but it'll be quicker if you just accept that I know you lied. So come out and let's talk like actual human beings."

Nothing. The monitors and fluorescent lights hummed her only answer.

"Oh, come *on!*" She headed for one of the other doors. "You think I won't come looking for you? This is a *huge* place, but I've got nowhere better to be. You really going to put us both through this?"

Still nothing. She moved out into the hall and began opening doors.

Well, *most* of the doors. So far as she knew, Grigory still lay atop the desk in one particular office, slowly rotting away beneath his makeshift blanket of curtains. She decided that, for the nonce, she was prepared to assume her mysterious hacker wouldn't pick that room to hang out in.

With each step, her head worsened. The hallway began to tilt.

"Please!" She winced at her own shout. "I'm not your enemy. I need your help, that's why I'm here! I don't have any..." The faint thump as she pushed yet another door open sounded like artillery going off behind her face.

"Any..."

Cynthia dropped to her knees, sobbed once, tried to catch her head in her hands, and blacked out before she hit the floor.

She could barely think, except to wish she hadn't woken up. Her skull felt like an overinflated balloon, and she wanted it to pop already.

"Right next to you."

Cynthia dropped a hand off the sofa—sofa?—and groped blindly at the carpet. Medicine bottle, syringe. Either her Vicodin and morphine, or somebody had gone through a lot of trouble to make her think they were. Right now, she didn't much care which.

It took almost a full minute of fumbling before she got the lid off the needle and the needle into her thigh. Slowly, torturously slow, the pain faded. She almost sobbed again.

The morphine, in turn, made her a bit drowsy, a bit loopy, but adrenaline kept her mostly coherent. Groaning, she sat up and pried her eyes open.

She was, indeed, on a sofa, in one of the offices. Same chairs, same desk, same computer as usual.

Her two pistols sitting on the desk beside the computer was less usual.

The man standing behind that desk, gazing at her through dark shades and cradling a shotgun, even less than those.

Young, at least comparably—upper twenties, maybe?—and heavyset. He wore a purple shirt which popped dramatically against a very dark complexion. He'd probably been cleanshaven and bald when shit hit the fan; now his face was surrounded in many weeks' worth of scruff.

"Thank you," she said.

"Yeah, well. Once I figured you were for real, couldn't just leave you there. You sick?" He pointed a few fingers at the syringe. "Diabetic?"

Did he not read the labels? "Tumor."

"Damn. Sorry to hear that."

"Yeah." Then, since she couldn't think of anything better to go with, "Cynthia Han."

"Lucas. Lucas Cook."

"Nice to meet you, Lucas. Again."

Silence for a time. Cynthia gazed at Lucas. Lucas, as best she could tell behind the shades, gazed aimlessly at the wall beside her.

"So," she said finally, holding up the syringe for emphasis, "You obviously brought my gear in from the bike."

"Not all of it. Just the meds and whatnot."

"I... Was this all of it?"

"Other than some over-the-counter shit, yeah."

"Fuck." She'd been so out of it when she hit the pharmacies a few days ago... Cynthia knew she'd found only a few doses, but she'd forgotten—or never noticed—*how* few.

"That for pain?" Lucas asked.

"Yeah. It doesn't get that bad *too* often, but when it does..."

He nodded, lips pursed in contemplation. "So," he said finally, "I've been here a long time. Had a while to look around."

"Uh, right?"

"This place was full of nerds under shitloads of stress. And if I learned anything working with computers my whole life, it's that nerds under shitloads of stress have got to *un*stress."

"Not entirely sure I follow."

Lucas snickered. "What I'm saying is, I found so much weed in all these offices, in desk drawers and coat pockets and shit, we could start a grow house that'd give Willie a run for his money. I don't smoke, so you think it'll help, you're welcome to it."

Cynthia laughed. She couldn't help it. For all her desperation, all her pain, it'd never even occurred to her as an option—not that she'd have known where in Houston to find the stuff even if it had. "I may very well take you up on that. Thank you. Again."

He shrugged, looking almost embarrassed. "Ain't even a thing. Been a while since I had anyone to talk to. So, you want to tell me how you got back here? Or the rest of your story? We never got too deep into it last time."

Why not? "Sure. You may want to sit down, though. It's not short."

He nodded—and though he was smooth about it, subtle, confident, Cynthia noticed that he reached back, feeling around for the chair instead of so much as glancing behind him.

She finally understood the shades he wore, why he hadn't any idea how the prepackaged morphine injections were labeled.

How he'd avoided falling under the influence of alien writing on the obelisks.

"If I *had* turned out to be hostile," she said, hoping her tone was friendly enough to convey what her expression couldn't, "were you just going to aim for the sound of my voice and hope you got lucky?"

Lucas started, and his mouth went almost diagonal, struggling between a scowl and a rueful smile. "I ain't *completely* blind. Right now, this close? You stand out enough, sort of a blurry blob against the rest of the blur, for this bad boy to do the job."

"Heh. Fair enough, I..." For the first time, Cynthia fully focused, really paying attention, on the shotgun. "Wait one fucking minute!"

For all that he couldn't see what had snagged her attention, Lucas was no idiot. "Don't even. Ain't like I knew those fuckers weren't going to come looking for me once they had you. Look," he continued, softening. "I'm sorry. I covered him back up, even prayed over him. But I had to protect myself."

"Yeah." Cynthia breathed deep, twice. *Not like Grigory would've objected. He'd probably have yelled at us for leaving the shotgun with him in the first place.* "Yeah, okay." She blinked. "How were you able to track him—or us—on the monitors?"

"Put my face close enough to the screen, turn the brightness and contrast high enough, I can manage."

"Fair."

Cynthia lay back, stretching out across the sofa once more, mulling over how much of the story to offer, wondering how much he'd even believe.

In the end, though, he'd already seen—*lived through*, she corrected herself—the end of the world. No reason he shouldn't accept, or shouldn't hear, the lot of it.

So that's what she told him. With only a few breaks, to go grab a few drinks from the café and a quick run to the restroom, she ran down every bit of what she'd been through since that first awful morning on the ISS.

When it was finally all done, Lucas's first response was a long, drawn out, "Fuuuuck."

"That's accurate, yeah."

"If you told me all this shit two months ago, I'd have called you crazy."

"If I'd told you all this two months ago, I would've been."

"Heh." He leaned back in the chair, taking a long chug from a Dr Pepper she'd brought him. "So, not that I got any problem with the company, but why're you back here?"

"Your turn first, Lucas. How'd *you* wind up here? You've heard my story..."

"Yeah, fair. Ain't as dramatic as yours, though. Guess you already figured out why those Goddamn obelisks don't fuck with my head?"

"Wasn't too hard to piece together, no."

"Okay, so..."

In the hours following impact, as the world spiraled into madness, an online network swiftly formed, made up of people who—mostly for physical reasons, such as Lucas's legal blindness, but some mental as well—had proved unsusceptible to the obelisks' influence. They observed, horrified and helpless, as those with firsthand experience, and then others exposed by the ubiquitous lenses of news and social media, up and vanished from their lives. In a day or two, nearly everyone in these makeshift chats, forums, and sub-communities found themselves alone.

Some stopped communicating, leaving Lucas and the others to wonder forever what had become of them. Some went in search of answers and never returned. Some announced they were taking their own lives. Many simply panicked or fell into despair, wailing and screaming for a life they couldn't possibly regain.

But others buckled down, focused on learning all they could. They gathered every news report, every scrap of rumor, that hit the Net before those who'd reported them fell under the obelisks' sway. And they discussed where they might go to find more information still. It hadn't taken long to come up with the idea of hacking into government departments—the military, the NSA and FBI, and, yes, NASA. Not many were skilled enough even to try, and those who were had little hope of success, but it seemed the best way to uncover anything more.

Then, less than three days after impact, without anyone to run and maintain the plants, the power grid died. Among the other, far more immediate concerns, it meant that nobody would be hacking anything—and that the network, these people's last link to their fellow survivors, was gone.

Which left him, Lucas had decided after another couple of days, with only one option.

"You did *what*?"

He shrugged. "Figured I was closer to NASA than anybody I'd been talking to, and I couldn't do shit at home. So I packed up my gear and hit the road."

"But..." Cynthia felt foolish, arguing against something he'd already done. She still couldn't help it. "That's, what, thirty miles?"

"I mean, more or less. Ain't like I was going to get run over. Highways were empty by then. And when I got tired, had my pick of houses or apartments to crash in."

"Jesus Christ."

"Anyways, took a while to learn all the systems, but time wasn't real pressing, so..." He concluded with a second shrug.

"Well, I'm glad you stayed. I think I told you last time, you can help me. It's too bad you weren't able to learn anything, but maybe with my help we—"

"Uh..." Lucas reached around, scratched the back of his neck. "Now, that' ain't quite what I said."

Cynthia sat up, turning to face him directly. "You said," she reminded him, "that we weren't going to like the records if we found them. That nothing showed up on RADAR or satellite cams."

"Yeah, that's... true-ish."

"'Ish?'"

"Hey, y'all could've been anybody, after anything! Besides, we barely got to talking before you got called out, remember?"

"All right. So what *do* you know?"

"I know there's something fucking *huge* out there. Probably that ship you told me about, that, uh, Cathedral. Felt it once myself, like the whole world shook. Might've been the same night it passed y'all in La Grange."

"Okay, but that's not really—"

"I'm getting there!"

"Sorry."

"That's the only time it came close enough for me to feel, but it ain't the first time it came through here. It showed up in Texas same night y'all came down from the ISS."

"How can you possibly know that?"

"Same way I can track the thing," he told her with a wide grin.

Cynthia could almost have mistaken the pounding of her heart for that same ship passing overhead once again. "How?! You said it didn't show up..."

"Not unless you know how to look." He rose, leaned the shotgun over one shoulder and—groping around a bit on the desktop—collected Cynthia's pistols and stuck them in his jeans.

"I don't suppose..." she began, watching the operation.

"We're getting there," he said, "but we ain't there yet."

Since arguing wouldn't exactly be good for the burgeoning trust, and since she shouldn't be needing the weapons in the immediate future—she hoped—Cynthia grunted and went along with it.

Only after he'd collected the hardware did Lucas also produce a white folding cane from behind the desk. Sweeping his path with a casualness born both of long use and familiarity with his surroundings, he led her from the office.

From the hall they passed into the courtyard outside, where the chill wind insisted on delivering just enough rancid stench from Clear Lake's frock of corpses to make her sick all over again, and then back into an adjacent structure. The brief trek finally ended at... another office.

This one, however, proved unique. It wasn't just the used

and rumpled cot, the laundry piled in the corner, the cornucopia of empty plates and open cans, though those were enough to identify the room as the hacker's sanctum.

No, it was the extra equipment plugged into the desktop computer. A second laptop, frankly more cutting edge than anything NASA would readily spring for, sat beside a few additional bits of chunky hardware the likes of which Cynthia had never seen. Curious, she crossed the room and leaned over for a better view.

"Big one searches for satellite signals," Lucas said. "Smaller one's a Braille display for when I have to read something more complicated than the text-to-speech can deal with."

"Okay. Show me."

He squeezed around her, thumped down in the chair. A few quick keystrokes woke both computers, and then exited from the security system through which he'd no doubt witnessed her collapse.

A swirl of colors on a gridded map appeared behind the vanishing window, and Cynthia would have smacked a palm to her forehead if she hadn't been too afraid of reviving the headache.

"Of course. I'm an idiot."

"You've been running from actual aliens, a psychic, and motherfuckers strapped like the NRA owes *them* money. Me, I've been sitting on my ass pushing buttons. Don't sweat it."

Still, it seemed so obvious. Something *that* big, so massive you could just *feel* it in the sky above you?

Sure, maybe some unearthly tech kept it cloaked from radar, invisible to camera. But the *atmosphere around it*, pressure changes, shifts in the wind as it passed? Any functioning local weather station would detect those, let alone NASA.

As Lucas had said, you just had to know how to look.

"Have you gone back?" Cynthia asked, forcing herself not to reach over his shoulders for the keyboard. "Tried to backtrack it, or find any patterns, or—?"

"All that, yeah. First thing, once I figured all this out. Bastard's made a whole shitload of trips across the state, but no flight or schedule patterns I can find."

The exhausted astronaut began to deflate.

"But…"

And straightened again. "But?"

"I can shove my face all the way against the screen, still only so much I'm ever going to make out. So you look at this, tell me what you see."

A few more taps and clicks. The image on the monitor flickered, greens and oranges and yellows swapping places and patterns.

"The day after y'all landed," Lucas told her.

Cynthia knew well how to read weather and atmospheric radar, and it didn't take her long to pick out one peculiar pocket of movement and pressure moving against prevailing conditions. While pinpointing the vessel was impossible—she could, at best, narrow it down to a broad area, miles in diameter, via the evidence of its passing—she watched as it drifted into the heavy hills of northwest Texas, just shy of the panhandle.

And then she watched as it moved away again. But…

"Hang on a minute."

"Ha! Thought I might've just imagined it."

"No, there's definitely something… Run that back again, would you?"

She watched a second time, a third, and only then was she sure. The effects of the Cathedral on the weather and winds were subtle, difficult to define, and of course completely beyond the bounds of anything Cynthia had seen before. So much other data, so many natural phenomena had to be filtered out and ignored, and then the impact of natural conditions on what remained taken into account. Still, she no longer had any doubt.

"It's smaller," she said. "It's a *lot* smaller."

"What do you figure it means?"

"It means," Cynthia told him, her excitement at having a clear path washing away the last trace of her drugged malaise, "that somewhere not too far from the Wichita River, the aliens left part of the Cathedral behind!"

Chapter Fourteen

Headlights diluted to inky pools in the gloom, engine the only sound for miles save for the limp breeze and soft rain, the old Honda crept along US-287.

The atmosphere in the car thickened with every mile, choked with worry, impatience, fear—to say nothing of the general awkwardness of strangers thrown together, two people who had long since exhausted the topic of their common concerns and weren't certain they cared enough to delve deeper into the personal. Lucas leaned back, lost in thought or perhaps even dozing, as Cynthia hunched miserably behind the wheel.

This had all seemed like a much better idea, back at Johnson. Their efforts at narrowing down their destination—tracking weather and wind, examining topography, even watching the movement of herds and flocks, where the overcast allowed and the satellites were positioned just right—had electrified them. Cynthia had finally felt she was making genuine progress.

The feeling had soured only a little when Lucas announced, partly out of burning curiosity and in part because he had literally nothing better to do, that he was coming with her. She hadn't expected it, worried his disability might slow her down or get him in trouble she couldn't handle. Then again, he'd already helped her find answers she couldn't have found alone, and he *had* done his best to care for her after she'd collapsed.

They'd grabbed the first set of car keys they found in a desk drawer, transferred their supplies to the Accord, and hit the road.

Given her prior travels in this desolate landscape, she hadn't anticipated a fun trip, but the highway marked the start of genuine misery.

It wasn't just the need to avoid the obelisks, though that would have slowed her down enough. Cynthia had built up a solid tolerance to the painkillers she'd taken over the past months, but the marijuana they'd acquired at NASA was something she hadn't touched since college. It kept the headaches at bay so far, but she felt sluggish, submerged in something, and didn't dare trust her reflexes. Even unable to see the scenery drifting by, Lucas expressed his dissatisfaction with their progress more than once, until Cynthia told him in no uncertain terms that the topic was closed unless he wanted to take the wheel.

The emptiness, the sheer isolation, gnawed at her as they continued, disturbing in ways it never was before. More of the pot's influence, maybe? Or because she shared the experience only with a man she didn't know?

Or due, perhaps, to what awaited at the other end.

Cynthia began to fret over being the only car on the highway, to worry at the attention they might attract. They were the only source of light, of sound, for miles. The Cathedral, the Crooked Men, the New Covenant, or God knew who else, what other desperate survivors... Any or all of them could loom suddenly from the gray, shooting or grasping, shouting or shrieking, and while Lucas had finally deigned to give Cynthia back her guns, she didn't feel in much condition to use them.

And she was so tired. A journey of more than four hundred miles, the drive would have taken over six hours under normal circumstances. For her, it took nearly three times that, forcing them to stop and break into a motor-court motel for a brief and fitful sleep.

For all her worries, nothing came at them. No Hunters. None of Lamb's people. And while she swore she spotted movement, a few running or lurking figures near the outskirts of Dallas, they'd come nowhere near the car. If they were survivors, as opposed to figments of her waterlogged imagination, they'd wanted only to be left alone.

She was coiled so tense and tight by the time they neared the Wichita River she almost wished someone *had* attacked them, just to relieve the pressure.

Lucas jolted in his seat, startled—or perhaps awakened—by an abrupt turn from paved street to rough dirt road. The Honda bounced, tires scraping, unhappy in an environment for which it had never been bred.

"What's up?" the hacker asked.

"We're here. Ish."

He grunted, settling back. For all their efforts at NASA, they still had nothing more precise than a general vicinity. They'd followed the weather and the map as far as they could. Now the plan devolved into "wander around and look for anything out of the ordinary."

Which, given that one of them had to beware of obelisks and the other couldn't look for anything at all, posed something of a challenge.

Cynthia pointed the wheels down first this dirt road and then that, taking the turns as they came. The terrain rose and fell, dropped and climbed, very much like the Hill Country further south. The poor car chugged along as best it could, but she felt its struggles at every slope.

Worse still, even the small, private roads left miles of rolling fields and towering hills unexplored between them.

"This isn't going to work," she announced, pulling abruptly into a small side-path that led to a locked gate. The "Private Property" sign canted forward where one of its four brackets was missing.

"So what, then? I don't know about you, but I ain't out here for the scenery."

Cynthia stared at him, then chuckled despite herself. "Guess you did more or less have the same view back at Johnson, huh?"

He grinned. "Pretty similar."

"I think we're going to have to do this on foot."

And that was the end of that grin. "You shitting me?"

She waved a hand at the broad property beside them, then sheepishly dropped it into her lap as it occurred to her what she was doing. "There's just too much open space between these roads, Lucas. We're never going to find anything from the car. Look, if you want to stay here, I get it. I can't ask you to go wandering around in the wilderness. We can—"

"Hell with that! I said I was coming with you, and I am. You just got to slow up for me, is all."

Part of her wanted to ask if he was sure. Part of her wanted to argue that she *should* go alone. She decided both parts were disrespectful. "All right. I mean, honestly, it's just going to get darker out there anyway. You'll probably do better out there than I will."

"Yeah, probably."

She chose not to ask if he was kidding, instead killing the ignition and grabbing for her leather jacket.

They spent a few minutes with the doors open, assembling everything they figured they'd need and dividing it into packs. With the engine off, Cynthia heard the distant rush and ripple of the Wichita over the whispering winds.

Those, and nothing else. No night birds, no coyotes, none of Texas's winter insects. She and Lucas might have been the only living beings for miles around.

"I wish," she muttered, hefting a bright camping lantern and casting about in the puddle of stark-white light, "we had a clue where to start."

"Hills."

"Huh?"

"Where are the hills thickest?"

Cynthia wanted to sink into the earth and felt grateful he couldn't see her face flush. "Because where the hell else are you going to hide something that big." She sighed ruefully. "You sure you're blind?"

His answering smile was wicked. "You sure you ain't?"

She chose to spread one of the maps she'd picked up across the trunk instead of responding to that. A bit of study, and she started off toward what it claimed was the nearest bit of dramatic topography.

Started, and stopped. "Do you, uh, need me to guide you or anything? Keep your hand on my shoulder or anything?"

Lucas thought it over, twisting his cane. "Take a few steps."

"Um. Okay." She did so, listening—as she was certain he was—to the winter grass crunching underfoot.

"I think we're good. Don't go sneaking off, don't shirk on the conversation, it shouldn't be a thing. Just stop if I shout and keep it slow."

So it went, slow indeed. Despite the warm clothes, Cynthia shivered, and again it wasn't just the cold. The world felt empty. More than empty, *absent*, as though everything beyond the radius of her lantern had just gone. The gurgling of the river, a comfort at first, gradually faded to one more part of the background, leaving her with nothing. She tried to keep up an ongoing conversation, but the effort wore heavily on them both, until it was easier to let her footsteps and an occasional "How you holding up back there?" do the work.

The night became ink, an endless puddle through which they waded. The hills swam in those waters, great beasts looming near enough to terrify before drifting away. More than once Cynthia stumbled, even fell a couple of times, despite the lantern. She'd been right: Tapping ahead with his cane, accustomed to feeling his way through foreign territory, sensing the pitch and yaw of the earth beneath his feet, Lucas proved steadier than she did.

The stress, the silence, the fear of what she might find—or what she might miss, or what might find her—chipped away at Cynthia's calm. Her skull throbbed, but she didn't dare take anything that might dull her senses, throw off her balance.

A third time she tripped, nearly twisting her knee, and found herself lying at a sharp angle rather than flat. She'd landed on the slope of a hill, a hill that—despite her lantern, despite her every effort to look in all directions at once—she hadn't even realized they were passing.

There she stayed for countless moments, grunting enough to let Lucas know she hadn't vanished but otherwise ignoring his increasingly worried questions. Tears burned her eyes, bile the back of her throat.

The fuck was she trying to prove out here? What was she going to do, wander dozens if not scores of square miles, in hopes of stumbling across their goal? Even during the day, dull and overcast and dust-choked, it would have been lunacy! At night? What the *hell* had she been thinking trying this at night?

You weren't, a voice—not even her own, but one that sounded an awful lot like Clarence Walker's, even if it didn't talk like him—told her from somewhere behind her brain. *You were confused, and you were scared, and you were damn well* stoned, *and it didn't so much as occur to you that you were not only engaged in a fool's errand, but going about it in the dumbest way imaginable.*

She wanted to tell it to shut up, but couldn't really be bothered.

Do you even know, it pressed on, *how to get back to the car?*

Of course she did!

Didn't she?

Cynthia raised her head, looked around.

Did she?

She was going to get herself killed out here at this rate, save Lamb and the Hunters the trouble. If it hadn't been for Lucas, she wasn't sure she'd even have cared.

Maybe it wasn't the pain or the drugs that had her so turned around, making such bad choices. Maybe the tumor was finally making its move. Damn thing had certainly taken its time about it, if so.

Furious at herself and wallowing somewhat in her misery, Cynthia didn't notice at first that they were walking again.

When had she forced herself up? Put one foot in front of the other? She had no memory of it.

No memory of choosing a direction, either, but they weren't headed quite the same way they had been. The chill breeze was coming at her dead on, now, not blowing against one cheek.

Figures.

Well, if she'd deliriously set off on some random tangent, she could turn off it just as easily. At least make this wild goose chase more comfortable, get the wind out of her face.

Yet she didn't. For another few dozen yards, she forged stubbornly forward, holding to her course without the slightest idea why. Exhausted bullheadedness? Did the new mix of drugs render her brain so sluggish that it took this long to translate decision into action?

Cynthia froze in her tracks, gawping, nearly stunned by the abrupt shift in sensation.

Or had she sensed this on some reptilian level while still too distant to consciously notice, and come this way deliberately?

The pain was gone, smothered once again by that familiar numbing blanket across her thoughts.

Almost familiar. She thought, just maybe, it felt ever so slightly different this time, a new "flavor" to the creeping anesthetization. A separate... accent.

Or was it different, after all? It might just be that she'd never had THC in her system when encountering it before. She could be entirely wrong. She might feel out its edges, seek out the center as she had before, and just more Hunters waiting for her. She bit down on her urge to call out a warning, to take Lucas by the hand and flee.

Instead she said, "I think I know how to find them."

"You maybe feel like expanding on that?"

"Not really. But if you hear me scream, run."

It took until after midnight for Cynthia to get a sense of the sensation's borders, to make her way inward. A gelid slush, teetering indecisively between rain and sleet, oozed over them, turning the crunch of the grass underfoot into something squishier. She stumbled along with an arm around Lucas's shoulder now, less because he needed the extra guidance than because they both welcomed the shared body heat.

"Ain't been this close to a woman in a while," he joked through chattering teeth.

"Don't get your hopes up, Lucas. Or anything else. You're not my type."

"Too Black or too blind?" he challenged.

"Too male."

Lucas missed a step, jolting them both—and then burst into near-hysterical laughter. His guffaws echoed from the distant hills, and he leaned heavily on Cynthia, shoulders heaving, until he finally caught his breath.

"You feel like sharing?" she asked.

"Just..." He waited out another fit. "Just my life, is all. Only woman I meet after the end of the world, and she's gay. That's some Twilight Zone luck, right there."

Cynthia rolled her eyes even as she swallowed a chuckle of

her own. "Keep walking, Henry Bemis."

"Who?"

"Never mind."

It slowly emerged from the shadows ahead. It might or might not have been shaped like just another hill; Cynthia couldn't tell. It stretched too far beyond and too far above the reach of her electric lantern to make out its full dimensions. It sloped like a hillside, albeit a steep one, had its own bends and folds and protrusions as if it sought to emulate the surrounding terrain.

But no hill or mountain anywhere in Texas reflected an obsidian black the way this did.

Not metal, precisely. She might almost have described it as glass-like, though it wasn't quite that, either. It was a substance—even after all she'd seen, all she'd learned, Cynthia found herself reluctant to entertain the notion, but it was the only one that fit—not of Earth.

"We're here," she whispered.

"Figured that," Lucas said, "when you gasped and stopped walking. What is it?"

"Let's find out."

They'd gotten a whole two steps nearer when the ground began to shake, setting them both stumbling.

No. *Not just the ground*, Cynthia realized, falling to one knee amidst the spastically twitching grass, the puffs of frozen soil that leapt and danced about her. *Everything* vibrated—the earth, yes, but also the falling rain, even the wind itself. A dull rumble permeated the world, sinking deep into blood and marrow.

She'd felt this before, though not so closely. Teeth clenched to keep them from knocking painfully together, she forced herself to look up.

From behind the artificial hillside, *something* rose into the night sky. Too far beyond the reach of her feeble illumination, it was nothing but a shape, a deeper and more solid blot against the darkness of the night.

A *massive* shape, stretching beyond the bounds of sight in all directions just like its grounded counterpart did. Still she watched it, struggling to make out any detail, any hint of its nature.

And then there was light.

Intensely, painfully, impossibly bright, a strange green-white erupting from the vessel hovering above. Cynthia cried out, raising a hand and turning her face from the blinding radiance. Stronger than the brightest day she could remember, she'd seen nothing comparable since before returning to the dust-clouded Earth, had genuinely forgotten that such brightness was possible, what it felt like. Even Lucas recoiled from its intensity.

All of which brought her blinking, watering eyes back to the synthetic hillside—a hillside that had begun to open.

No hinged door, no sliding panel. The substance flowed, peeling unevenly apart like two separating pools of condensation on a cold glass. From beyond the new aperture shone another light, not nearly so intense as the one above but still dazzling in its own right.

Into that aperture, silhouetted by that light, a figure stepped.

Chapter Fifteen

"尊贵的韓小姐，欢迎您的光临."

"I…" Whatever Cynthia had expected to hear, whatever she might ever have *imagined* she might hear, that wasn't it. "I'm sorry. I don't… I don't speak Chinese."

"Oh." The backlit stranger sounded uncountably disappointed.

"We, um. I mean, my mother wouldn't allow it in the house after my father died. English only!" she added with a passable imitation of her mom's accent and a forced chuckle.

Why am I telling him all this? Am I that *nervous?*

"Besides…" She nearly stumbled over the words, now, so rushed to get them out. "That, uh, that sounded like Mandarin? Even if I spoke… If Mom hadn't… We're Cantonese. So I still probably wouldn't…" She shrugged helplessly.

"I see. Pity."

That's what it was! Not nerves—well, yes, nerves, a lot of nerves, but not *just* nerves! The stranger's disappointment, even just the few syllables she'd heard of it, put her in mind of her mother and Commander Walker both.

"Well," the man continued, "it's hardly important. I was only greeting you, Ms. Han. You, too, are welcome, of course, Mr. Cook."

"I even want to know?" Lucas asked.

Cynthia grunted. "Telepathic."

"Ah, sort of."

The stranger stepped forward even as the light behind him dimmed a little bit, revealing himself to be a man in his fifties or sixties, his face just a bit wrinkled, his hair white. His features would have suggested to Cynthia that he was Chinese even if his greeting hadn't, and if his charcoal suit represented what his life had been like before, he'd been a man of means and status.

"My name," he told them with a shallow bow, "is Zheng Xiaowen. It is my privilege to welcome you both to the Cathedral. If you will please come with me?" He turned on his heel and stepped into the light, clearly presuming they would follow.

Nearly bent double with doubt, and certain Lucas must feel the same, Cynthia did so. Her nose and throat began to itch, irritated by an atmosphere that somehow combined aspects of identifiable familiar odors—machine oil, tree sap, ozone, blood, gunpowder, salt—without reproducing any of them in their entirety.

"Do not concern yourself with your shoes," their host joked as the sensation beneath their feet turned from uneven and grassy to perfectly smooth.

Footsteps. The tapping of Lucas's cane. Even the swish and occasional squeak of their jackets. All normal, all expected, but something was off, something Cynthia couldn't initially put her finger on. It all sounded *flat*, somehow.

No echoes. She could sense the space around them, even though her eyes hadn't yet adjusted to the brightness, but not one sound echoed.

"So." Marching ahead, gaze turned downward in a futile attempt to escape the lights, she felt she ought to say *something*. "You're human, Mr. Zheng?"

He laughed from up ahead—but not far up ahead. He was, Cynthia realized, holding himself to a slower gait so as not to outdistance Lucas. "Quite human, I assure you."

"If you know anything more about us than our names, you'll understand how you being a human on their side might be a problem for us."

Zheng's chuckling stopped. "You don't know who the sides *are*, Ms. Han. Perhaps you might hold any declarations of enmity until you do. But yes, I understand how I might 'be a problem.' I fear you may find much of what you'll be seeing problematic, until you hear us out."

Cute that you think I'll feel otherwise after *your bullshit*. It didn't feel like the time to voice such sentiments aloud, though.

Of course, in this place, with these *creatures*, maybe she didn't have to.

"What did you mean 'sort of' telepathic?" she asked instead.

"It's not quite... We will get to it, I promise. I can tell you that they are as curious about you as you are about them. You're different, but not so different that the Disciples cannot feel the touch of the others on your dreams, woven into the substance of your thoughts."

It was the sheer casualness of the comment that got to her. She swallowed, mouth suddenly dry. "The others?"

"The Wayward and the Enigma."

Well, that was helpful.

The lights had dimmed further and her vision had adjusted somewhat, allowing Cynthia to finally make out more than the barest impressions of her surroundings.

But not much more. Something about the peculiar hue of the illumination interacted with the dark, not-metal/not-glass walls so that it faded, absorbed before it could spread. It was bright, but contained; she could see clearly, but not far. The effect was disorienting, surreal.

They were in a hallway, perfectly straight, devoid of side passages or recognizable features. An artery without flaw, beginning to end. It couldn't possibly be an efficient use of space! She ran her gaze along the wall, up to where it met the ceiling...

Blinked, hard. Tried again, this time to examine where it met the floor.

It didn't, exactly. She saw no seam, not even any real curve. It looked as though the wall and the floor—or the wall and the ceiling—sloped together gradually, so gradually as to be all but invisible, until they melded into one another without angle.

Except they *couldn't.* So subtle a curve would require dozens upon dozens of feet, maybe more, to link one surface to the other, and the hall was no more than a few yards wide.

Shuddering, she shifted her focus back to the substance of the wall itself.

In brighter light than she'd had outside, she could see, too, that some sort of striation ran through the substance. Lighter streaks than the rest of the material, it vaguely resembled an extended and more monodirectional pattern such as one might find in high-quality marble, mixed with the efforts of a particularly OCD spider. The striae were long, almost unfathomably. She could see no end to them, ahead or behind.

They reminded her of something else, but it wouldn't come to mind.

At no point could she spot a source for the green-white illumination. It was just *there*.

Another wall sealed the passage ahead, impeding further progress. Zheng stopped before it.

"My apologies," he said. "I would prefer you not have to experience this until after we've arrived at our destination and had the opportunity to explain. Unfortunately, what's behind here occupies too much of the Cathedral for us to avoid it.

"You will probably want to touch something. It is *vital* that you do not, no matter how tempting or what you think you might accomplish. As I said, there is much happening here you do not yet understand."

Silence, a heavy-lidded gaze, and Cynthia realized he was waiting for an acknowledgment. She was tempted not to offer it, not to promise to leave alone something she just *knew* wasn't going to make her happy—but the fighter pilot and astronaut in her comprehended all too well the importance of, as one of her instructors had put it, "Not fucking with anything you don't know how to unfuck."

"Okay," she said.

Lucas added, "Yeah."

Zheng said nothing, gave no signal Cynthia could see. Nevertheless, the wall opened, peeling, pulling, drifting apart just as the exterior entryway had done. Again, however, she saw the process much more clearly this time. Saw those peculiar striae stretch and bulge, pulling taut here, relaxing there, and she knew what had nagged at her about them.

Muscle fibers. They reminded her of muscle fibers.

Could the whole vessel work that way? Reshaping itself at whim? It would explain the entry hall, straight and without access to any other part of the Cathedral because, for the moment, it didn't need to be anything else.

Then she looked through the gaping aperture and forgot all about the surrounding walls.

"What?" She assumed Lucas reacted to her strangled gasp, but she had no thought, let alone breath or effort, to spare in response. "What is it?"

Cynthia darted forward a few steps, pushing past Zheng, oblivious to his disapproving glare or a few under-his-breath words in Mandarin. It was probably best he'd made no move to physically restrain her from passing him by. She might have broken his jaw.

Unlike the hallway, the lighting here was such that she could see for a distance—perhaps because the open space had no walls to absorb that light. It was impossibly huge, the chamber beyond. No, not a "chamber." The only justifiable term was *cavern*, for all that it was artificial. It couldn't be less than a thousand feet on all sides, and hundreds in height. Rings of balconies and protruding walkways rose high above, forming multiple partial levels.

And so far as Cynthia could see, the entire vast space was practically full.

In row after tightly packed row, stacked toweringly, impossibly high, stood countless capsules. Roughly brick-shaped, with rounded corners, they glinted dully in the antiseptic lighting, their color a murky, organic gold somewhere between unpolished amber and the oxidized sebum of an infected blackhead.

Limbs formed from the walls and ceiling, bonelessly flexing with the pull of those fibrous striae, occasionally emerged to probe at one capsule, or to carefully slide another from this column to that, all to no purpose Cynthia could fathom. Some were simple prods, poking or perhaps taking samples; others assumed the form of inhuman hands, bristling with finger-like tendrils that wrapped and carried capsules in a serpentine embrace. Other than those, she saw no machinery, no equipment of any sort. Just more capsules, and more beyond those.

She could scarcely begin to guess how many there might

be. So massive was the chamber, so tightly packed the capsules, they could well number hundreds of thousands, maybe more.

And contained in each one, visible as no more than blurred shapes within the ugly, glutenous substance, was a human body.

Cynthia moved toward the nearest with a wordless cry, one hand outstretched, now deaf to Lucas's increasingly desperate questions.

And, until he put himself between her and the nearest row of capsules, to Zheng's objections.

"You were warned, Ms. Han! You mustn't touch anything!"

That outstretched hand abruptly wrapped about Zheng's tie. "You fucking bastard! Is this what they came for? To collect our dead? And you're *helping* them?! Tell me why I shouldn't—"

"Who said," he asked, aiming a vaguely offended scowl at her fist, "that they were dead?"

"Wh-what?"

"This facility contains one million, thirty-seven thousand, three hundred and eleven men, women, and children. And I give you my word that every last one is alive."

Cynthia fell back, staggered to the depths of her soul. "How... how can...?"

"I did tell you we had a great deal to discuss."

"I want to see."

"That's not possible at this time." Zheng straightened his tie and slid the tip back under his coat. "It's unlikely that your interference could harm anyone, but not entirely impossible, and the Disciples will not allow that. I gave you my word, and for now, you will have to accept it.

"Now, come. We're almost there."

Again he walked, and again Cynthia fell in behind him, struggling to absorb everything she'd just seen and heard.

"You can't just leave me hanging like that!" Lucas snapped. "I can't do shit if I you don't tell me what's happening."

"Yeah. Sorry." Stumbling over the details as she tried to take in everything around them, she filled him in.

"Jesus."

"I don't think he'd approve, frankly."

"You buy it? You think they're alive in those things?"

She'd wondered that herself, but now that he asked... "I don't know Zheng, but his face when he said it? And I don't think they'd bring us in here just to lie to us. What'd be the point? Yeah, until he gives me reason not to, I think I believe him."

From the underside of an overhead balcony, another tendril extruded itself, condensing into semi-solidity and writhing silently toward another stack of human cargo.

Zheng halted at what appeared to be a random spot along one wall. "Stand close, please."

As soon as they'd obeyed, the floor around them separated from the rest and they began to rise. The wall beside them rippled and flexed as it lifted them up.

And up.

Until they had finally passed beyond the upper reaches of the artificial cavern, through another sudden aperture in the ceiling, and found themselves in a much smaller chamber.

Smaller on a purely relative scale, of course.

The illumination in here was dimmer, once more creating that peculiar "isolated puddles of light" effect. Unimpeded, Zheng moved toward the room's other side, to stand beside a peculiar pedestal. It appeared to be formed of the same substance as the rest of the Cathedral, but its upper surface was coated in a layer of a yellowish semi-solid muck similar to the capsules below. The room seemed to be otherwise empty.

Cynthia started to ask a question, which transformed into an abortive yelp as the wall behind Zheng moved.

No, not the wall. Something *behind* it.

The surface, she realized, was strangely transparent. Whatever lurked beyond was partially obscured, as though viewed through cloudy water or thin ink. Only the parts of it that came right up to the "window" proved visible, and only when in motion.

All she could tell was that it was enormous, somehow fibrous, twisting and writhing against itself, and continuously pumping, flexing. Her mind crafted an image—rightly or wrongly—of great muscular lengths, almost a cluster of fleshy trees, intertwining with one another, even as they beat in erratic patterns like a failing heart.

One creature? Multiple? The merest limbs or other fragment of an entity so very much greater than she might imagine? Any guess would be sheerest supposition.

As it had done increasingly often of late, her bewildered brain seized first on perhaps an unduly trivial query. "Wait. If they're that big..."

Zheng waited for her to gather her thoughts.

"The passage we came through was sized for humans!"

"Yes. That's all it needed to be now."

"O...kay, then." Haltingly, digging for the right words, she described what she saw to Lucas as best she could. Again Zheng politely waited for her to finish before speaking.

"We can talk here. I'm afraid, as nonbelievers, this is as far into the Cathedral, or as near to the Disciples, as you're permitted to come."

The thing behind him pulsed.

"How much higher could we go?" Cynthia asked. "We've got to be near the, uh, 'hilltop' by now."

"You saw a portion of the Cathedral in flight, Ms. Han. It's since reattached itself to the remainder."

"I didn't hear or feel anything!"

"You wouldn't have, not with their technology. Nor would you find so much as a seam between the two parts if you looked now. They've fully merged."

She slowly nodded. "So they—you—leave behind the, what, cargo hold? When you're cruising around looking for whatever you're looking for. I guess even alien tech gets better gas mileage with less weight."

"A bit simplistic," Zheng said, "but essentially accurate."

"That's what you said about the al—uh, the Disciples being telepathic. When do we get the less simplistic but more accurate versions?"

"We'd prefer to start with you, Ms. Han. You're different. You *feel* different, to them, than most humans. Why?"

Cynthia crossed her arms and glared.

"They want to know why you have such a negligible reaction to the Scriptures."

You call that level of pain negligible?

"They want to know about your experiences with the Enigma. And with the Wayward."

She thought, given what she knew, she could guess who they meant. Still she said nothing.

The writhing of the thing behind the translucent panel slowed.

"Do you intend not to cooperate?" Zheng asked. For the first time, he sounded a touch impatient.

A touch dangerous.

"Takes two to cooperate, Mr. Zheng. The 'co-' might have tipped you off."

"I'm not certain I unders—"

"Why have they *done* this to us?! They've killed *billions*! What do they want? Why in God's name are you *helping* them?" She clasped her hands behind her back so he wouldn't see them shake. "You give me answers, *then* I'll give you some! Not before!"

Now it increased, the twitching, twisting, coiling, sliding, until she imagined she could hear the serpentine trunks of tissue—or whatever those were, those lengths of meat and muscle she could barely see, attached to Heaven only knew what—scraping against one another.

And then she felt it, a feathery brush inside her skull, ghostly fingertips rifling the edges of her thoughts. Nothing so gross, nor so violating, as Lamb's assault had been, but the sensations were definitely distant cousins. A dagger of agony pierced her brain, then faded just as swiftly, before she could even cry out, leaving a persistent but thankfully dull ache in its wake.

Zheng craned his neck as though someone had called his name, then jammed his fingertips into the semisolid film on the panel. A grimace flashed across his face. He turned to face the thing—or things—in the inky murk behind him. Now and again he gestured with his free hand, as though emphasizing a point, but he spoke not a word.

When he finally did address Cynthia and Lucas once more, the skin beneath his eyes had sunken as though he'd missed a full night's sleep.

"My apologies, Ms. Han."

"Yours?" she challenged. "Not theirs?"

"They do not... have a concept of apologies, precisely. They are unaccustomed to misunderstanding, and this isn't a transgression severe enough to require atonement. So you'll have to accept mine, I fear."

"Anyone want to tell me what we need an apology *for*?" Lucas asked.

"An unintended offense," Zheng said. "The Disciples are unaccustomed to asking for what they want to know, or waiting for it. It's just not how they communicate, how they think. They meant no intrusion."

Cynthia felt disinclined to let it go. "Intended or not, it's crowded enough in my head already. I don't need anyone else in there."

"Understood. For what it's worth, they can't read human minds very well, and yours less than most. They learned nothing from you that you haven't already shared."

"Hm." She paced a bit, watching the peculiar motion behind Zheng from the corner of her eye. "So they *are* telepathic."

"That's a bit simplist..." Zheng caught himself and smiled. "Forgive me. It's a habit. And," he admitted, "an excuse. These concepts are difficult to..."

He stopped, staring down at the yellowed goop. "The Disciples... do not view, or interact with, the universe as you or I. Their senses, and yes, their communication, occur on an entirely different... Let's call it 'psychic plane.' They see things we don't, miss things we would consider blatant, and their thoughts... touch. Even meld."

"Sounds like telepathy to me," Lucas said.

Cynthia nodded. "Ditto."

"'Telepathy' implies a level of deliberateness, an *ability*. This just *is*." He scowled. "I'm sorry, this is, as I said, difficult. I'm trying to translate, not even from another language, but from concepts that aren't conveyed by speech at all. I'm afraid this may be the best I can do."

Lucas's cane tapped the floor, producing almost no sound, as he approached the podium. "Seems *you* understand them just fine. In fact, you seem *real* comfortable with all this."

"I am one of the fortunate few to have been gifted with enlightenment, yes. I know how bad this all looks. How bad it all *is*. But I also know what's at stake."

She should have gotten there first. It all fit so neatly, and she'd had far more direct experience. Cynthia, however, was still thrown by the mental probing, by the lingering pain, so it was Lucas who made the connection.

"Goddamn obelisks got you, too, huh?"

Cynthia sucked in a long, ragged breath. "Son of a bitch."

"The Scriptures didn't *get* me, Mr. Cook. They enlightened me."

"That's such a crock of shit—!" Cynthia began.

"Enlightened me into secrets far beyond anything mankind would ever have discovered on our own," Zheng insisted. "Into the True Faith."

She could *hear* the capital letters.

"So, what? Only the chosen few get to learn the 'Truth'? Do you have to sign over your bank account and mortgage to be told you're special? Do—?"

"It was meant to be a gift to all of us!"

Whether it was the sudden shout or the tears that followed, Cynthia's tirade faltered.

"It was meant to lift us up," he continued, wiping at his eyes, clearing his throat. "Every people, every nation. Not to... Not to do this."

Again he glanced back at the entity beyond, which now hung nearly motionless, obscured in the liquid shadow. Again Zheng coughed, then pressed his hand harder into what Cynthia was coming to think of as some sort of relay.

"The obelisks came to us—sorry," he corrected, "to *them*— many tens of thousands of years ago. The Scriptures brought truth and understanding, the ecstasy of the Progenitor's grace."

"The what?" Lucas asked, but Zheng didn't appear inclined to halt his recitation.

"A world torn and divided came together, united by the new faith, a divine revelation so holy it touched every mind, every soul.

"And following behind the obelisks came the Disciples of the *prior* world, as alien to the new believers as the current Disciples seem now to you. They spoke of the history of the faith, its sacred paths and precepts, all that had occurred since the universe's purist truths were scribed into stone that is not stone, so very long ago."

Zheng's gaze had gone unfocused, though whether he'd grown lost in his own story or was, perhaps, speaking in part on behalf of something other, something else, Cynthia wouldn't dare speculate.

"So it had gone, from the Beginning." Again the capital letter was fully audible. "For millions of cycles, billions of years, before all but the eldest stars were anything more than atoms and dust in a nearly barren universe. We have no notion who or what the first Disciples might have been, whether they found the Progenitor or It found them.

"And no, Mr. Cook." He snapped out of his fugue. "They don't call It 'Progenitor.' That's the closest word I can come up with for the concept as they communicate it. That is, the closest but one, and I don't believe you're ready for me to use that one yet."

God. He's talking about "God."

"It sang in the minds of its Disciples, and they sang Its praises in turn, and their lives, their world, were blessed. For eons. Eventually, however, the Progenitor grew weary. It had always been drawn to water—or, well, let us say, to oceans, whether they were quite water or something else. The first Disciples found It a world, a world of placid seas and towering crags. The Progenitor pulled that world around It, as a blanket, and slumbered, while the Disciples began the long, laborious process of carving their truth into the great pillars."

Cynthia almost vomited again. Sweat broke out along her gaping jawline, and she staggered to Lucas's side, leaning on a startled shoulder before she could collapse.

She'd paid the recitation almost no mind. Oh, she listened, took it in, but had dismissed it as the ravings of a zealot who, except for his particular religion coming from a bit farther away, was much like any other. It might have explained the

"Disciples'" motives, but it was none of it fact.

Except... Except she'd *seen* that world, hadn't she? First, when she'd spent too long staring at that obelisk, what felt like a lifetime ago, and again when Lamb had invaded her thoughts, threatened to crush her mind.

It could still be delusion, part of the message carried in the Scriptures, part of Lamb's obvious madness.

But it had felt so very real.

"We don't know by what means they instilled the Truth within the Scriptures, nor how they constructed the obelisks. We know only that it is the obelisks themselves who decide when a civilization is nearing its end, when it is time to move on, to spread their gospel to new worlds. It is they who guide themselves, who choose their destination, where the truths and the beliefs they carry imprint themselves on the hearts of the newly blessed. The Disciples merely follow, often in stasis for hundreds or thousands of years, so that they may guide the new believers in turn, as their precursors guided them."

The technical part, the astronaut part, of Cynthia's brain was racing. Whatever propelled them, whatever protected them in their flight at what had to be near relativistic speeds, was a technology so unlike anything humanity could even conceive that it didn't resemble technology at all. She wondered if it had been those forces, whatever they were, that had shut down the cameras on the ISS, on the satellites, that had created that unprecedented interference.

Perhaps contemplating the mechanical conundrums allowed her to avoid speculating on harder, far stranger questions.

So it took a moment for her to catch up with what Zheng said next.

"And so has the cycle continued, unbroken, flawless, world after world, species after species. Until Earth.

"Until us."

Chapter Sixteen

Comprehension proved as brutal an intrusion, a violation, as anything the Disciples, the obelisks, or Joshua Lamb had ever done to her. Understanding, not only of Zheng's words but their implications, forced itself on her. She didn't want it. She couldn't escape it.

"Something went wrong." She'd no intention of whispering, she just couldn't dredge up the strength for anything louder.

"Yes," Zheng said, crying openly.

"It went wrong, and we... We only got pieces. Irresistible need, your Goddamn religious ecstasy... And the home of your *fucking Progenitor!*"

"Yes," he repeated. "Even before Its slumber, It spoke to them, touched them, from beneath the waves."

"Oh, God." Lucas's cane clattered to the floor as he, too, reached understanding. He followed seconds later, falling to his knees, sobbing. "Jesus God..."

Cynthia moved to kneel beside him, one consoling hand laid on his arm, the other collecting his cane. Not merely out of sympathy, not even because she, too, needed human contact, but because focusing her efforts on Lucas was all that kept her from genuinely attempting to murder Zheng.

"You *bastards!*" All the loathing, all the hatred in the world found purchase within that hiss. "Families, children, *billions* of people!" Waterlogged, sinking, choking and gasping and *smiling their euphoric smiles* as they drowned, as they watched their siblings and parents and loved ones and infants drown... Cynthia gagged, and only her refusal to appear weak in front of the Disciples and their quisling allowed her to choke down her rising gorge.

"It wasn't supposed to happen this way!" Zheng insisted, pleaded. "It's *never* happened this way! The Disciples are as horrified by this as we are! They brought us a gift, brought us enlightenment! They—"

"They tried to *brainwash* us! To force their beliefs on us, take away our free will! How the fuck is that better?! How can you defend that?"

"It's not 'brainwashing,' Ms. Han! It's revelation! They offered us truth!"

"That's what you've been *programmed* to think!"

"Because it's *true*! You can't understand!"

"*I* can't...?" She stopped herself, wincing as the pain in her head flared despite the general numbness proximity to the aliens normally brought.

Another intrusion, another attack? No, that didn't feel right. It was the stress, the emotion, the shouting. That she felt it even here couldn't possibly be a good sign.

"The writing itself is... is psychic," she said, forcing herself to calm, to face it all as intellectually, unemotionally, as she could. "The Scriptures aren't just a description of the faith, it's *embedded* in them. And for whatever reason—maybe that 'different mental plane' stuff you were spouting—we're not... compatible." The words were bitter, poison to be spat out.

"That's the conclusion the Disciples have reluctantly come to, yes," Zheng agreed.

"'Come to'?" Lucas protested, his own voice raw. "Y'all didn't figure that shit out soon as people started marching into the fucking ocean? Thank you," he added when Cynthia pressed the cane back into his hands.

"You must understand..." the old man began.

"Aw, shit, here we go."

"The Disciples never felt the *need* to examine the Scriptures before now. Their actual nature, I mean, not the words. For billions of years across countless worlds, they accepted that the truth of their contents was divine revelation. The notion that there might be a mental element—a telepathic one, if you must—never occurred to them. Nor would it have seemed out of place if it had, since that's how they communicate. They've done more analysis of the obelisks in the past few weeks than has been done since before there was a planet Earth, trying to understand what went wrong!"

I was right. Fanatics are fanatics, from any world. Cynthia would have cheerfully died, in that moment, if she'd any idea of how to take the Cathedral with her.

Through a fierce grimace, she asked, "So what have you learned?"

Zheng glanced back, as though seeking permission. "Not much more than we knew in the first few days," he confessed. "Humanity's... lack of compatibility is a near thing. You know what happened to most of us, but a few seem unaffected at all, a few appear to have been, ah, damaged. And a small number, like myself, received revelation as intended."

She kept herself from objecting, squeezed Lucas's arm in a signal to keep quiet. It wasn't a point worth arguing. They'd get no further than they had the last time.

"When the Disciples realized it had all gone wrong, they tried to intercept people before they reached the shore, physically prevent them from drowning themselves. I fear they didn't manage to save many, relatively speaking, but they tried."

"Those are the people downstairs?" Cynthia asked.

"Yes."

"They're, what? Asleep? In some kind of stasis?"

"Effectively, yes. The Disciples have been working on them—non-intrusively and non-harmfully, I assure you!—to try to correct the problems. They believe it's been long enough for the compulsion to walk into the sea to have faded, no matter what else has or hasn't worked, but they aren't certain. Even if it has, they'd rather not release the survivors until they can ensure that it won't simply take hold of them again the next time they encounter the Scriptures."

Lucas sneered, carefully rising to his feet. "But y'all ain't trying find a way to *protect* them from the Scriptures, or get the obelisks to move on."

"I told you, the Disciples don't command the obelisks. *They* decide when—"

Cynthia, too, stood up. "Bet it never even occurred to you to consider it, though. Even after all you've done, keeping us from dying and otherwise leaving us the hell alone isn't enough for you, is it? You said it yourself, you're trying to 'correct the problem.' You're still looking to convert the rest of us."

"It's still necessary! For the greater good!"

"Oh, fuck—"

"Humanity must be enlightened!" Zheng insisted. "And not just for our own sake!"

"What's that supposed to mean?"

"If you were paying attention, you'll remember I said the obelisks decide to leave as a civilization is approaching its end point. It's unlikely that any of the prior faithful, of any race, still survive elsewhere in the universe. If we can't shepherd the human race, not only into survival and replenishing itself but into the faith, belief in the Progenitor could die right here!"

Cynthia stared at the old man, and she swore that, despite his blindness, Lucas did the same. "Boo-fucking-hoo," she said when she finally managed to find her voice.

"What she said," Lucas added.

"You can't understand," Zheng repeated.

Cynthia nodded. "You're Goddamn right."

Silence, then. The inky darkness swirled behind the wall.

"So what's with the Hunters," she asked. "If you guys want us alive to worship your precious Progenitor, who're *they*?"

The inky darkness swirled faster.

"I think that's probably enough for now," Zheng said. "I've told you a great deal. It's your turn to answer a few—"

"Hell no."

Zheng blinked. "Pardon?"

"You're the ones who dropped out of the sky and killed most of us, and you're the only source of answers I've got. You're done when I say you're done, and *then* I'll think about taking a few of *your* questions."

"That is unacceptable, Ms. Han!"

"Sue me." She crossed her arms for emphasis. "You can't

read our minds well enough to get the information you want. Certainly not *mine*, and Lucas doesn't know all of what you want. And yes," she bulled on as Zheng drew breath to speak, "you can do some unpleasant things to me. Maybe even get me to talk eventually. Except that, one, that'd take a lot longer than just telling me what I want to know. And two..."

She reached under her jacket. "Maybe you figured we couldn't do a lot of damage, or maybe you just didn't think of it, but you didn't disarm us when we came in." The barrel of the Taurus was grotesquely cold against her temple. She couldn't help but flinch, but it didn't stop her from thumbing the hammer back.

"Oh, fuck," Lucas muttered.

"I don't have too long anyway," she said, and hoped the quaver as she spoke wouldn't ruin the effect. "I won't pretend I want to pull this trigger, but it's going to get a lot more tempting if that pain starts up again."

Zheng watched her for a time, saying nothing, then once more turned to consult with the presence behind the panel.

"Put the weapon down, Ms. Han. If you'll commit to answering our questions, we'll address the rest of yours first."

The hammer clicked again as she carefully lowered first it, then the weapon. Lucas began breathing again.

"When you speak of 'Hunters,' I believe you mean the Wayward."

Yeah, I figured that's who you meant.

"They are... Well, to be quite candid, they are an embarrassment. The Disciples' great shame."

You mean besides killing over seven billion people?

"A small but, ah, significant faction of Disciples decided that, if most of us reacted so poorly to the Scriptures, there must be something unholy about humanity itself. So when a few people *didn't* perish under the influence of the obelisks, they felt their calling was, well, to finish the job. The others tried to convince them not to, but..."

Cynthia waited for him to continue, only to gradually realize he wasn't going to. "Okay, but who...?" She played it back over in her mind, brow furrowing. "You're saying the Hunters—the

Wayward—*are* Disciples?" Then, at his nod, "But…" Her gaze flickered to the movement beyond, the enormous shapes she could scarcely make out, then back to Zheng.

"Yes. They are the same."

"But the Hunters look human! Well, sort of."

"You have seen how the Cathedral operates. In its own way, it is almost alive. Shaping and reshaping itself, sprouting what limbs or tools it requires, absorbing them back when the task is done. With the proper application of that technology, the Disciples can, within limits, do the same to themselves. They're able to get closer to us, this way, even if they don't truly understand the whys and wherefores of the forms they've chosen."

She couldn't follow it, not really, couldn't picture such towering, writhing things sculpted and *compressed* to the shape of a man. She accepted it, because she'd learned too much not to, but that didn't mean she truly understood.

"If they're trying to kill us all," Lucas protested, "how come they're coming after us on foot, stabbing us and whatnot? Y'all must have shuttlecraft and blasters and shit."

"They *did* take the Cathedral's probe vessels, Mr. Cook. Most of our weaponry, also. And they slaughtered over half a million survivors in the first week."

Cynthia felt sick again, and Lucas choked.

"But we didn't carry many weapons. The Cathedral is a holy vessel, not a warship. Nor were the probes intended to fly for long without returning for refueling. They've long since expended all such advantages, and a very good thing for everyone that they did!

"Some have even attempted to return, having decided the task is hopeless without such tools. Or perhaps as a way of gaining access to the survivors in stasis below. Either way, the Disciples refused them entry. Their actions are unforgiveable."

"*Their* actions?" Cynthia would have thought she'd moved beyond the capacity for shock, for outrage. "You're just letting them hunt us down! Even if you don't give a shit about us in general, you said you need us!"

"We do," Zheng said. "But the Wayward, however

misguided, are fellow Disciples. You are not, at least not yet. We won't aid them, but we won't raise arms against them."

"Oh, *that's* convenient."

"I am trying to be patient, Ms. Han, but your accusations are growing tiresome. The Wayward have the same difficulties and impediments we do, without the technology of the Cathedral to mitigate them. They don't understand you. They don't see the world as you do, and don't recognize the significance of many details when they do. They can only sense humans if they're relatively near, and not with precision. Most of the remaining survivors across the world should be safe."

Cynthia stepped forward until they were separated only by that control panel or communications relay or whatever it was. "They're getting better at it. Maybe because they're more human, but they're learning. I've *seen* one starting to figure out the differences between separate cars, just for starters. And they're *enjoying it*. They're *playing* with us."

"What? That's not possible. This is a religious duty for them, nothing more."

"Maybe it was. Maybe for most of them it still is. But not all of them." The Flannel Man's mimicked words, the trophies and the body parts left deliberately behind... Oh, she knew an enemy's taunts when she saw them!

"Impossible," Zheng insisted again.

"Is it? Ask your friend back there. Ask it what happened the last time any of its kind squeezed themselves into someone else's shape to go hunting."

Zheng's lips curved in a condescending smile. "That would be a foolish question. No such thing has happened before. Not with a shape so drastically different from their own."

"So how do you know what's possible?"

The smile faltered. "Perhaps," he said, sounding troubled, "now really would be a good time for you to answer some of our questions. Starting with your own experiences involving the Wayward."

She was tempted to refuse out of sheer stubborn spite, but decided she'd be pushing her luck. "Any chance we can get a few chairs brought in?" she asked.

Two simple columns, the right size for use as stools, coalesced from the floor. Suddenly, Cynthia wasn't sure she wanted anything to do with them, but refusing now might offend someone. She guided Lucas to one, gingerly lowered herself onto the other.

"All right. I think there was one nearby when we were crossing the Hill Country, but the first one I ever saw was in a hospital in Austin..."

For long minutes she described each and every encounter, and God, had the first really been only weeks ago? She described, of necessity, the deaths of her friends, and every detail she thought to gloss over, to avoid summoning to mind, Zheng questioned until she had no choice. She had no conscious memory of crying, but her cheeks and chin were wet before she was through.

So many dead. So many friends lost.

Lucas rose, as she described JD's murder, to stand beside her. She adored him for that.

Even reliving the grief and horror, though, her mind sought answers, and she found herself wondering: Why didn't the Disciples share that terrible movement, that unearthly film-skip stutter, that the Crooked Men possessed? Was it something to do with the process, whatever it might be, that folded and compressed them into humanoid shape?

Or maybe they *did* share it. Could it be that the creature observing them *did* move the same way, that something about the murky fluid or the translucent barrier—or both—obscured it from her?

In the end, she decided it didn't matter enough to ask. They had too much else to discuss.

By the time she'd concluded the last of her stories, the horrid ambush into which she'd led Carlos and his people, Lucas had returned to his seat and Zheng's face had passed briefly through an almost frighteningly eager expression before he'd regained control.

"Well," he said, with a nonchalance so forced it nearly shattered, "tell us more about this New Covenant you escaped from."

"Are we still playing games, Mr. Zheng? You don't care about the New Covenant. You want to know about their leader. Joshua Lamb. Your 'Enigma,' am I right?"

"I must admit, we don't know his name. But we believe so, yes.

"You see," Zheng explained, "a very, *very* few people—we think no more than ten or so, across the whole planet—had a different sort of reaction to the Scriptures. It seems to have partly elevated their minds, bringing them nearer the Disciples' own level. For most of them, it's a small thing. A bit of insight into those they're speaking with, fragments of knowledge they shouldn't have and don't recall acquiring. This man, however, this 'Joshua Lamb'…"

Cynthia took that as a cue and described everything she'd seen—felt—Lamb do, everything she'd heard he could do. Zheng grew ever more concerned as she spoke, and even the creature behind the wall twitched in apparent agitation.

"It's not merely the Wayward he can hide from," the old man said then. "We've been aware for some time that he has a sizable population of followers, but even knowing very generally where they are, we've been unable to pinpoint him."

"That's what you were doing a few days ago?" she asked, thinking back to that night in La Grange. "Searching for your Enigma?"

"And multiple times before that, yes. Nor is he just hiding from us. We believe—that is, the Disciples believe—that he's occasionally managed to infiltrate their own mental conversation. Not deeply, and not for long, but enough to anticipate us, to learn more about our efforts than we would prefer.

"And he's hostile to us. That much we know for certain, not just through those sporadic psychic brushes, but because he's tried to destroy one of the obelisks! But we've no notion of how this happened, or what his limits may be."

"Before he… he tried to kill me," Cynthia said, "he told me… Told me he wasn't sure he *was* Joshua Lamb anymore. That something else had waited in the Scriptures themselves, or in the psychic energies they hold."

"What?!"

"Yeah. He thought it, uh, woke up when exposed to humanity. And that it had chosen him as a new... host, I guess? That it gave him his power, and a greater understanding of the Scriptures than you all have."

"Ludicrous! Utter nonsense!" Zheng literally flailed his free hand, and Cynthia thought she'd never seen anyone so offended. "The man's clearly been driven insane by whatever happened to him!"

"Okay, but how would you know that? You just told me that you've got no idea how he gained these powers and that nobody's really tried to study the obelisks for about a zillion years."

Zheng stared, jaw clenched and one eyelid twitching.

"I'm not saying I believe it," she continued. "Convincing me Lamb's a nutcase isn't exactly a hard sell. I'm just saying, you don't really *know*, do you?"

"We know he's dangerous," the other said stiffly. "To you and to us both. And we think that studying him, and his unique condition, might just be the key to figuring out how to keep the Scriptures from harming people anymore."

"And that's what this is all really about, isn't it? You need me to help you find him."

"You *do* have good reason to fear him, to want him gone."

"True," Cynthia admitted, "but he's also the only thing protecting people from the Hunters. And you."

"Do you really want a reborn human civilization under the rule of Joshua Lamb, Ms. Han? That might be close to a worst-case scenario for your goals *and* ours. And that's assuming he doesn't get worse. That his powers don't continue to grow or drive him to further madness. If they do..."

Cynthia lowered her head, pinching the bridge of her nose. "Look, this has all been a lot to take in, and you're asking me to... to choose the lady or the tiger for at *least* a few hundred people, and just maybe the whole human race!" *And might just be two fucking tigers, for that matter.*

"It's a truly awful situation," Zheng acknowledged. "If there were anyone else..."

"I'm not asking you to find someone else. Just... Is there somewhere I can sleep on this?"

Along the back wall of the room, the floor shifted once again. Two rectangular platforms congealed from the glossy substance of the chamber, followed swiftly by a small quantity the dull golden jelly. It climbed the sides of the cots in chunks, moving in fits and starts, a reverse image of oatmeal poured from a bowl. Finally it reached the top, forming a thin layer of cushioning atop the hardened surface.

At the same time, a narrow wall rose up to block one corner from view, leaving just enough room to squeeze around it.

"Any facilities you may need are there," Zheng said, removing his hand from the panel and pointing toward the new wall. "Please relax, as best you can, and we'll continue this in the morning." He left them, then, with a brief bow. The wall behind him revealed no further movement, though whether the thing had truly departed or simply drifted back and gone still, they had no way to tell.

Shaking, Cynthia stood and guided Lucas toward one of the two "beds," poking with distaste at the cushioning. It felt consistent enough that it shouldn't leave bits clinging to skin and hair—probably.

She worried briefly about being consumed in the night, added to the countless bodies in stasis below, but if the Disciples had wanted to do that to them, surely there were easier, faster ways.

"Think they're still listening?" Lucas asked.

"Probably? Not much we can do about it either way."

"True that. So what're you going to do?"

"God, I don't know." She flopped down, wincing at the gloppy *squish* beneath her. "I'll be damned if I'm going to leave King Joshua in charge, but letting the rest of the human race be *mind controlled* into worshiping some alien thing a billion light years across the universe isn't exactly an acceptable Plan B, you know?"

"Heh. No shit." After a moment of silence, he spoke again, far more softly. "You figure any of it's legit?"

"I figure *they* believe it, and they have the power to make *us* believe it. That's all that matters."

For another hour or so they talked, hashing and rehashing, coming to no new conclusions, until sleep finally claimed them. Time and again Cynthia awoke from sweat-drenched nightmares of distant suns and endless seas, of empty cities across the globe, of tendrils burrowing into her skull to consume her every thought, each of the writhing things with Lamb's face. And each time she fell back asleep with the same panicked questions.

The lady or the tiger.

The tiger or the other Goddamn tiger.

Until she woke up convinced it was morning, though she couldn't see the sun.

Because this time she awoke with a plan.

Chapter Seventeen

This was a bad idea.

The whole plan was nuts, built on a foundation of desperation and lies, but Cynthia hated no part of it more than this.

From atop one of the towers of Houston's renowned Galleria, she stared through binoculars at the New Covenant-occupied hotel. At least they were still there; she'd been worried about trying to find them again. She saw fewer vehicles on the street, more armed sentries on balconies and nearby buildings. Lamb's people had fortified themselves something fierce since she'd been here last, and she doubted it was due to her escape.

They'd had good cause, too. Her head had gone briefly numb no fewer than three times on their drive in. The Hunters might not have laid siege yet, but they knew where to find the New Covenant, were massing for *something*.

She almost wished they were closer. Cynthia lowered the binoculars, pressing thumb and forefinger against tightly closed eyelids. The frigid wind and the rough gravel were bad enough, but those she could have ignored.

The pain, however, had started back up after they'd left the Cathedral's surroundings, and not even her various medications had been able to quite knock it out again. They dulled it enough for Cynthia to ignore what remained, to function close to her best, but complete relief now required dosages so high as to render her useless.

She was getting worse. No stopping it. No slowing it down.

But that was okay. If her plan worked—hell, even if it didn't—it would be over soon. Over on her own terms, and with meaning. As final chapters went, she could do a lot worse.

Right now, though, she'd have welcomed a touch of numbness.

And some news! She chewed her lip, unaware it had chapped and split in the cold, and looked again through the binoculars. Getting Lucas killed was *not* part of the plan.

He insisted he was sure, time and again, and anyway she'd no other option. The New Covenant would have shot her down before she got two words out, but they didn't know him, and he hardly looked like a threat. Still, watching him slowly tap and feel his way, block after block, had been nerve-wracking; watching them surround him, guns drawn, shouting questions as they hustled him inside, had been agonizing.

And then, for more than an hour, nothing.

The wind shifted. Leaves and old paper stampeded across the streets below, made blurry and abstract by the gloom, perhaps racing for shelter from the dust-thickened rain Cynthia could feel building in the air.

The side door to the hotel drifted open. Lucas emerged, surrounded by half-a-dozen others. She saw his lips move through the lenses, saw one of the others respond.

He stopped a few steps from the entryway, raised a hand, and waved.

His *right* hand.

Cynthia continued chewing her poor, abused lip.

It should be fine. Right meant that Lamb had agreed to speak to her, that she wouldn't be shot the instant she approached. Left would have meant run the very fuck away.

Could she trust it, though? She trusted *him*, but what if Lamb had somehow picked up on their signal? He wasn't supposed to be able to pull that kind of obscure detail from someone's head, but she didn't *really* know. What if Lucas was being coerced, or emotionally manipulated?

Get ahold of yourself, Cyn.

This had to happen. This was the plan. All they could do was kill her.

Cynthia stood, put away the binoculars, double-checked her pistols—just in case—and made for the stairs.

The New Covenant soldiers did not, in fact, shoot her as she approached. Neither, however, did they attempt to hide the fact that they really, really wanted to.

Cynthia caught herself as they all but slammed her into the side of the building, a shock of pain running down both arms. Fingers and knuckles dug into her skin as they roughly searched her, stripping her of not only her weapons but her flashlight, the binoculars, the car keys, and everything else she carried. A vise of a fist clamped on her shoulder, spinning her around to face her "hosts" once they were through.

"Ow," she said. Then, "Hey, Vivian. How's things?"

The MP5 in Vivian's hands visibly trembled. "You have no idea how much I want to shoot you."

"So, not good, then?"

"You killed almost thirty of us, you bitch! Including Carlos!"

Already freezing, Cynthia suddenly couldn't quite feel her face. "Wait, what? You didn't even have that many people chasing—"

The other woman's fist in her solar plexus ended her protests. Cynthia dropped to one knee, doubled over and gasping.

"Hold up!" Maybe he couldn't see it, but Lucas clearly recognized what had just happened. "You ain't supposed to—!"

"Shut up!" Vivian knelt at Cynthia's side, every word a snarl. "They followed him back. Found us because of *you*. If not for Joshua, they'd have slaughtered us all."

"I'm sorry," Cynthia managed between gulps. "Had no choice. Had to... get out. Lamb tried... to kill me."

"Then you should have fucking let him. He knows what he's doing." Vivian rose. "Get her up and bring her inside before I really lose my temper and forget our orders."

A pair of equally pissed-off guards all but carried Cynthia inside, though she was walking under her own power again quickly enough.

The New Covenant had been busy since she'd fled. Most of the windows were barricaded, wooden planks or furniture nailed over them. Several outer rooms were wired with alarms and explosives, more furniture and even parts of cars had been turned into makeshift machine gun nests, and every guard post was equipped with cans of fuel and at least one flamethrower.

Cynthia still didn't think it'd be enough, not if the Hunters came in any significant numbers, but she didn't figure anyone would appreciate hearing that right now, least of all from her.

And maybe she was wrong. *Something* held the creatures at bay.

"Cynthia?!"

No doubt summoned by whisper and rumor, people crowded the foyer and then the hallways through which they passed. Most were New Covenant, no happier to see her than Vivian and the guards had been. The call, however, hadn't come from any of those.

"Natsuhiko. Love what you've all done with the place."

Her escort wouldn't let the man too close, but while they scowled at his presence, they made no effort to drive him off or keep him from speaking. Marcus, too, materialized from the throng and followed in their wake, shaking his head in bewilderment.

"I was sure I must have heard wrong," the other astronaut said. "No way even *you'd* be crazy enough to come back here!"

She honestly couldn't help but laugh. "Were you not paying attention all the time we've known each other?"

"Cynthia, this isn't funny. You have no *idea* how much these people hate you. What were you *thinking*?"

"No," she admitted. "It's not funny. But it's important. You'll understand when I…" They marched her through the doors, back once more into the dining room. That Lamb was seated at the center of the long table, exactly where he'd been the first time, came as no surprise at all.

The figure beside him, however…

"Jesus Christ," Cynthia whispered.

Ethan's face had been battered until it *resembled* batter. Although the coloration of the bruises and the scabs on his lips and scalp suggested he'd been healing for a few days, one eye and one cheek remained so swollen he appeared lopsided. His jaw sagged a bit, not broken but perhaps fractured on one side. Bandages wrapped his head, and while Cynthia couldn't see clearly enough to be certain, one of them looked like it might literally be holding his left ear in place. His hesitancy as he reached for a cup of water, the way he slumped in the chair, spoke of agony all over his body, perhaps cracked ribs.

"In my expert medical opinion," he said when he saw her staring, only mildly slurring, "it's not nearly as bad as it looks."

"Or as bad as he deserves," Vivian spat, "after what he did to—"

Lamb rose from his chair. "Please, let's not rehash old disagreements just now. Not when we have new ones to discuss. Sit down, Ms. Han."

She obeyed, though she could scarcely tear her focus from her old friend. She wasn't even sure she disagreed with Vivian, not after what she'd learned, after what he'd done. Still, after having known him for so long, it hurt to see him this way.

One of Lamb's soldiers, a tower of a man who reminded Cynthia of a meaner Michael Clarke Duncan, guided Lucas to the chair beside her.

"My people were not happy with the order to bring you inside alive," Lamb told her flatly. "And despite my abhorrence for unnecessary violence..."

Yeah, right.

"...I must confess to a brief temptation not to give that order. So I do hope that whatever you've come to say, it's as important as your friend Mr. Cook claimed."

It had been easy, when concocting her plan, and on the drive back toward Houston, for Cynthia to dismiss most of the danger to herself, to lean into the fact that she was dying anyway. Here, though, in a room surrounded by people who really would happily shoot her, she found her back itching, her shoulders hunching at every fidget.

Hoping none of that showed in her tone, she asked, "How much *did* Lucas have to tell you to get me in here?"

Lamb sat, frowning. "That you had been inside the Cathedral. Actually *spoken* with one of the Heretics' collaborators. And that you'd asked him to leave the room for much of the discussion you had with them!"

Indeed she had, after they'd awakened that morning. It had

resulted in the second-most difficult argument she'd waged in that unearthly place.

"Yes, I did."

"Leaving aside the fact that them letting you go doesn't incline me to trust you, for you to speak with them behind his back doesn't suggest that *you've* got a great deal of trust in your new companion."

Lucas snorted. He'd raised a similar objection.

Cynthia shook her head. "And I'll tell you what I told him. It wasn't about how much I trust Lucas. It was about how much I trust *you*."

Several angry mutters sounded to either side, but Lamb leaned back and fiddled thoughtfully with the cylinder at his neck.

"I see," he mused. "You wanted to be sure I could sense he was telling the truth when he said he didn't know all the specifics. That I would *have* to hear them from you."

"I'd prefer to live long enough to see it all through," she said sweetly.

"We could make him tell us where to find them," the large guard threatened from behind her, beside Vivian. "Come up with our own plan."

A second snort from Lucas, who then tapped the handle of his cane lightly against the side of his shades. "Any of this look like a fashion statement to you? I ain't leading anybody anywhere. Anyways, they're expecting Cynthia. Nobody else is getting inside."

"They know you're hostile," Cynthia picked up the thread. "And I promise, as much ordnance as you've gathered, it's not enough to blast your way in and still do enough damage to take them out, even if you *could* find them.

"Besides, you'd be killing human survivors. About a *million* or so."

Now she had everyone's attention. "What?" Vivian asked, a single, sharp breath.

"I mean, I didn't count, and I suppose they could have been lying about the precise numbers, but I saw a *lot*."

Vivian sounded dazed. "Why would they keep so many of us alive?"

Cynthia kept her focus on Lamb, giving him a flat stare that she hoped fully conveyed her intended meaning of *I damn well know you already knew all this.* "The obelisks are their holy writing, yes, but they weren't just trying to share it. It's no accident it got into our heads.

"They were trying to *convert* us. Psychically, by force. This whole thing was a Goddamn missionary pilgrimage. When it all went to shit, they gathered as many of us as they could, stopped them from drowning themselves, and have been trying to find a way to... fix the problem."

"All quite fascinating," Lamb said, "but it doesn't explain what they want from you. Or what you want from us."

"They want us to survive, Lamb. They want us to *thrive*. Without us to carry their torch, their whole faith peters out. And that's how we are going to fucking destroy them."

Just the two of them, now—cancer-stricken astronaut and psychic cult leader—back once again in the office. Nobody else, on either side, was happy to be cut out of the conversation, but Lamb had wanted privacy, and what Lamb wanted, he got.

It wasn't quite so neat as it had been last time Cynthia was here. The door hung loosely on makeshift hinges, and the furniture had been rearranged.

The alterations didn't make her any happier to be here. If she closed her eyes, she could feel the carpet against her cheek, Lamb's brutal intrusion in her head.

"You did know, didn't you?" she challenged as soon as her backside hit the chair.

"That the Scriptures had been intended to convert humanity to the Heathen's apostasy? Yes, I knew. If you're going to whine at me for everything I understand but haven't explained to others—let alone to *you*—that growth in your head will kill you *long* before we're done."

"Charming."

"I'm really very close to done being polite with you, Cynthia."

"And to think," she muttered, "I'd decided you're the *lesser* evil."

She caught him blinking, confused for the first time. "Explain."

"They want us to survive," she repeated. "To rebuild civilization. Okay, great. You, me, them, all on the same page with that one. But not under their control, not forced to take on their beliefs and smile while we're reprogrammed.

"So they've got to go. And you're the only one with the manpower and firepower to help me do it."

"You just said my arsenal wouldn't be sufficient. I actually have stores of explosives you haven't seen, in addition to the trucks, but nonetheless, I agree with you. So what are you proposing?"

"I convinced them," she said, settling back in her seat, "to give us Houston."

"I'm sorry, you *what*?"

"Long as you're not challenging their religious precepts, they're actually pretty reasonable, or at least the humans working with them are.

"They want us to rebuild. The New Covenant, frankly, isn't big enough to do it yourselves. Maybe there's a few million other survivors scattered throughout the world, but the operative word there is 'scattered.' There is exactly one population of humans left big enough to actually make a go at it."

Lamb leaned his elbows on the desk, fingers steepled. "The survivors in the Cathedral."

"Right. Based on a few tests the Disciples—"

"Heretics!"

"*Whatever.* Based on some tests *they've* run, they believe the survivors have been in stasis long enough for the compulsion to have faded. They won't just try to drown themselves all over again. I convinced Zheng and his, uh, masters that they should release everyone. Let them start working on rebuilding a single large city. It's better for us—humanity, I mean—and we'll all still be in one general area if they... need to gather us again."

Lamb understood instantly. "In case they need to *modify* us so that the Scriptures work properly next time."

"Uh, basically."

"They can't have believed for one second that you'd be okay with that!"

"They didn't." Cynthia locked gazes, and only her left hand—which she kept clenched on the arm of the chair, hopefully out of his sight—shook at the memory of what he could do to her if he felt too overtly challenged. "Not any more than you believe I'm okay with you being in charge once they're gone. They know I'd be trying to find a way to prevent them converting us, just like you have no doubt in your mind that I'll be looking for a way to push you out once this is all said and done, and just like *I* know you're going to try to have me eliminated when this is all over. But they aren't worried about it, because they don't think I can do it. Just like you don't."

"My, we're being forthright today," he said, eyebrow raised, though he denied none of it.

"No reason not to be. We both know where we stand."

"Yes, we do. I'm still not certain how any of this helps us get rid of them, or how we're supposed to settle a population that big in a city still full of obelisks."

"We're not. They're going to remove the obelisks from Houston."

And that had been the *most* difficult argument, by far, she'd waged within the Cathedral.

Lamb was on his feet, snarling, and Cynthia felt the first twinges of his power in her mind. "You're lying to me, Ms. Han! They don't command the obelisks, they follow them!"

Already knew that, too, did you?

"That's exactly what Zheng told me," she said, clinging to composure by her fingernails. "And then, when I suggested that they could make an exception, collect just a handful of the obelisks like cargo, he said that might even qualify as heresy."

"'Might'?"

"I don't think even the thing he was communing with knew for sure. They've never so much as considered it before."

"And what did you say to that?"

"I said they'd never wiped out most of a race with their Scriptures or stared down the barrel of the possible end of their religion before, either."

Lamb calmed, though he didn't yet return to his seat. "That worked?"

"I mean, not at first." Just remembering the shouting back and forth threatened to feed the headache. "I don't even want to *hear* the words 'heresy' and 'blasphemy' again if I can help it. At the end of the day, though, the longer they our let infrastructure decay before releasing the survivors, the fewer of us survive, and the less chance we have of rebuilding anything that can last, or being able to, ah, repopulate. And the longer they keep the survivors in a medical stasis that wasn't designed for humans, the more likely something goes wrong. I finally got them to see that."

"And just that? Nothing more?"

Cynthia snorted. "Look at me, Lamb. I don't exactly have anything to offer them, do I?"

This was it. One deception in a torrent of truths. This was where everything might fall apart. If he had *any* means of sensing her lie, if he could read her thoughts or emotions even slightly more than he'd implied, or hell, if her performance simply wasn't up to par…

If Lamb wasn't convinced, however, he gave no sign. "All right. What's your plan?"

"They're going to start gathering the local obelisks in another day or so, but it's going to take them a good long while. Most of the Cathedral's cargo space will be left behind, full of humans, and you know how big the obelisks are. They can only transport a few at a time, in the hangar space they used for their smaller probe vessels. Once we see where they make their first few, um, pickups, we should be able to guesstimate which ones are likely to be the last."

"Okay?"

"And then we use the intervening hours to rig those obelisks to hell and gone. Bet your tons of explosives prove a *lot* more effective going off inside the ship than they would trying to punch through from outside. Especially since I'm sure even their funky tech's got to include *some* fuels and complex mechanisms that'll contribute to a large boom."

For a few breaths he genuinely gawped at her, before

bursting into laughter. "Oh, Cynthia, you are *far* more devious than I gave you credit for."

I really, really hope that's true.

"You told me that a number of your people can approach the obelisks safely," she said. "Either immune, or they've already been affected as much as they're going to be. They can lead the demolition teams. In the meanwhile, you, me, and a small force head to the ground-bound portion of the Cathedral to free the survivors."

Lamb's grin crumpled into a suspicious frown. "Why?"

"Uh, because they're not planning to release everyone until Houston's clear, and if we *do* manage to pull this off... Well, they may feel like they need us, but do you really want to count on them holding on to that attitude once they realize we've blown up the rest of their ship and most of their friends? We need to have everyone out before they get pissed enough to want payback!"

Among other reasons, but you don't need to know those.

"No, I got that part of it. I mean why you and me specifically?"

"Oh. Me, because only I know where they are, and I'm not telling anyone until we actually get there. I have no intention of becoming superfluous. Second, for related reasons, I have no intention of letting you out of my sight while we're executing this plan."

"Why, Cynthia, don't you trust me?"

"And third," she said, refusing to even pretend she was going to answer *that*, "I don't know how many of the Disciples—or Heretics, or whatever you want to call them—we'll find in the cargo section. We may need you to counter any, well, psychic attacks, or efforts to pinpoint us for their human soldiers."

Lamb finally sat back down. For a long while he stared at the wall off to Cynthia's right, saying nothing, until, "You're hiding something from me, beyond their location. I don't need my gifts to tell me that."

Shit, shit, shit, shit...

"Of course I am. I'm already working on how to deal with you when this is over, and I'm sure you're doing the same. We're not friends, Lamb. We're barely temporary allies. Right now, we share a common enemy, and that's fucking it. We can work together despite that, or we both lose everything right here."

She had, in fact, said very much the same thing to Zheng Xiaowen when she made her deal with *him*. If this whole thing didn't go down perfectly, she would have at least one very powerful man *exceedingly* pissed at her.

Another long pause, then. "Fair enough."

Oh, thank God.

Again he stood. "I'll start giving the necessary orders, get things moving."

"One last detail," she said.

He froze, halfway around the desk. "Yes?"

"I want to have a word with you about personnel…"

Chapter Eighteen

The hotel had that whole "boot-plus-anthill" vibe going. Cynthia had tried hard to avoid thinking of it in terms of that old cliché—given the forces arrayed against them, casting herself and the others in the role of ants felt frighteningly prophetic—but she couldn't help herself.

An endless chorus of running footsteps, buzzing voices, and clattering tools swept the halls. Almost all of Lamb's people were involved in preparation, to one extent or another, though few had been fully briefed on what they prepared *for*. He and Cynthia had agreed it would be better if nobody could accidentally let the truth slip out—verbally or just in their thoughts—should they somehow encounter one of the enemy, however improbable.

Perhaps ironically, Cynthia herself had no specific duties for now. The overall plan was hers, and she'd lead a major part of it, but nothing happening this moment required her attentions. She'd taken the opportunity for a substantial dose of painkillers and a restless nap, but now that she was up, she figured she might as well make herself useful.

And spend a bit of time with her own people. Odds were good she might not have another chance.

Marcus was head-down with Vivian and several of Lamb's other lieutenants, working out logistics and what amounted to troop movements. He didn't need her interrupting. Instead, she made her way to the second-highest floor of the garage, where the New Covenant had set up a workstation well away from everyone else, and with multiple layers of concrete separating it from the bulk of the explosives. That arsenal had, as per Lamb's boast, proved larger than Cynthia knew. In addition to several additional truckloads of C4 and ANFO beyond what she'd seen, it included an assortment of grenades, mines, explosive shells, and even a small selection of missiles for the helicopter gunship.

She felt the glares that lashed her skin, her nerves, like switches and whips. The New Covenant might have accepted Lamb's decree that she was a necessary ally in the coming conflict, but that didn't mean a one of them had forgiven her.

Well, that was fine. She wasn't feeling too generously toward them, either.

Several long tables had been lined up, allowing dozens of people to work on various stages of setup. At one end, chain, rope, polyester ratchet straps, duct tape, powder-actuated nail guns—everything necessary to affix even the heaviest payloads to the obelisks. (Lamb had assured her that the nail guns should suffice to penetrate the outer layer of stone, at least until that stone began to "heal." It would be long enough.)

At the other end, the end she moved toward, a vast array of electronics, wires, and—the reason for the workstation's isolation—blasting caps.

Natsuhiko glanced up from his efforts and nodded a greeting. Downing, glasses pushed atop his head and the ring of his miniature screwdriver around one finger, did not, as he was wrists-deep in timers. Lucas sat beside them both, waiting. Every now and again, one or the other of them would press a detonator and a wire into his open hands, and he would twist the one around the terminal of the other.

"Looks like fun," she said, looming over Natsuhiko's shoulder.

"Does it?" Downing asked, still without looking up. "'Cause it's not."

"Well, I'll make a deal with you. Next time, you come up with the plan, and I'll set the frequency on all the detonators."

"Your largesse knows many bounds."

"'Largesse'? Who the hell have you been talking to while I was away?"

Natsuhiko carefully set down his own detonator and rubbed at his forehead. "Cynthia, are you sure this is a wise idea?" He and the others Cynthia trusted had been told, while not the entirety of the plan, a good deal more than most. "You really think the Cathedral's just going to *not notice* thousands of pounds of explosives strapped to the obelisks?"

Downing finally turned her way, the same question writ large in his expression.

"I really do," she said, "Look, we already knew the aliens don't see the way we do, and based on what *I* saw inside, a whole lot of their procedures are automated. And the weight shouldn't make a difference. Those things have to weigh, what, thousands upon thousands of tons."

Lucas frowned. "Yeah, see, that's the part I ain't happy about. If they can carry those massive things, you think we got enough explosives to make a dent?"

"What I've seen of Lamb's arsenal should make a *very* big bang. Plus he says he's got even more, plus whatever they're carrying in the way of fuel... And the obelisks should help direct the force into the ship itself.

"I know," she said, hands raised in supplication, "it's not foolproof. It's a risk, a big one. Soon as any of you offers up a better plan, I'm all for it."

"And what *of* Lamb?" Natsuhiko asked, voice low. "Are you so sure his is the right side to take in this?"

"Trust me." It wasn't an answer, not really. She knew it, they knew it. She couldn't give them a better one—for more reasons than they could ever guess.

Downing grunted and returned to work. Natsuhiko and Lucas both nodded, though neither appeared thrilled.

"Look, guys—" she began.

"Cynthia?"

She straightened, fists clenching, at the call from behind her. "I told you," she said without turning around, "I have nothing to say to you. I thought I was pretty clear."

She'd certainly tried to be. When he'd first approached her, after learning that she'd insisted he be assigned to the work details she was overseeing, when he'd thanked her for getting him, however slightly, out from under Lamb's thumb, she'd held nothing back.

I didn't want to see you beaten any more. I owed you that much. But that's it. We're through. You'll follow instructions when I have them passed to you, and otherwise we're going to have absolutely nothing to do with each other.

Ever.

"Yes," Ethan said. The sadness and the hurt in his tone very obviously came from more than his physical wounds. She didn't care. "Yes, you were very clear."

"Then go the fuck away."

"Cynthia, listen."

"I said—"

"I fucking heard what you said!"

All work, all speech, ceased throughout the workstation. Everyone watched, shocked but also fascinated. More than a few couldn't entirely hide their smirks.

They want us to get into it, Cynthia realized. *See two people they hate beating on each other.*

"I'm not here as your friend," Ethan said, visibly struggling to calm himself.

"I could've told you that."

"I'm here," he continued, "as a man under your command who has something important, and relevant, to show you. They haven't told you everything."

Shocking. Cynthia sighed, long and loud.

"All right, Doctor Bell." He flinched at that. *Good.* "Lead the way."

If she thought she felt the weight of everyone's hatred as she'd walked the halls earlier, she knew better now. The two of them, the murderer and the child molester, side by side? She all but choked on the loathing that wafted across their path.

After a few moments, they approached the conference rooms the New Covenant had set aside as an infirmary. Still Ethan continued, wending between various cots and salvaged equipment, until all that remained was a door that, so far as Cynthia knew, opened into one last, smaller room.

A New Covenant soldier, complete with M4, stood before that door.

"That's far enough, Doctor Bell."

"Move. She needs to see it."

"She's not authorized—"

"I'm authorizing her. I'm still one of the few doctors here, whatever else you think of me. Get out of the way."

"I can't do that."

"Then shoot us."

The guard's mouth worked. "I—"

"You can shoot us, which I'm sure you're ready to explain to Lamb. Or you can try to subdue the both of us together. Or you can stop wasting time and *move*."

He moved. "I'm going to report this to Mr. Lamb."

"You go do that."

Cynthia watched the man leave, then followed Ethan through the door. "All right, what'd you need to show *Jesus fucking Christ!*"

It lay on the room's single bed, bathed in the light of a cluster of lamps that had been dragged in from unused rooms. Not just its arms but its legs bent up and inward, curling toward its chest like a long-dead spider's. Cowboy hat, sunglass, boots, had all begun to flake away into shreds of dried, dead tissue, exposing only deeper layers of the same substance beneath. Several fibers of that not-quite-flesh dangled, stiff and brittle. The entire body was gaunt, even shriveled.

Hunter jerky, she thought, biting back a crazed giggle.

She wandered from one side of the bed to the other, studying. Fascinated, horrified. The usual hot, chemical scent was all but gone. She smelled mostly dust and dried leaves.

"We found it behind an abandoned car half a block over," Ethan told her. "Not long after the attack."

"What happened to it?"

"We're, uh, not entirely sure. We thought maybe one of the flamethrowers injured it badly enough that it died before getting away, but it doesn't appear to have any overt burns. It's possible," he admitted, though he blatantly didn't want to, "that something Lamb did to it proved lethal."

"Lamb?"

"This was one of the two that confronted us—uh, him—personally. Until he drove them away. Maybe."

"Yeah, I'm going to need you to expand on that."

Ethan crossed his arms. "So now you're talking to me?"

She whipped around to face him. Had she been any nearer, her hair might have left welts across his cheeks. "Don't you *fucking* start!"

In a near monotone, he described the encounter—the Cowboy, the Flannel Man, Joshua Lamb, and Ethan himself, powerless to do more than watch and pray. And he described his concerns and his doubts as to what had actually happened on a psychic level he could never comprehend.

Again she examined the dead creature, chewing over all she'd been told. If Lamb *did* have the power to kill the Crooked Men with a thought—even delayed—was that a good thing or bad? And if he didn't, what the hell had happened?

"How long did it take to decay like this?" she asked.

"Um. It didn't. This is more or less how we found it. It's lost a few flakes, that's all." Then, "Why are you giving me that look?"

"Let me guess. Lamb decided not to let most of the people here actually see the body?"

"Yes," the New Covenant's prophet said from the doorway. "Lamb did." He stepped into the room wearing a flat, unfriendly expression. "In fact, my orders were very specific, were they not, Doctor Bell? *Nobody* was to be allowed in here without my authorization."

"She needed to know."

"That was not your decision to—!"

"I know now," Cynthia interrupted. "So save it, okay? My point is that Natsuhiko was with me when we killed the one in La Grange. If you'd let him in on this, he could've told you immediately that *that* one didn't shrivel up this way when it died."

Ethan blinked. "What?"

Lamb said nothing.

"It curled up like this, but it wasn't… shrunken. Desiccated." Even as she said the word, she knew. "It's probably hard to see, or you'd have found it already. But I bet that somewhere on this thing, there's a small wound. About…" She held her thumb and forefinger apart. "…this wide."

"What are you saying?"

It was Lamb who answered. "She's saying she believes one of the other Hunters killed it. And she's correct."

While she once again had to swallow a chuckle, this time at the shock plastered across Ethan's features, Cynthia couldn't even pretend to be surprised. "You knew all this already."

"I did."

"And you decided once again to keep it secret from your people."

"I did. They know what they need to know, when they—"

"When they need to know it, yeah. I can't imagine why you need alien powers to get people to trust you." Ignoring Lamb's flicker of irritation, she continued, "Too bad you can't tell us *why* they're killing each other now. That could be useful."

"Who says I can't?"

She stared. He smiled.

Cynthia gave in first. "Are you planning to tell us?"

"Are you planning to be a little less insulting to me in the future?"

"Not particularly."

She at least had the pleasure of watching his smile fade.

"I told you before, Lamb. We're not friends and we don't have to like each other, which is good, because we're never going to. We have a common goal, that's it. And since this is my plan, I need to know this shit. More to the point, you need me to know it! So let's have it."

In the corner, Ethan seemed to be having a small fit.

"We're going to have one long, last talk about this when everything's over and done with, Ms. Han."

Cynthia swallowed once, waited until he wasn't looking to wipe the sweat from her palm on her pants leg, but said only, "Fine by me."

"The good doctor," Lamb said, his anger gone as though it had never been, "thinks I'm unaware that these two creatures had some manner of disagreement before they fled. I believe that this one here wanted to warn the Cathedral about me."

"They already know about you," Cynthia protested.

"They know *of* me. They don't understand what I am. What I *truly* am."

Oh, here we go.

"These Hunters caught a glimpse of it. Of the power I wield, the ageless psyche that has joined with mine. They saw that my faith is greater than theirs, that the understanding and enlightenment I've been granted goes beyond what they could ever hope to possess!"

"You're insane." She never knew if she'd spoken aloud or merely thought it, but either way, he failed to hear.

"But if the Heretics knew, if they were warned what they face? They might abandon their pride, call the Hunters back to defend the Cathedral, seek to smooth over their conflict, stand together as one. And most of the Hunters, ever faithful to their flawed beliefs, would obey. The other? The one you call the Flannel Man? It couldn't have that. It cannot abandon the hunt. It hates us too much. Adores the excitement of the kill too much."

"How could you know all this?" Ethan asked.

"I was in direct contact with them, Ethan! And that was enough. Every day that passes, the gifts and the knowledge granted me by the Scriptures grows. Every day our final confrontation draws nearer, my connection with the minds of the Hunters and the Heretics grows, too. As does my certainty in what God needs me to do about them."

Or maybe just your delusions and your ego.

Could she dismiss it, though? For all the mad ranting, some of the details lined up. She was the one who'd told Zheng some of the Crooked Men had grown enamored of the hunt, taken it beyond a religious duty to be performed swiftly and efficiently and then left behind. And she'd seen the cruelty of the Flannel Man herself. If any of them were to slaughter another just so it could keep killing, it would be that one.

But she couldn't know, could she? Not for certain. And if this plan was have the best odds of working—the *whole* plan, not just the part she'd shared with Lamb—she needed to know for sure.

"I've heard this all before," she said.

Lamb went still, even as Ethan's jaw sagged.

"I beg your pardon?"

"Your wild claims. Your ranting."

Ethan visibly winced. "Cyn, maybe you should—"

"No, by all means," Lamb interrupted. "Do continue."

Her head began to tingle, and she knew she stood on the precipice, that the slightest additional nudge might push him—or her—over.

"What's this great enlightenment of yours?" she demanded. "What do you know that they don't? What makes them 'heretics'?"

Lamb glared, then smiled, turned away.

"I know them better than anyone else who hasn't already succumbed to them, Lamb! How much can you possibly understand if you can't even make *me* understand?"

He continued toward the door, reached for it. Stopped.

"You are not a subtle manipulator, Ms. Han." He pivoted to face her once more. "But you want to understand? Fine. Let's seek revelation together, you and I."

She refused to take a single step back, standing her ground no matter how many instincts roared at her to retreat. Even if she failed to learn more of his beliefs, his motivations, the worst she'd face would be another torrent of fanatical gibberish. He wouldn't turn his power against her, not yet.

Probably.

"What do you suppose the Progenitor is?"

"Umm." Not what she'd expected. "The Disciples believe it's some sort of god incarnate."

"Yes, I'm aware. What do *you* think it is?"

Cynthia took the opportunity to pace, so far as the room permitted, as though in contemplation. It took her out of his direct path.

"Some sort of psychically powerful creature, I'd guess. Powerful enough to make other telepathic races think it's divine? Maybe it's as old as they think, or maybe there's a line of them."

"Logical. I'm glad you've given it some consideration. But you've no idea *how* old, Ms. Han. Nor *how* powerful."

"You're not going to tell me you believe it's actually a god, too!" she insisted.

Lamb ignored that. "There's a reason that the nearest linguistic match for their conception of it is 'Progenitor.' It was the first, or at least among the first."

"First what?" Ethan asked nervously.

"Sentience, Doctor Bell. In this corner of the universe, at least."

Cynthia had long believed Lamb was mad. This was the first time she *wanted* him to be. "That's not possible. It would have to be *billions* of years old!" Zheng had claimed it was that ancient, of course, but she'd dismissed it then as pure religious dogma.

"Billions upon billions. With the power to rewrite whole races with a thought. Tell me, does that sound like something you would revere?"

"Fear," she admitted without hesitation. "If I believed all this, it would be something I would fear."

"*Exactly!*"

She couldn't help but jump at his shout. He'd approached to within a few steps, his gaze feverish.

"So did the ancients, Ms. Han. And under the guise of worship, they did something about it.

"'Disciples,' the fools call themselves. They follow the Scriptures that were implanted in their minds, and they do not question, because they were *programmed* not to question. So it has been, species after species, planet after planet, to the beginning. Even I don't know if the deception was deliberate, or if their understanding was corrupted through the eons, but it's a lie. Their faith, their veneration, all of it."

She waited, on edge, short of breath, and she had to remind herself in every pause that she heard a twisted religious doctrine through a diseased mind, that she could take nothing he said as truth. Had to remind herself because, while he spoke, it all sounded so impossibly, frighteningly real.

"The prayers of uncountable souls, Ms. Han, Doctor Bell. Of a million races across space and time. Psychic energies, collected and channeled by the obelisks, and projected back to one single world in the depths of reality's eldest corners. Not to honor and venerate the Progenitor, nor even to appease it, *but to keep it in slumber.*

"The Heretics are not worshipers of the Progenitor, though they *believe* they are. They are its *jailors*."

Cynthia found herself perched on a small stool near the bed that served as a bier for the dead Hunter, without memory of sitting down. Across the room, Ethan leaned hard against the wall, nearly hyperventilating.

Whatever she'd thought Lamb had to say, whatever secret she'd expected him to reveal about the Disciples' faith that even they purportedly didn't know, wasn't even close.

"Or at least," he concluded with a sudden smile, "that's what the very first Disciples intended when they carved the Scriptures and imbued them with powers and entities of their own. Who's to say who's right, really? The story should certainly make for a good way to drive them to despair if I can get into their heads, though. Maybe stop them in their tracks."

It was, at that. She didn't buy any of it herself, of course.

Then why are your hands trembling, Cyn?

"And what about you?" she gasped out as he made as though to leave. "I know their faith, and I understand what you know—" *or think you know* "—about their faith. But what do *you* believe?"

"I believe…" This time when he turned the handle, he didn't halt himself, stepping through the open doorway. "I believe that you still have a great deal of preparation to oversee. Good afternoon, Ms. Han."

Chapter Nineteen

E ven without the demon of now-constant pain gnawing on
her skull, Cynthia's anxiety would have been more than
enough to nauseate her.

At every step, the plan presented her with ever more ways
it could go wrong, a swiftly narrowing path to victory. When
she and the New Covenant convoy had departed the hotel,
beginning the multi-hour drive toward the Wichita River and
the hill-cradled nest of the Cathedral—and her head had almost
instantly fallen numb—she'd come near to panic.

The Crooked Men were gathered, watching. She couldn't
pinpoint them, couldn't guess at their numbers, but they lurked
nearby. Ready to attack the convoy? To attack the forces left behind,
who waited for the first sign of the Disciples so they might guess
which obelisks would be the last ones gathered? Both?

She'd pull muscles in her back, her neck, squirming against
her seatbelt, trying to peer in all directions from the passenger
seat of the blocky, rust-speckled van. All she got for her troubles
was more pain as she caught sight of an obelisk emerging from
behind a downtown skyscraper.

Yet no assault came, either against them or, according to the
frequent radio checks, those who remained behind.

"Relax, Ms. Han," Lamb had finally ordered from the back
seat.

"You're not even a *little* worried?"

"I expect if they were going to attack, they'd have done so.
They don't like dealing with groups this big. They don't like
dealing with *me*. And I suspect most of them remain concerned
over what happened to their dead brother."

"*Or* they're just waiting to figure out which group is weakest, since you've just split your forces."

"They can't tell. I can't hide the fact that we've separated, but I can still cloak us well enough that they shouldn't be able to measure our numbers, or be certain which group *I'm* a part of."

"You think."

"God will provide," he'd said with a contented smile.

Whether it was Lamb, God, or something else, he'd been right. Hours later, the convoy had halted a couple of miles from the Cathedral, lying in wait within a small valley, and still no attack had come. Cynthia had left the van, paced, kicked at the frozen soil, returned to the van, fidgeted, tried and failed to strike up a conversation with Natsuhiko and Downing, sat down again, stood up again, triple-checked her weapons and ammunition...

The dark skies rumbled. Clouds swirled. Dirt and gravel danced across the earth. And somewhere above, the Cathedral— or at least a portion of it—drifted by on its way to collect the first of Houston's obelisks.

Finally!

That didn't mean it was time to move, though. Not yet.

At Lamb's order, Vivian checked in regularly with their people back in the city. A couple of hours after the Cathedral had departed—within the atmosphere, the Disciples were either unwilling or unable to fly their vessel any faster than the casual glide they'd seen so far—New Covenant spotters watched as three obelisks on Houston's southeast side floated upward, illuminated and apparently lifted by a sodden green energy that somehow made the observers feel *greasy*.

More crackling, staticky shouting back and forth over the radio, guesses made, numbers added up. The Cathedral reappeared over the hills, sinking out of sight behind the most dramatic peaks to set down its holy cargo before beginning its second trip.

Lamb and Vivian put their heads together over the radio, giving further orders, listening to additional reports, combining what they'd observed with Lamb's vague premonitions. Finally, everyone was satisfied they knew which selection of obelisks would most probably be last on the list—and roughly how long it would take the Disciples to get to them. In Houston, the other half of the New Covenant set out to affix their bombs to the chosen targets.

But here, in north Texas, they waited still. Cynthia knew they must, knew *why* they must. It was her plan. She still thought she might just lose her mind.

The afternoon and much of the night dragged on. The Cathedral appeared, disappeared, reappeared, again and again. Everyone napped in shifts, though Cynthia found, between her impatience and her pain, that sleep was difficult to come by, even harder to keep hold of.

Until, at last, they received the report they'd been waiting for. All sections of Houston but one had been cleared. Only the obelisks now laden with New Covenant explosives remained.

"We'll head out now," Lamb said. "Gather just outside the cargo bay. I can make sure none of them sense our presence. As soon as the rest of the Cathedral departs on its last run, we'll move in."

Of the several dozen soldiers he'd brought with him, he assigned ten to remain behind, to spread out and guard the approach, watching for Hunters, for the early return of the Cathedral, for whatever unanticipated dangers might present themselves.

"Doctor Bell," Cynthia said, "you're with them."

"I... what?"

"I want you on rear guard."

Ethan sounded not merely disappointed, but frightened. "Why?"

"Because it's a way you can be useful without me having to deal with you!" she snapped. Then, only a little more gently, "And because if anything goes wrong, I'd like you healthy enough to come in and clean up the mess." She cocked a head toward the others Lamb had ordered to stay behind. That group, too, included several New Covenant medics.

"But..."

She nodded, understanding. "Downing, you're with him, too."

The engineer hissed and literally stomped over to her. "Why do *I* have to fucking stay with him?!"

Because I don't want to deal with your irritating ass, either! "Because the New Covenant folks actually like you, for some reason. Bell's less likely to meet with an accident if you're with him."

Lamb and Vivian, both near enough to overhear, chuckled.

"Maybe he should," Downing spat. He did, however, wander back over to the others, shaking his head and muttering.

Vivian collected several radios and distributed them. "Good luck, Joshua," she said, taking up position with the rest of the rear guard.

"We don't need luck," he replied. "We have grace. But," he added, "I suppose luck wouldn't hurt."

A nod to Vivian, another to Cynthia, and he set off, more than twenty of his people following behind. Cynthia offered Natsuhiko a wan smile, and the two of them fell in as well, marching into the darkness.

"All right, people!" Vivian called out before the main force had fully faded from sight. "Everyone pair off! Eyes and ears, and if you spot *anything*, you report it to me before you do a damn thing! We're on channel four on the presets.

"Doctor Bell, Walther, you two are together. You know, in case of *accidents*." She pointed past a nearby rise to the copse of dark, looming trees beyond. "You're that way."

"Anything could be hiding in there!" Downing protested.

"Then I suggest you find them before they find you." She walked away, spouting orders and directions to the other pairs.

The doctor and the engineer exchanged glances. "After you," Ethan said.

"Fuck off."

Ethan shrugged, checked his pistol—the New Covenant hadn't tried to make him take part in this mission unarmed, but they weren't about to give him heavy weaponry, either— then returned it to his belt. He clicked his flashlight on and advanced, Downing following a few steps behind.

Other than Downing stumbling as they maneuvered

around the knoll, having failed to realize how far the slope extended, they traveled in silence for minutes, halting at the edge of the copse. Somewhere within, a night bird broke off its song halfway through at their approach.

"I'm sorry," Ethan said, gazing into darkness.

"Huh?"

"For being weak. For disappointing everyone. I'm sorry."

He finally turned. The beam of the flashlight was more than enough to illuminate the utter revulsion on Downing's face. "Yeah. And I'm sorry for how I treated you *before* I knew what a fucking asshole you are."

Ethan wasn't certain whether the sudden chill came from the increasing wind or his companion. He stepped into the trees, hoping to get out of the path of both.

Sticks and grass crunched underfoot, and Downing cursed as branches snatched at his sleeves.

"Why don't you turn your flashlight on instead of relying on mine?" Ethan asked.

"Why don't you shut the hell up instead of, you know, ever talking again?"

More minutes passed. *Probably no more than seventy or eighty thousand*, Ethan groused internally. *Funny, it feels longer.*

"Downing, listen—"

"*You* listen, God damn you! Where the fuck do you get off apologizing to *me*? You haven't even got the—!"

"No!" Ethan hissed, spinning and actually raising a finger to the other man's lips. "*Listen!*"

Now that both had fallen silent, Ethan was certain. In the distance, filtered through the largely bare branches, he heard the rumble of an engine, maybe more than one, punctuated by the squeal-hiss of heavy brakes.

"Trucks?" Downing whispered.

"Sounds like. But why? Did Lamb have them trailing behind the convoy? And if—"

"Sorry, boys." All but invisible in the gloom, Vivian stepped from the trees behind them, MP5 raised. "Afraid we didn't tell you everything. Guns on the ground, please. *Slowly.* Two fingers only."

Downing's blinking behind his glasses gave new meaning to owlish. "What? Vivian, why—?"

"Now!"

Ethan and Downing carefully removed their pistols and dropped them to the grass.

"What now?" Ethan asked.

"Now, I'm exactly half sorry. I actually like you," she told Downing. "But him, I've wanted to kill for a while now."

"Wait, that's it? You're just going to shoot us?!" After all Ethan had seen, all he'd experienced, this blurry tableau felt more unreal than anything else. He couldn't quite wrap his head around it. "You hate me that much?"

"Well, yes, but that's not why." Even in the faint glow of the single flashlight, the barrel of her weapon gleamed. "None of you were getting out of here alive, but you might have had a few more minutes if Han hadn't insisted you stay out here on guard." She shrugged. "If either of you want to turn around, feel free."

"You don't want to do that," Downing said. For all that his voice shook, he sounded quite certain.

Vivian snorted. "And why's that?"

"Because I'm damn well not going out alone. I spent most of my prep time working with the explosives, and since we were going into battle, I thought I might help myself to a couple." He raised his hands, palms outward—to reveal the narrow length of metal dangling from a small ring wrapped about his middle finger. "How fast can you run?"

With a squeak somewhere in the back of her throat, Vivian dove behind a cluster of gnarled roots, lying half exposed along the hardened soil.

Downing hit the ground almost as rapidly, scrambling for the pistol he'd dropped.

He found it, shaking hands slapping at it, struggling to scoop it up...

Realizing no detonation was forthcoming, Vivian rose, turning, MP5 rising...

The engineer managed to shove a trembling finger into the trigger guard and squeezed off shot after shot.

He was no marksman, nor had Downing ever fired a weapon at another human being. The first three bullets flew wide.

The fourth and fifth punched through flesh and bone a fraction of a second before Vivian could pull her own trigger. She coughed once, a sound more indignant than pained, then toppled to lie draped over the roots.

"What the *fuck*?!" Ethan demanded.

"We need to go. We need to not be here when her people come to see what the shooting was about."

"But what the *fuck*?!"

"Come *on*!"

They scrambled deeper into the trees, as fast as the rough footing and the darkness would permit. Downing grabbed Ethan's light and switched it off, something the doctor himself would have done if he'd been thinking straight.

After several minutes and a great many more stumbles, trips, bruises, and scrapes, they finally stopped to catch both breath and bearings.

"*Now* what the fuck?" Ethan asked.

Downing nodded, and promptly vomited all over the nearest tree trunk.

"I killed her. Oh, Jesus, I shot—"

"Just like she was about to do to us. You did what you had to."

Downing kept shaking—Ethan could tell that much even in the dark—but his breathing slowed.

After giving him another moment, Ethan said, "So was it a dud? How did you know?"

"Huh? Was... was what a dud?"

"The grenade!"

"Oh." Downing covered his flashlight with his hand and turned it on. The fleshy glow barely spread a few inches, too dim to be seen from any distance. He smiled, his chattering teeth reflecting pink. "No grenade."

"Then what..."

Downing turned his other hand over. The ring about his finger was a keychain; the length of metal in his palm, the tiny screwdriver for his glasses.

"You're crazy," Ethan breathed, fighting the sudden urge to piss himself.

"Didn't have a lot of time to plan, did I? You should be—"

Again they froze as the night burst into new sound. Not trucks, this time, but very nearly as familiar.

"That can't be good," Downing muttered.

"We need to warn Cyn!"

"Right!" The engineer scrambled for his radio. They'd worked this out with Cynthia in private before leaving the hotel, in case of emergencies: She would keep her own radio set to a different frequency than the New Covenant, in case the others needed to reach her, to tell her of any threat to the plan. "Uh, what channel did we agree on?"

"Seven! Aren't you supposed to be good with numbers?"

Downing ignored that. The dial clicked. "If she's still in the middle of the group, everyone's going to know we had this arranged."

"Call her!"

"Right. Cynthia? Cynthia, this is Walther. Emergency! Do you read? Cynthia?"

Nothing. Static, with an occasional broken echo of Downing's own messages.

"Try again."

He did. And again.

"Is her radio not set to seven?" Ethan demanded. "Or is something interfering?"

"How the shattered ceramic fuck do I know?!"

"Well, we have to do *something*!"

They did. Knowing full well that the terrain and the jealous darkness would take every opportunity to trip them up, that they had every chance of arriving far too late to make a difference, they ran.

One final time, the sky shuddered and the earth trembled. The alien thing passed unseen overhead, fading briefly behind the hills, then moving south once more. Moving to collect what should, one way or another, be the last load of Houston's obelisks.

After a night and more spent in waiting, Cynthia and the New Covenant, and perhaps humanity itself, were on the clock.

Cynthia, who had been here once before, who could feel by the soothing blanket muffling her pain that they were near, led the way with Natsuhiko at her side. Lamb and his soldiers followed behind, pouring from between two small hills, a newly diverted river of flesh and bone and so very many guns.

Although she'd know him only a few days, she wished Lucas were here. Approaching the Cathedral without the one person who'd been at her side last time felt, however superstitiously, like a poor idea.

It gleamed dully in the glow of two dozen flashlights, a wavering pool of visibility as though reflecting some of the lights, absorbing others. Closer they came, and closer, and still the sloped wall of the Cathedral sat unmoving, its occupants showing no awareness of the enemy's approach. Lamb's confidence that he could cloak their presence from the Disciples as thoroughly as he had the Hunters appeared well founded.

And it probably would have been, if the Disciples hadn't already known they were coming.

"No matter what happens next," Cynthia hissed at Natsuhiko, "follow my lead!"

"Oh, God, Cynthia, what did you do?"

As before, the wall peeled open, condensing in reverse, to reveal the bright but sickly illumination beyond. Zheng Xiaowen and three more of the Disciples' human brethren stepped into view, all armed. They carried hunting rifles, perhaps less threatening than the New Covenant's military hardware, but effective enough.

Of course, they were only four against almost thirty—until they weren't.

Floodlights snapped on across multiple hilltops, bathing the New Covenant in near-blinding white. Men and women, zealous adherents of the obelisk Scripture and fanatically loyal to the Disciples, aimed their own rifles and pistols downward. In a span of seconds, the stealth advance was not merely exposed but surrounded by a high-ground force more than half again their size.

"If everybody would kindly hold quite still," Zheng announced, "we can avoid any unpleasant outcome."

If only in confusion, rather than acquiescence, everyone obeyed. Everyone but Cynthia and a stunned Natsuhiko, whom she dragged along by his wrist. The rogue pair made a dash for the Cathedral's newly exposed ingress. Not only did none of Zheng's people take a shot, Zheng himself stepped aside to let them pass.

Once they'd cleared the line of fire, Zheng continued. "We only want Joshua Lamb. Turn yourself in, and nobody needs to get hurt here today. Not even you."

His hands empty of weapons and held away from his sides, if not precisely raised, Lamb stepped from the center of his people, ignoring their cries and protestations.

And he laughed.

"Oh, Ms. Han, I'm almost impressed. Was this your scheme all along? Lure me out here so they could take me?"

In was, indeed, precisely that. The last bit of the plan, the final argument that had convinced Zheng and the Disciples to go along with removing the obelisks from Houston, the detail she'd kept even from her friends, lest Lamb somehow pull it from their thoughts.

They wanted him. Not just to eliminate a threat, but to learn the extent of his power. How he'd gained it, what enlightenment he could truly provide, if any, about their own faith.

To determine if, by studying him, they could "fix" the disconnect between the Scriptures and the surviving humans.

And Cynthia had gone along with it, just as she'd gone along with the New Covenant, because she didn't intend to let any of it happen. Use Lamb to destroy the Disciples; use the Disciples to destroy Lamb.

Now they were here, yet so much could still go wrong. None of the New Covenant would reveal the presence of the bombs on the final obelisks, would screw up their one chance to be free of the alien influence, and Cynthia was fairly certain the Disciples had neither cause nor time to dig that knowledge out telepathically, if they even could.

Lamb himself, though? Was he mad enough, spiteful

enough, to torpedo his people's future because of her betrayal? She didn't *think* so, but she'd been wrong about him before. She'd expected him, in fact, to react with anger to this setback, to rant and scream and, with any luck, open fire so that Zheng's people would have no choice but to follow suit. She'd hoped he'd be too *dead* to remain a threat.

When it became clear she didn't plan on answering, he called out again. "You hate me that much, do you?"

"It's not about hate! It's about not leaving a monster like you in charge. But yes! Yes, I do!"

Angry rumbles and the shifting of weapons sounded among the New Covenant, but still nobody took that first, fateful action.

To Zheng, she snapped, "He's never going to surrender! You can learn what you need from an autopsy!"

"We don't know that. I will take that option only if I must."

God dammit!

"It's very rude to whisper about me when I'm right here!" Lamb called out.

Cynthia began to sweat despite the chill. *Why isn't he more upset about this?*

Far off in the night, five shots rang out, followed instantly by shouts and accusations from the gathered crowds. Barrels rose, fingers tightened.

"No!" Zheng shouted, stepped forward, rifle held over his head. "Hold fire! Hold fire!"

Lamb, too, had taken a step, but he said not a word. Instead, his features tensed in concentration. Through the numbness in her mind, Cynthia felt a faint touch, water lapping at the edge of a gentle pond. Spreading from Lamb, like a ripple in that pond, the yelling faded and expressions softened.

The emotional fuse that had so nearly set off the entire assembly sputtered and died. Cynthia didn't know which worried her more, that he'd once again short-circuited the last step of her plan, or what those distant shots might mean.

For several minutes the two leaders spoke to their people, offering reassurance, working toward calm, insisting that—no matter how things appeared—it would all turn out right in the end.

"Please!" Zheng finally shouted, all but begging. "Just cooperate! Send your people home. I don't want to hurt anyone! There are so very few of us left."

"There are." He smiled, broadly, and what gleamed in the floodlights was the grin not of the lamb, but the wolf. "And now, even fewer."

The world erupted.

Chapter Twenty

They came in fast and low, skimming the treetops. Two similar shapes, whirling blades and heavy steel, one in dull camouflage all but black against the night, the other in incongruous orange and white.

They came in fast, and they came spitting fire.

The Coast Guard Jayhawk slewed sideways at it passed overhead, bringing its lone armament, a belt-fed machine gun in the starboard door, to bear. Bullets chewed into the frigid soil, shattered a floodlight, and tore gaping rents into Zheng's people. The noise of its engines wasn't remotely enough to drown out their dying screams, nor the dust kicked up by its rotors sufficient to obscure the terrible view.

Cynthia felt Natsuhiko freeze beside her, saw Zheng and his nearest people had done the same. Instincts drilled into her through multiple exercises and genuine engagements drove her toward her friend, yanking him to cover.

From the second helicopter, the Black Hawk, came not a barrage of bullets, not at first, but a single flash.

Across the small valley now turned battlefield, a hilltop occupied by Cathedral forces vanished in a roaring torrent of flame.

Now fully illuminated by the inferno below, the gunship rotated. Machine guns mounted on pivots in both doors raked the edges of the blast zone for survivors, but those weren't the weapons that caught Cynthia's attention, made even her freeze up, if only for an instant.

The Black Hawk's stubby wing attachments—the External Stores Support System, hardpoint mounts for all manner of peripherals—were packed tight with Hellfire missiles. The shot that had obliterated the hilltop had been only the first of almost a score.

In the valley, the New Covenant opened fire on the demoralized enemy, all diving for cover or staring in horrified paralysis at the death raining down on them from the sky. And in the midst of it all, head upturned and hands still raised to his sides, drinking it in like the finest music, Joshua Lamb stood still as the obelisks.

Cynthia fired at him and then, not waiting to see if any of her wild shots struck home, dragged her friend deeper into the Cathedral, hunting frantically for shelter she knew was nowhere to be found in this long and featureless hall.

Except it didn't remain featureless.

Gasping, choking on emotion and ambient dirt, Zheng staggered in behind them and slapped a palm against the wall. A patch of that glutenous sludge seeped from within and formed around his hand. An instant later, portions of the wall peeled open, revealing narrow alcoves, perfect shelter to avoid—and return—fire.

He said nothing to Cynthia, merely looked her way, and then ducked into one, his rifle raised. Cynthia shoved Natsuhiko into another and followed, her own carbine at the ready.

Despite the cacophony outside—the gunfire, the explosions, the cries—Cynthia heard Zheng muttering across the way, a litany repeated over and over. She couldn't properly understand the Mandarin, of course, but the tone was enough to provide the gist of it.

Come on... Come on...

If he was waiting on more of his people to take shelter here, he was doomed to disappointment. When the first group appeared in the entryway, Cynthia recognized them as New Covenant.

She fired, burst after burst until the M4 ran dry, ducking back to avoid having her own head taken off. Zheng, perhaps also out of ammo, waited for a lull in the action before diving from his niche, arm outstretched, toward the panel of sludge. He meant, Cynthia assumed, to seal the entrance entirely.

A second hand slapped into it at the same time as his own.

Lamb and Zheng locked gazes, unblinking. Cynthia felt, without knowing how, that a battle as fierce as the one outside now took place within. She glared at Lamb, would have charged him if not for the cluster of his people who had followed him in. Her trigger finger itched.

"Gun?" she asked Natsuhiko.

He shook his head. "I think I dropped it when the missile hit. I'm sorry."

"Swell."

"Downing and Bell?"

She glanced at her radio. It was, indeed, set to channel seven. And they must have seen or at least heard the helicopters coming. That they hadn't warned her, combined with the shots they'd heard...

"I'm sure they're fine," she lied.

In watching the two men at the end of the hall, Cynthia also had a good view of the fire-consumed night beyond. Thus she saw, quite clearly, when something vaguely human-shaped leapt from the treetops to snag the open doorframe of the Jayhawk. The helicopter sagged to one side at the sudden weight.

The cry came over the radio from at least five voices at once. *"Hunters!"*

Above, the crew of the Jayhawk opened up with small arms, not nearly sufficient to hurt the thing struggling to climb in there with them, but enough to knock it loose, send it plummeting to the earth below.

Lamb spoke from his throat, lips and jaw scarcely moving. "You know what to do."

The New Covenant survivors clustered together outside, weapons bristling in all directions. As the Black Hawk sent hundreds of rounds of suppressing fire into the tree line, its Coast Guard counterpart began to circle. Using a series of spray nozzles attached to tanks or cannisters that must have been placed on board for just this purpose, the crew drenched the surrounding terrain with... Well, Cynthia didn't know precisely what. But she'd have bet what little she still possessed that it was flammable.

Then, as the brightly hued helicopter climbed, escaping the conflagration to come, the Black Hawk once again rotated in place, launching Hellfire after Hellfire at the earth.

Even when flying her own combat missions, Cynthia had never seen anything quite like it. Explosion upon explosion, enhanced by whatever fuel or accelerant they'd sprayed, obliterated whole acres of woodland, of open prairie, of hillside. She flinched from the heat, face covered in sweat and eyes stinging, and could only imagine how it must feel to the men and women outside. It was like standing in the heart of an erupting volcano.

She had no idea how many of the Crooked Men had followed them, whether they'd attacked now to protect the Cathedral, because they'd needed the first detonation to pinpoint the humans through Lamb's protections, or because they'd only just finally arrived. But even if none had perished in the firestorm, they would think long and hard before making another approach.

Which was, Cynthia realized, probably why the helicopters were here. Even if Lamb had anticipated her betrayal, as now seemed probable, she couldn't imagine he'd have arranged this degree of air support for that alone.

A gasping, rattling sigh sounded from the end of the hall, though Cynthia wasn't sure whether it had come from Zheng or from Lamb. The former went statue-stiff, the latter had begun to shake.

She had no idea who was winning.

No idea, until the wall at the *other* end of the hallway opened, providing a clear path to the stasis pods and the remainder of the storage bay beyond.

"Tell them," Lamb rasped, "to start unloading."

The soldier nearest him, the same large man Cynthia remembered from the dining room, passed the order along and then incautiously waved his gun at Zheng. "You want me to—?"

"No." It took a moment for Lamb's head shake to catch up with his refusal. "No, I can't control him for long. He knows these systems better than I, and has... allies in the network. But I want to make a point."

Another moment. Cynthia leaned out, trying to see better, then ducked back as a single bullet winged her way.

And then Zheng turned his face toward the wall. A small section of the substance, not metal and not glass, opened up, presenting a depression only inches deep. Zheng stuck his face in it.

"No!" Cynthia risked sticking her head out once more. "Lamb, you—!" She recoiled from another shot, but kept shouting. "You got what you need from him! There's no reason to—!"

Lamb grunted, giving a final mental command to Zheng, who gave a final mental command to the vessel.

The hole closed with a sharp, wet crack. Slowly, clinging to the wall through exposed fluids and the hollow sinuses of his skull, Zheng's body slid downward, leaving a long and glistening smear in its wake.

"That," Lamb announced, sounding much more himself as he removed his hand from the panel, "is what I think of the Disciples. I wanted it to know."

"It?" Cynthia asked from within the niche—largely to distract herself, keep her roiling gut under control.

"There's only one here. Hiding upstairs, where you first spoke to Zheng, I should think. The rest are all aboard the Cathedral's other half. You might as well come out, you know."

"I think we'll stay back here a little longer. It's cozy. And there are fewer bullets."

She couldn't see him anymore, not from her current angle, but she heard the rustle of his clothes as he shrugged. "Up to you. But I would imagine you'd rather be shot... than burn."

Lamb barked further orders before she could ask what the hell he meant. A band of his people advanced, scouting the cargo bay. From what he told them, she had the impression he— or rather Zheng, under his influence—had opened a stairway to the upper level, where he'd earlier taken Cynthia and Lucas via rising platform.

Another command, and someone slapped a radio into their leader's waiting hand. "Emmet? Get down here and start unloading. Reese, how're you doing on missiles?" A pause, then,

"All right, land and reload. I want you back overhead before the fires fade. Everyone else, clear a landing zone, and stay sharp! I don't want you shooting any of Viv's people, but nobody else gets close!"

Shouting from inside, shouting from outside. The dull roar of both choppers touching down in the valley.

Nobody came to try to pry Cynthia and Natsuhiko from their bolt-hole, but neither did either of them feel confident in stepping out.

Her mind raced, struggling to keep track of everything. When equipped with Hellfires, it was common practice for Black Hawks to carry additional missiles as cargo for quick resupply, so that part of what she'd overheard made sense. Presumably, then, "start unloading" had been directed to the crew of the Coast Guard Jayhawk, but unloading what?

People began tromping past the niche, visible for barely more than a step in the narrow sliver of hallway Cynthia could see. First one way, arms laden, then the other, emptyhanded, and back again. It took her a few moments to figure out what they were carrying.

Cylindrical tanks, initially. Cynthia presumed those held more of the fuel or accelerant they'd used to feed the conflagration outside. Then several stacks of white, clay-like bricks, presumably held back from the obelisk team's munitions.

No. No, even he can't be that crazy!

But she knew, then, what he'd meant when he'd said she would burn.

"You can't!" She didn't even care, now, that it might get her shot. Cynthia rushed from the side passage, Natsuhiko—after a sharp gasp—following behind. "You can't do this!"

Indeed, many of those passing by laid down their burdens to reach for their guns, but Lamb forestalled their firing with a gesture. "Not only can I, Ms. Han, it's absolutely essential."

The tension visibly drained from everyone around them, as every member of the New Covenant within the hall resumed their tasks. Indeed, if they cast any further glances Cynthia's way at all, they were dim and uncaring at best.

"What are you doing to them?" she demanded.

"Just a bit of a nudge. Dampening their curiosity, enhancing their trust in me. I've already told them this is necessary, but it's a big ask, even coming from me. I'd as soon not have your questions sabotage their acceptance."

"Acceptance? *Acceptance?!* That's the future of the human race you're about to murder!"

"Oh, of course it's not. There are plenty more survivors out there. It'll take some time to find them, but we'll manage."

She honestly hadn't thought he could surprise her anymore. Now, slumping back against the wall, she almost laughed at herself for thinking so. "You're going to kill over a million people." The words barely meant anything. She couldn't entirely absorb them, even as she spoke.

"Yes."

"For God's sake, *why*?"

"That's why. For God's sake." Then, apparently responding to the incomprehension that she knew must be written all over her, "The Heretics have been working on these people for weeks, Ms. Han. Some might already have been reconditioned, ready to absorb the Scriptures as Zheng and his brethren had. I can't risk that."

The sounds of the chaos around her faded, muffled as though through cotton, and her vision blurred. She only scarcely heard Natsuhiko, from just behind her. "I don't understand."

"You want to wake it up," she whispered. "You lunatic, you believed every word, and you want to *wake it up*!"

"Of course I do! Can you imagine? A god, a *true* god! None of the fairy tales we've been raised with, no faith without reward! A creature older than half the stars in the sky, with the power to craft whole species, to shape worlds! And all beholden to me, for finally freeing It. To *me*!"

"But *this* is just a story, like all the others! It's not literally true! It can't be!"

"It is. I know. The mind in the Scriptures made it quite clear."

"You mean the same way the obelisks made belief in the Progenitor 'quite clear' to the Disciples? To every other race for millennia?"

"That's different. I went deeper. I learned the truth."

"Or you just got a higher fucking dose! Please! However sure you are, what if you're wrong? *What if*? There are over a *million people* in that bay! Lamb... Joshua... Jerold. Please!"

For an instant only, his brow furrowed. For the narrowest sliver of a second, she thought he might relent.

A detonation shook the Cathedral. Cynthia screamed despite herself, expecting a rush of heat to be her last sensation.

Nothing else happened.

"That wasn't for the bay," Lamb said without trace of hesitation or doubt. "Just a smaller charge, for the *thing* upstairs. Had to make sure it didn't have any way of stopping everything once it starts."

Whatever they'd done, it was dead. Cynthia knew that for sure as the numbness in her head faded, allowing rivulets of pain to leak through. She wanted to sob. "Why am I still alive?" she demanded.

Lamb shrugged. "I wanted you to know what you'd made possible. Now that you do?" He reached behind him, produced a small Beretta.

Don't close your eyes. He doesn't get the satisfaction.

But the subsequent shots, four of them, sounded before he'd aimed the weapon, echoing from outside. They, in turn, were followed by a chorus of shouts, and then the constant, brutal pounding of the Black Hawk's machine guns.

Chapter Twenty-One

In everyone's moment of distraction, Cynthia lunged.

She had no more idea of what might be happening than anyone else. It didn't matter.

With everything she had, she cracked an elbow across Lamb's jaw, grabbed him by the wrist as he staggered, and twisted. The New Covenant leader slammed to the floor with a bone-jarring thump.

Cynthia turned the other way, his pistol in her hands, and opened fire in quick bursts of two or three. All around her, Lamb's people dropped, still reaching for, or struggling to raise, their own weapons.

Shouting and footsteps sounded from the cargo bay as the remaining handful within the Cathedral came running, drawn by the commotion. Throwing herself against the wall and dropping to one knee, Cynthia kept shooting. An MP5 that had recently belonged to one of the men she'd shot opened up from behind her as Natsuhiko appeared at her side.

The frame locked open on the Beretta 92, its magazine empty, but not before the pair of astronauts had dropped every last member of the New Covenant who'd entered the alien craft.

Unfortunately, they hadn't all been dropped hard enough.

A second MP5 spat a three-round burst. Natsuhiko cried out, spinning in place before toppling to the floor beside her.

Cynthia rolled backward, only barely clearing the path of a second burst and leaping to her feet. His jaw misaligned, clearly broken, and his gaze bereft of all remaining sanity, Lamb swung the weapon toward her as she lunged.

A fierce backhand knocked the submachine gun from his grip—and then Cynthia was on her hands and knees, vomiting bile at the agony in her head.

God, not again, please!

That she could think that clearly, that she wasn't already dead or at least oblivious to the world, could only be due to the presence of the Hunters. However repelled by the flame and the detonations, they hadn't fled far. It would do her no real good, though, would buy her, at best, an extra minute of helpless agony.

Still she tried. Tried crawling toward him, reaching for him, or at least she meant to be, thought she might be. She couldn't be sure. Couldn't have done anything if she reached him, couldn't remember why she was *trying* to reach him, couldn't entirely remember who she was, not through the pain.

He didn't gloat. Couldn't move his jaw well enough to gloat. The satisfaction of that, she held onto even as all else began to fade.

Gagging and choking on his own blood, Natushiko forced his arm up and over his chest and squeezed his trigger.

Strange, curving cracks shot through the wall where the bullets hit, nowhere near Joshua Lamb. Cynthia didn't think her friend had the mental wherewithal to aim, let alone the physical strength. They served well, however, to startle, to distract. Lamb jumped, his attention split, and her own torment waned.

Screaming aloud, Cynthia staggered upright and slammed the full weight of the empty pistol into Lamb's throat.

Or rather, into the tiny vial hanging at his throat.

It might have been the shock and pain on their own, or perhaps it was something about the bits of obelisk gravel that, along with glass shards, were driven into his flesh. In either case, whatever concentration and whatever power he'd brought to bear shut down. All the pain, save for the ubiquitous lingering ache, vanished from Cynthia's head.

Lamb gurgled at her, his expression slack. One hand clutched at his shredded neck, the other reached for her.

Cynthia brushed that hand aside, took hold of the cord on which a few broken bits of the vial still hung. Her grip tight, she stepped past him—and then knifed forward, hauling Lamb off his feet and up on her back.

Glass, gravel, cartilage, and bone ground audibly before the cord finally snapped. Joshua Lamb slapped limply to the floor, throat torn and eyes blank. One hand twitched feebly, spasming like a dying insect.

Cynthia had already forgotten him by the time she landed on her knees beside her friend. She lacked anything clean to serve as bandages, or sufficient hands to put pressure on every wound, but she wouldn't leave him. After all this, all they'd been through, she wouldn't let Natsuhiko die alone.

"Cynthia! Cyn!"

She recognized the voice before she realized it was calling her name.

Covered in dust, dirt, and sweat, Downing and Ethan jogged in from outside. Both halted, taking in the peculiar substance and even more peculiar angles of the hall. They stood dazed, however, by more than fascination. Cynthia had seen expressions like theirs many times before, during her Air Force days. She'd worn it herself, on occasion.

These men had done things today they'd never done before. They'd killed—nastily, violently. She knew, without asking, that they'd walked past the New Covenant sentries, just another two of Vivian's rear guard. Walked past and over to the Black Hawk, with its paired machine guns...

Much as she disliked one and had grown to hate the other, she idly wished she had either the time or the energy to make it easy for them.

Instead, she went straight to business. "Did you get everyone?"

Downing flinched, looked sick.

"Most of them," Ethan answered. "Some scattered. They'll be... Oh, Christ." He dropped beside her, examining the fallen.

Natsuhiko still breathed, but they were shaky, shallow gasps. His eyelids fluttered.

"Can you help him?"

He continued looking Natsuhiko over. "He's in shock," he

finally said. "But if I can stop the bleeding and stabilize him..."

"If Lamb's people kept them properly stocked," Cynthia told him, "there should be emergency kits in both choppers. If you need painkillers, my own supplies are in the van."

Ethan nodded, brusquely pointed where she and Downing needed to put pressure to keep Natsuhiko from bleeding out, then ran. The engineer took his place, wincing as he pressed his hands against bloody wounds.

"What happened out there?" she asked him.

Downing's incredulous glance, first at the hall around them, then at Lamb's twitching body, said more eloquently than words that he felt the question should be his. Nevertheless, he answered, telling her of Vivian's intent to kill them, his clever ruse—clearly a source of no small pride—and the sudden appearance of the helicopters.

"Wait. Stop." Cynthia suddenly felt so very cold. "You called me?"

"Yeah. Tried a couple of times."

She glanced at her radio. Channel seven, as they'd agreed. Could she have missed it, in the chaos? It was possible, but the other possibility was horrifying. She had to be sure.

Ethan had returned by the time she looked up. He crouched and set to work on Natsuhiko with bandages, medical adhesives, and IV tubes. One of the few remaining Dilaudid syringes lay beside him, in case the patient woke up.

"Downing, go outside and call me," she ordered

"But—"

"*Now!*"

Grumbling, jumping at every flicker or sound in case it might be a New Covenant survivor or a Hunter, he wandered out into the light of the slowing fading fire.

He called. Cynthia got nothing but static.

"What's wrong?" She could only imagine how pale she must seem, to elicit such concern from Ethan even as he struggled to save Natsuhiko's life.

"It must be something to do with the Cathedral," she whispered. "Even right outside, through an open door, I can't get a clear signal. No wonder I didn't receive when you tried earlier."

The doctor shrugged. "Okay, but what's it matter now?"

He didn't see it. He hadn't thought it through. Her answer was frantic, a near shriek. *"The bombs are on a radio detonator!"*

Roughly fifteen thousand feet above the hills and plains, roads and woodlands, the Black Hawk tore through the dark Texas sky. It shook, rattled, alarms screaming as, every few minutes, Cynthia pushed the engines beyond listed maximum power, risking overspeed as long as she dared before cutting back to let the systems cool down.

Even assuming it survived the trip, the chopper would need substantial service before it could safely fly again. That was okay, though. Whether everything went right or wrong, this was a one-way trip.

Cynthia didn't want to be here.

Leaving the Cathedral cargo bay while New Covenant survivors remained unaccounted for had almost proved too much. A quick check confirmed Lamb's people hadn't set any timers before thing went wrong, but she and her friends had neither the time nor the manpower to remove all the explosives, all the fuel. If anyone came along determined to finish what that psychic psycho had started...

But she'd had no choice. She couldn't salvage the plan from there. She just had to hope that, without Lamb's "gifts" nudging them along, messing with their emotions, his surviving followers wouldn't be so quick to commit a million murders.

She'd never been fond of flying helicopters, either; had only minimal experience with them. It provided neither the comfort nor the confidence she'd have felt in the cockpit of a Warthog.

The constant shuddering drove further waves of pain into her skull. She'd wavered once they'd passed beyond the range of the assembled Hunters, scarcely able to hold a straight course, but she'd only allowed Ethan to provide her a few pills. They barely dulled the edge, but anything stronger and she might not be safe to fly.

Might not be able to do what had to be done. Because while this might be the last place she wanted to be, she understood, finally and completely, why she was here.

Behind her, Natsuhiko lay strapped to a cot, swathed in bandages, multiple medications running through his veins. Ethan crouched beside him, futilely bracing himself against the Black Hawk's unpredictable rocking. He'd done, Cynthia had to admit, a remarkable job. His patient's bleeding had stopped, his breath was slow and even. He might suffer the aftereffects of his injury for months, years, maybe the rest of his life, but he *had* a rest of his life.

Whatever else Cynthia might have to say about her former friend—and that was a great deal, little of it positive—Ethan remained a skilled doctor.

Downing sat beside her, multiple half-crumpled maps spread over his lap, cursing viciously at and into the radio.

"No good," he said to her, shutting the channel with an angry flick of a switch. "They don't want to tell us anything without talking to Lamb first. I've tried telling them he's, uh, otherwise occupied, but..."

Cynthia's head pounded.

"I thought we already knew which obelisks were left," Ethan called from the back. "Didn't we have all that figured so we'd know which ones to wire?"

"We know which *cluster* of obelisks are left," she replied. "But we don't know which of those the Cathedral's already picked up! If they get to the last one before we—"

"Hey!" the radio crackled. "Cyn, Walther? Y'all read me?"

"Lucas?" Downing nearly punched himself in the lip, grabbing for his headset. "That you?"

"Who else? Heard your last transmission, and I think I got what you need."

"Great! I... Wait. No offense, but how do *you* know which obelisks are left?"

Static, for a long moment. "Same way I'd know if I *could* see, dumbass. Listening to everyone else."

"Oh. That makes sense."

"Cyn? You on this channel, too?"

"I'm here," she said, banking a bit to port.

"Listen, y'all need to watch your backs out there. The team on the last obelisk? They reported in, said they were packing it up, but they never showed back at the hotel."

She and Downing exchanged looks. "Understood."

"All right, get that map open..."

Cynthia set them down in the westmost lot of Zube Park, near the concession stand and the soccer fields. To the north, across Little Cypress Creek, she could just make out the miniature train that once carried children and parents in long loops around the property, now covered in grime and already beginning to rust. East of that, an array of partial pits and frameworks where construction on new buildings had begun but never progressed.

And rising high in the center of that unfinished work, the most important of the countless alien obelisks.

She began unstrapping herself, then turned as she felt the weight of her companions' stares. Downing and Ethan had gathered close, both so clearly wanting to speak without the first notion of what to say. She forced herself to smile through the pain growing worse with every moment.

"Yes," she told them, for what was far from the first time. "I'm sure. It's the only way, and you know it."

"I know," Downing said, extending a hand for her to shake.

Her fingers had just touched his when she felt a piercing, familiar sting in her thigh.

"Not *quite* the only way," Ethan said, pulling back the now empty syringe.

"What...?" She was already starting to fade, though her confusion and her fury worked hard against the morphine coursing through her. "What...?"

"I think she means *what the fuck?!*" Downing shouted, face purpling with bewildered fury.

Ethan smiled. "Keep an eye on them, Walther." He reached into the bag at Cynthia's feet, removed the detonator, and slipped from the helicopter.

Cynthia struggled to rise, fell back. She'd grown so accustomed to the stuff, she should be able to shake off the worst of the drowsiness in minutes, even with the Vicodin already in her system—but minutes were more than she had.

She saw Downing watching her, worry and rage and

indecision a thick mix on his face. Then, growling, he opened his restraints and raced after the doctor.

Slurring syllables that were meant to be profanities, Cynthia closed her eyes, took deep breaths, counting the seconds until she could move.

Chapter Twenty-Two

"**Y**ou fucking bastard!"

Ethan had been running across the park, stumbling in the gloom, gaze downward not only to watch his step but to avoid the alien writing. He had thought he was alone.

Now he spun, startled, to see Walther Downing pounding up behind him. The engineer had removed his glasses—probably to protect himself from the obelisk—but his vision remained clear enough to pinpoint Ethan.

The doctor was *not* happy to see him. "What are you doing? You left them alone! You *whoa!*"

He ducked Downing's wild haymaker, launched a quick jab in return, just enough to stagger the other man, make him back off.

"What are you doing?" he asked again.

"What are *you*?" Downing demanded in turn, rubbing his chest where he'd been hit. "What do you think this is, your big moment of redemption? Wipe away all your sins in a big Hollywood self-sacrifice?"

"Um." Ethan felt his face flush. "We both know it's better this way. Cynthia shouldn't have to—"

"Cynthia's dying, you fuck! Slowly and painfully! She was ready! She *wanted* this! You're not saving her, you're *stealing this from her!*"

Ethan looked away, detonator twisting in his grip.

"But you," Downing continued, relentless, unyielding, stepping close again until Ethan could all but taste his words, "you're weak. We're going to need doctors in the new world, Bell. More than almost anyone else. You could have helped."

"Nobody would ever trust me again."

"So what?! Yeah, you'd have to face some punishment, probably have someone looking over your shoulder at all times to make sure you... But you deserve that! You still could have saved lives! Taught others to save lives! You're not doing this for Cynthia, and you're not redeeming yourself. You're just too much of a coward to face the consequences of what you've done. You're pathetic."

"Walther, look..."

"I don't fucking want to hear it!"

"No!" Ethan pointed violently at what had caught his attention when he'd turned away, flinching from the other man's barbed truths. "*Look.*"

From behind a small heap of dirt and rock, where the workers had been digging a foundation for the new structure, protruded an arm. An arm that, even through the thick wool of its coat sleeve, was visibly gaunt and shriveled.

Downing's breath came fast, bordering on hyperventilating, but he drew his pistol. "Head for the obelisk," he ordered.

"But—"

"No time! Go!"

Indeed, even without the Crooked Men, their time was short. The air began to vibrate, the dark clouds overhead to swirl, with the approach of the Cathedral.

Ethan ran. Again he kept his gaze down, and still he stumbled several times—once falling flat on his face, where only sheer luck kept his thumb from jarring the detonator early. Only when he'd come within a few yards of the obelisk, when he couldn't have read the engravings even by craning his neck as far as it would stretch, did he risk looking around.

He saw neither Hunter nor Downing, only the column of stone before him and an empty park, its detritus dancing and the waters of its stream rippling as the unseen craft drew ever nearer.

Several tools and components lay scattered about the obelisk's base: wires, a set of wrenches, a few near-empty plastic sacks, a nail gun. He could only assume they'd been dropped in panic. He ignored them, examining the stone itself, and the various bulging sacks of AMFO and bricks of C4 strapped all over the lower thirty feet of its height.

Could he squeeze under one of those straps? He tugged at it. It was tight, as it had to be to hold the bags in place, but maybe he could loop an arm through it, at least. It might be secure enough to...

Something dropped from above, where it had clung to the obelisk as he only wished he could. Dropped to slam into the ground behind him, and rise, lurching, flickering, looming, to its feet.

Ethan turned, trembling, detonator nearly falling from his grip. He already knew what he would see. Even in its sudden plummet, he'd recognized the lines and colors imprinted across its torso.

He stared into that checkered pattern now, then upward into the blank, featureless expanse of fleece.

The Flannel Man cocked its head, silent for only a few seconds before bursting into a torrent of burbles and shrieks.

And amidst that torrent, *"Face the consequences! Face the consequences! You're pathetic..."*

"Just do it," Ethan whispered through quivering lips. "You don't have to rub it in."

The inhuman thing leaned in, until its face—or lack of face— was inches from his. *"Rub it in..."*

It raised a gloved hand, palm splitting to extrude that horrid talon. This close, even that small movement proved stuttering, sporadic. Rivulets coated the jagged thing, rivulets of an oily sheen part liquid and part tendril, oozing free only to drip and dance and writhe across the surface before burrowing back inside through separate cracks and pores.

Ethan retreated, stumbling on loose rock. The Flannel Man watched him go without pursuing. Its wet, mucous burbling quickened, deepened, and the doctor could only imagine that it laughed at his feeble efforts.

It's not fair! He recognized the lament as childish, even as tears streaked his cheeks. *I shouldn't even have to be here! They used me, it wasn't my fault!*

Another step back. Apparently, that was far enough.

From within the deeper shadow of the nearby trees, Downing opened fire.

He jogged forward, a pace or so every two shots, and at this range most of those shots even landed. The Flannel Man ignored the first few, finally staggered with the remainder of the magazine, so that it stood with its back nearly against the obelisk itself.

Otherwise it scarcely seemed to notice, and its laughter— or whatever that hideous bubbling represented—grew harsher still.

Downing stared at his empty pistol, then over at Ethan, and finally scoured his surroundings, searching for a miracle.

The nail gun lying near his feet hardly qualified, but it was all there was.

While the doctor stood, still paralyzed, Downing scooped it up and charged with a wordless shout. It was, Ethan had to admit, one of the bravest acts he'd ever seen.

Or would have been, had Downing managed to follow through.

Mere steps from the Hunter and the obelisk, his courage failed. Maybe he just froze, understandable if ill-timed when faced with that inhuman horror. Or maybe, forgetting that much more than just his and Ethan's were at stake, he suddenly questioned whether Ethan was worth his own life.

Whatever the case, he halted just beyond arm's reach. His cry faded into gawping silence, his hand and the makeshift weapon it held dropped to his side.

And the Flannel Man reminded them both that human concepts didn't apply to it. Concepts like "arm's reach."

It knifed forward at the waist and seemed—although Ethan could never be sure, not with the creature's impossible motion—to fold *vertically*, from head to crotch, so that its right side stretched further than its left. Its hand slashed upward, the grotesque spike punching into Downing's jaw.

Not all of it, that would be too quick. Just a few inches, to start.

Blood flew from the wound and washed from between the man's lips in a slower, thicker tide, carrying bone fragments and several teeth knocked loose by the intruding talon. Downing screamed, wild and feral, through compressed and shattered bone.

The Flannel Man straightened, dragging its prey closer, pressing its weapon deeper by deliberate millimeters.

Downing raised a trembling hand and squeezed the trigger, over and over.

Gunpowder detonated and nails punctured alien tissue. Some barely penetrated, less effective even than bullets against the creature's dense musculature. But a few pierced the folds of the flannel shirt, or rather the thin membrane of flesh that had taken the shape of that shirt, and into the stone of the obelisk.

The Hunter's burbling became a prolonged shriek and it lashed out with its other hand. Downing's skull caved in beneath the blow, hanging misshapen and limp from his shattered neck.

Ethan screamed. The Flannel Man lunged at him—and came up short, dragged to a halt by the steel lengths pinning it to the stone.

They weren't deep, weren't secure, wouldn't hold long. God willing, they wouldn't have to.

From overhead came continuous artificial thunder, and a sudden sickly glow that bathed the obelisk without spreading further. The dirt at its base began to shift, falling away.

Screaming still, Ethan jammed an arm through one of the straps. He had no idea if he had the strength to hold on, not for the entire ride up, but he would damn well try—if only because, if he *was* dying here tonight, he refused to die alone at the hands of the Flannel Man.

It turned out he didn't *need* the strength. As the light reached its brightest and a peculiar whistling sounded in his ears, like a distant wind blowing over a narrow bottle, his weight seemed to fade. The obelisk rose and he rose with it, and he felt as though he would drift away, but not fall, if he were to release his grip.

The grounded receded into the darkness with startling speed, as the light never seemed to reach farther than the obelisk. He swiftly lost sight of the rubble, of the great pit where the obelisk had landed and the smaller one where workmen once dug, of Walther Downing's broken body that, even in death, had begun to twist and dry and *curdle* with the power of Flannel Man's venom.

The Flannel Man...

It tugged, shrieking, fingers pressed and sticking to the stone, dragging itself forward. One of the nails popped free, tumbled away to hover at the edge of the light. A second. A third. With each one, the creature inched that much closer.

He never saw the ship, too busy watching the deathly thing creep toward him, unable to tear his gaze away. He knew only that, without warning, the dark and empty sky around him was gone, replaced by something equally dark but, though massive, enclosed. Only below could he still see open air, and even that view narrowed as the Cathedral sealed itself.

Would he have gone through with it, here at the end, had he any choice? He wondered briefly, and he couldn't answer. He didn't want to die. He didn't want to live with what had happened, with everyone's contempt and judgment, but he didn't want to die.

The final nail tore free, the Flannel Man lurched forward, and life of any sort was no longer an option.

He wondered, oh so briefly, how Dana was holding up—and realized that he hadn't wondered about her, hadn't spared her so much as half a thought or a worry, in days.

Ethan squeezed his eyes shut and pressed the button.

The alien craft refused to behave as an earthly thing even in death.

For less than a fraction of a second, the hull at the base of the Cathedral bulged, bubbled, like microwaved skin, and seemed almost as though it might successfully absorb the blast. When it gave, it didn't so much split as separate, the material opening and condensing as it had before, but now all at once. That first detonation set off others, internal stores and systems, until the reaction spread through the vessel.

Only the first explosion, the bombs set by the New Covenant, produced visible flame. The others were pure force.

Blasted apart from a dozen spots, the Cathedral became a literal mountain of shrapnel and debris—and still, for an instant, it did not fall. Briefly held aloft by whatever energies it used to collect the obelisks, the chunks and pieces flew impossibly far and wide before finally plummeting to Earth. Entire nearby neighborhoods, fields, copses, were obliterated in the artificial hail that followed, but the park itself, and its immediate surroundings, were spared.

Spared of all but the obelisks.

Their surface cracked and pitted by the blasts, the trio of spires from within the hangar plunged downward, landing upright in a cluster that dug itself yards deep into frozen soil. There they would sit, far enough from the city center to pose no real danger, and slowly heal.

And one more thing, too, one last remnant, plunged from the sky to land near the park's edge.

Charred, slashed, and broken, its voice silenced save for a liquid rasp, the Flannel Man shambled to its feet. It must have been in agony, or whatever passed for agony among its kind, yet it stood motionless for long moments. What went through its mind, then? What did it think of the Cathedral's destruction, of the foul and unholy entities that had caused it? Did it mourn? Did it gloat? Did it care?

Could any human have made sense of *whatever* it felt?

Eventually it turned, lurching and twitching across the park toward the Black Hawk, still sitting where Cynthia had touched down, engines still active and rotors still spinning. Perhaps it sought survivors on whom to vent its rage, or perhaps it wished to check for further threat, or perhaps God Himself couldn't have interpreted its motivations. But it approached, blackened spots flaking where it, like the obelisks, had begun the long process of healing.

With a sudden jolt, the helicopter lifted mere inches off the earth and spun, driving the tail rotor into the creature's body.

The entire craft shook, nearly throwing Cynthia from her seat. She fought hard with the stick, with the anti-torque pedals, with the throbbing in her head, to keep it all steady.

Not particularly sharp, the blades didn't so much slice through the Flannel Man's flesh as rend, rip, and tear. The Hunter flew one way, flung aside by the impact, trailing broken bits and streamers of tissue. Several separate chunks flew another.

Designed to take enemy fire, those blades didn't break nearly so readily as a civilian model. Still, the impact with the dense creature bent some, cracked others. They whistled horribly as they spun, and the helicopter began to drift, rotating and slewing despite its pilot's best efforts.

But Cynthia would be *damned* if that thing was getting up and walking away!

Every muscle in her body ached as she was hurled against the restraints, forced her will on the controls. Until finally, *barely*, she'd muscled the failing machine into the open grass across the parking lot, dozens of yards away, and forced the nose back the way they'd come.

With a gasp of relief, she set it down. It wouldn't be flying again.

Far ahead, barely visible in the Black Hawk's lights, the Flannel Man rolled over, hauling itself upright.

The helicopter's ESSS held the two Hellfire missiles the New Covenant crew had reloaded before Downing and Ethan commandeered the craft, plus one they hadn't launched in their initial salvo.

Cynthia waited until the Flannel Man *almost* stood before firing all three.

The parking lot disappeared in fire. She knew it must be her imagination, but she thought she heard, *hoped* she heard, a final piercing shriek beneath the detonation.

She leaned back, pressing a hand to the side of her head, and waited. She knew the missiles were enough, that even a Hunter couldn't have survived, and the fading of the final touch of numbness left no doubt. Still, she meant to go and check, to see it with her own eyes, once the fire burned down.

And then what?

Rage and resentment seared her from within, hotter than the conflagration outside. She thought she'd hated the aliens, hated Lamb, but in the moment, the worst of her bile was reserved for Ethan Bell.

Her gaze drifted down to her own pistol, and she thought the barrel looked cool, welcoming. Certainly preferable to the weeks or months of pain the selfish bastard had left her.

And had she been alone, she might have done it, but she wasn't. Natsuhiko still needed help. She'd have to find a working car, get him back to the hotel, hope that even if what remained of the New Covenant chose to kill her on sight, they'd be more charitably inclined toward him.

Cynthia wept softly at the pain and the memories and the world, and watched the fires burn.

Epilogue

// ...and running within a few more weeks," Natsuhiko told her, shifting in his chair. Trying, she assumed, to find a comfortable position, one that didn't aggravate his pain. "Lucas says it should cover more than half the city to start with, and that we can connect the rest pretty quickly if we make the network a priority."

She said nothing, as had become her habit during most of her friends' visits. Every day it took more and more effort, and felt worth less and less.

Progress continued as she lay, helpless and seething, forced at the end to rely on others for *everything*, her resentment and loathing toward the dead man she'd once called friend having metastasized as thoroughly as the tumor in her head. Huge sections of Houston had power, now. They were coming to the end of their gasoline stores, true; after several months, the stuff had begun to break down. The kerosene and other fuels still had some time, however, and they'd managed to salvage quite a few solar panels from around the city. It would be enough to keep them going for a while. Long enough to get any of the nearby refineries running again? To complete the necessary construction, and clear the corpses, to turn the local dams and riverways into power plants? Well, they were certainly taking their best run at it.

But Cynthia couldn't help, and wouldn't be around to find out.

Around her, the hospital room actually sounded like a hospital room. Things beeped. Things pumped. Beside her, the IV dripped with a constant stream of dangerously excessive painkillers. She'd insisted, and the doctor—Cynthia couldn't recall her name—had decided no purpose could be served by refusing.

On her stomach, Lombardi yawned, stretched, turned around, and went back to sleep.

"Um." Natsuhiko twisted a heavy cane in nervous fingers. He couldn't walk without it, might not ever again. They weren't sure yet. Otherwise, he seemed fully recovered from his injuries. She envied him that—"recovery"—even as she pitied him.

Recovery meant he wouldn't escape any time soon. Not the way she would.

"Marcus is going to lead a convoy to Carrollton. Lucas says Wikipedia ran some of their servers from there. If we can bring them back up, stop having to rely solely on the scanning teams at the libraries, the local internet should become a lot more useful, a lot faster."

Now she did turn, concerned. She understood the importance of getting as much information to the survivors as possible, understood the difficulty and complexity of the rebuilding efforts, even confined to Houston. But...

"Sec..." She swallowed hard, cursed the growing interference between thought and speech. "Security?"

"Ms. Ogude believes that Marcus's people and policies should be more than sufficient while he's away. And you know Marcus. He wouldn't go if he didn't agree."

Cynthia nodded, stiff and painful.

Ogude, a Nigerian city planner whom they'd found among the survivors in the stasis pods, had swiftly proved herself knowledgeable enough to run the efforts at reconstruction and the city's nascent government. Cynthia didn't know her. She did, however, trust Marcus, whose own experience, and the fact that he'd led the team that finally returned and freed everyone from what remained of the Cathedral, had left him in charge of Houston's defenses.

So far, those forces hadn't faced any real challenges. Apart from a single scouting party that went missing, whose fate remained a mystery, no potential enemies or threats had materialized. If any Disciples survived the bombing, they kept to themselves. Bands of human survivors arrived, not to raid and pillage, but to join. And the Hunters... Well, everyone knew they still walked the Earth, but whether held at bay by the city's safeguards or merely biding their time, they'd so far left the new Houston population alone.

Not that Marcus had grown complacent or allowed anyone under him to slack. The city limits and its most populous areas saw constant patrols, traveling in groups of vehicles, armed with flamethrowers and explosives. Between those, constant city-wide drills, and regular contact—now augmented by the new, if limited internet—Houston was as safe as could be hoped.

It didn't stop Cynthia, didn't stop *most* people, from fretting.

"Ob..." she asked, or tried to. "Obel..."

"Marcus is taking some former Covenant people on his team. They'll be the ones driving. The obelisks shouldn't be a problem."

That only swapped one threat for another, so far as Cynthia was concerned. So far, however, most of the New Covenant had assimilated as well as anyone else. She didn't know if it was because Lamb wasn't playing with their heads any longer, or just because rebuilding society—even without him—is what they'd wanted all along.

She still didn't trust them, though.

It did, however, segue neatly into the one last topic she *did* want, need, to talk about. The hospital's only other permanent patient.

"Lamb?"

"Not long now."

"G... good." It was one of the reasons she'd held on as long as she had. She didn't want to go before he did.

The New Covenant survivors had found him, broken and unresponsive, in the cargo bay hall. While they'd managed to get a tube down his broken throat, he'd gone too long without a clear airway. His brain never recovered.

Neither refusing to treat him, nor a quick bullet in his head, would have gone over well with his former followers, and their cooperation had been vital to getting the first buildings up and powered, transporting and acclimating the confused, horrified, and often despairing survivors. So he lay in a room, several doors down, kept alive by the labors of machines. The doctors all said he would never recover. Cynthia, Natsuhiko, Lucas, and Marcus had agreed to make sure of it, to take steps if it ever appeared that he might.

Now he was dying, despite those machines, and Cynthia wished he'd get on with it already.

She didn't think she could stay much longer.

For a little while they talked, or rather Natsuhiko talked while Cynthia listened and, on very rare occasion, managed a word or two in response.

And then Lombardi—who had spent almost all his time in Cynthia's room for the past week—stood up, stretched again, and wandered up to her pillow. After almost a full minute of kneading, he lay down in a furry puddle with his side pressed against her head.

He'd never done that before. Cynthia and Natsuhiko stared at one another, and they knew.

Natsuhiko stood, braced himself on his cane and hobbled near to take her hand. His eyes glistened. "None of us would have made it without you," he told her, voice cracking. "You literally saved humanity. You won't be forgotten."

She squeezed his hand, blinked away her own tears, and said nothing.

"Do you want me to stay?"

"No. Th… thank you."

Lombardi looked up and chirped once, at the sound of the door closing behind Natsuhiko, then began to purr. Cynthia reached up, stroking him until her arm grew weak, her eyelids heavy, and she drifted away.

But not entirely.

Though surrounded by darkness, she felt a sense of place. Whether floating or standing—she seemed to be doing both, and neither—she knew there was ground beneath her.

And not just a sense of place, but also a sense of *presence*. One she recognized.

"Hello, Lamb."

Nothing.

One last telepathic link? Two dying minds, one of them psychic, connecting at the end? Is that how this was happening?

Did it *matter* how?

"I hope this means you're aware, even if there's not enough left of you to respond. I hope you've felt every ticking second. I hope..."

She felt harsh sand beneath her feet. Looked up to see that impossibly still alien sea, bathed in stark whites and faints blues by the searing star above. The great protrusions of stone, greater than any obelisk, grasping for that sky.

And then those waters were no longer still.

It breached the surface in a biblical wave, the Leviathan rising at the end of days. Upward it stretched, and upward, a pulsing, writhing thing of fibrous tissue and ocean sediment. Higher than the reaching monoliths and higher yet, until she could no longer see its end and it began to blot out the burning sun.

Faster it pulsed, and stronger, and Cynthia saw that it resembled not so much any sort of external tendril *but a single exposed nerve*, and the alien sun was not obscured so much as fading, fading...

And then she, too, was fading.

Cynthia Han had one final moment to wonder if she saw merely the last crazed dream of a dying zealot, or a vision of something more, before she was gone.

About the Author

When Ari Marmell has free time left over between feeding cats and posting on social media, he writes a little bit. He's been a storyteller since childhood, something he did frequently in lieu of schoolwork. His professional endeavors include novels, scripts, short stories, role-playing games, video games, and the occasional dirty limerick. He's worked with publishers such as Del Rey, Pyr Books, Wizards of the Coast, Titan Books, Aconyte, and now Crossroad Press.

Ari currently resides in Austin, Texas. He lives in a clutter that has a moderate amount of apartment in it, along with George—his wife—and the aforementioned cats, who probably want something.

You can find Ari online, if you're not careful.
Website: mouseferatu.com
Twitter: @mouseferatu
Facebook: facebook.com/mouseferatu/

Bibliography

Novels Available from Crossroad Press

Obelisks

Obelisks: Dust
Obelisks: Ashes

Other

The Iron Devils

Other Series Novels

The Corvis Rebaine Novels

The Conqueror's Shadow
The Warlord's Legacy
Mick Oberon Jobs
Hot Lead, Cold Iron
Hallow Point
Dead to Rites
In Truth and Claw

The Widdershins Adventures

Thief's Covenant
False Covenant
Lost Covenant
Covenant's End

Other Novels

The Abomination Vault (Darksiders)
Agents of Artifice (Magic the Gathering)
Ash and Ambition
Bloodstone: Awakening (Bloodstone) (forthcoming)
Gehenna: The Final Night (Vampire: The Masquerade)
The Goblin Corps
In Thunder Forged (Warmachine)
Litany of Dreams (Arkham Horror)

Curious about other Crossroad Press books?
Stop by our site:
http://store.crossroadpress.com
We offer quality writing
in digital, audio, and print formats.

Made in the USA
Middletown, DE
19 March 2024

51234022R00151